PRIDE WARS

THE FOUR GUARDIANS

BY MATT LANEY

HOUGHTON MIFFLIN HARCOURT

BOSTON   NEW YORK

hmhbooks.com

The text was set in Berling LT Std.
Series logo design by Sammy Yuen
Map art © 2019 by Jeff Mathison

Library of Congress Cataloging-in-Publication Data
Names: Laney, Matt, author.
Title: The four guardians / by Matt Laney.
Description: Boston ; New York : Houghton Mifflin Harcourt, [2019] | Series:
Pride wars ; [2] | Summary: Prince Leo's identity as a Spinner, once thought to be his greatest
curse, may become his greatest weapon when his devious cousin seizes control of Singara,
forcing Leo to flee into enemy territory.
Identifiers: LCCN 2018051353 | ISBN 9781328707383 (hardback) |
ISBN 9780358229421 (paperback) | ISBN 9780358055990 (e-book)
Subjects: | CYAC: Science fiction. | Princes—Fiction. | Ability—Fiction. |
BISAC: JUVENILE FICTION / Fantasy & Magic. | JUVENILE FICTION / Action &
Adventure / General. | JUVENILE FICTION / Animals / Cats. | JUVENILE
FICTION / Animals / Lions, Tigers, Leopards, etc. | JUVENILE FICTION /
Fairy Tales & Folklore / Adaptations.
Classification: LCC PZ7.1.L342 Fou 2019 | DDC [Fic]—dc23
LC record available at https://lccn.loc.gov/2018051353

Printed in the United States of America
DOC 10 9 8 7 6 5 4 3 2 1
4500758501

For my children
and in loving memory of my father,
David A. Laney

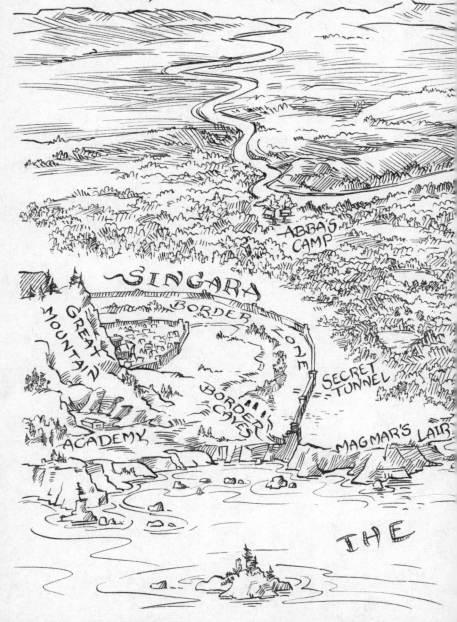

—— CHARACTER LIST ——

LEO the thirteen-year-old rightful Kahn of Singara.

ANJALI the captain of Leo's quadron.

STICK one of Leo's quadron-mates.

ZOYA Stick's twin sister and quadron-mate of Leo.

KAW a Panthera warrior.

ABBA/MU leader of the Panthera outcasts.

LAMASURA/THE BLACK TORTOISE one of the Four
   Guardians.

LI a Panthera warrior.

WAJID a Paladin of the Panthera, newly escaped from
   the Royal Academy of War Science.

URSUS a mighty grizbear, one of Leo's Jin.

LATHA a shape-shifting squirrel, one of Leo's Jin.

TAMIR Leo's power-hungry older cousin who has made
   himself the regent and ruler of Singara.

AMARA   Tamir's daughter and a general in the Royal Army.

ABDU   a Paladin of the Panthera.

NIMSHOOK   a draycon, one of the Twelver's Jin.

KAITAN   an elephamus, one of the Twelver's Jin.

TULA   a large reptilian creature, one of the Twelver's Jin.

JAKOBAH   an elder Paladin of the Panthera.

THE TWELVER/SUNIYAH   the Shakyah and leader of the Panthera.

YOHAN   a two-headed giant, one of the Twelver's Jin.

MAGMAR   a giant spider, the oldest and most powerful of the Jin outside the Four Guardians.

ENRIK   a humana, one of the Twelver's Jin.

JADEN/THE GREEN DRAYCON   one of the Four Guardians.

THE WHITE TIGER   one of the Four Guardians.

HASATAMARA/HELEL   the ancient demon trapped beneath the Great Mountain.

DAVIYAH/THE RED FIREWING   one of the Four Guardians.

PRIDE WARS

CHAPTER 1

Journey far enough into the unknown and you will
eventually encounter yourself.
— *Sayings of the Ancients*

I AM LEO, the rightful Kahn of Singara, and I am about to die.

Time of death: any minute now.

Cause of death: Maguar attack.

At the moment, I'm picking my way through a twisting tunnel with my quadron-mates: Anjali, Stick, and Zoya. This secret tunnel goes under the Great Wall to enemy territory. Torch light sparkles on the damp walls. Only a few meters of trail are visible before fading into darkness.

For the last hour, the tunnel has slanted downward.

Unexpectedly, the path gently rises.

"The trail is sloping up," I announce to my companions.

"That means we've gone under the Great Wall," Anjali concludes. "Welcome to Maguar territory."

That might be funny if death was not waiting on

the other end. The Maguar are not known for friendly welcomes. They are known for ripping our kind to shreds without a second thought.

We've seen the enemy only once, back at the Royal Academy of War Science. Wajid had been a prisoner at the Academy since the Great War twenty-five years ago. He was huge and monstrous. If all Maguars are like him, we're done for.

A blood-chilling roar blasts through this cramped passageway.

We freeze in our tracks.

"What was that?" Stick is in the lead position, carrying the torch. He'd be the first to face whatever beast is lurking up ahead. "Don't tell me that was a Maguar!"

"Unlikely," Anjali says. "Whatever made that noise is way bigger. Keep moving."

"Keep moving *toward* the big scary noise?" Stick protests.

"It's coming from aboveground," she argues, "not in the cave," as if that resolves the issue.

Anjali is our captain and leader. At sixteen, she's the oldest and the most experienced in the Science of War. She's smart, fearless, and fierce. Except for Kaydan, a general of the Singa Royal Army, there's no one else I'd want at my side.

Why are we leaving the safety of our homeland to enter enemy territory?

I need to get away from my older cousin Tamir, who made himself supreme military commander last night. The same night my grandfather, the Singa-Kahn and our true leader, died.

Grief claws at my heart. Losing him is like losing the sun and the moon.

What's more, Grandfather's death means I should be the Singa-Kahn. That's exactly why Tamir and his many followers want me dead. The land of our enemies is the best place to hide. Not even Tamir would dare search for me there.

"This place is darker than snake guts at midnight," Stick says, squinting deeper into the black throat of the cave. "And it's getting darker by the second."

"That's because your torch is dying, brick brain," Zoya retorts.

Zoya is Stick's sister. She's the largest of our group and also the quietest. But when she has something to say, it's usually worth hearing.

Then there's me.

I'm like most any other Singa, only shorter.

To look at me, you wouldn't know I conjure creatures from another world without trying, without even wanting it to happen.

I've kept this power hidden for most of my life . . . with good reason. Those who speak fiction are known as Spinners and are severely punished if caught. In my case, it's much worse. When fiction strikes, strange visions follow and powerful beings get stuck in our world.

Then I met Shanti, an old shepherd. He taught me that I'm not afflicted but gifted. He says I'm a door between two worlds. Such a gift, he said, is very rare. Even among Spinners.

"I see light up ahead," Stick reports.

It's true. And just in time. Our torch is little more than a glowing ember.

Ahead, a distant pinprick of light winks at us like the first star in the night sky. Our pace quickens, and the glimmer becomes a long golden finger pointing to the way out.

The roar returns. Louder this time. And stronger.

Stick stops, forcing us to bunch up behind him. "This is a suicide mission," he groans.

"We can't go back to Singara," I say. "At least I can't."

"None of us can," Anjali states. "We all know too much, beginning with this secret cave. If we go back, Tamir will do whatever he can to extract information from us about Leo and his whereabouts. Trust me. You're better off dead."

"And the Maguar will treat us better?" Stick complains.

"They didn't kill my mother," I say. "She's lived there ever since I was born."

Stick isn't convinced, but he won't get two steps past Anjali if he decides to turn tail.

He shrugs. "Okay, let's do this."

We trudge up the final stretch of cave and huddle under an opening. It's no bigger than the seat of a chair, but it beams like the sun itself in this dark underworld. When my eyes adjust, I see leaves dancing before a pale blue sky.

"Lift me up, Zoya," I say. "I'm going to look around."

Zoya hunches over and I climb onto her shoulders. She stands and my head pokes through the opening. I scan the landscape with eyes and ears, expecting to find the source of the terrifying roar, or maybe a horde of bloodthirsty Maguars closing in. But there are only chirping birds and the scents of pine, earth, and pollen riding on the breeze.

"All clear," I say, and hoist myself up.

In a few moments, we're all standing in a small field surrounded by trees, warming our fur in the sun.

The hole to the cave is hidden by tall grass and low-lying shrubs, practically invisible. I hope we can find it again when the time comes.

"What's that on your back, Leo?" Stick says uneasily.

Zoya moves behind me to see for herself.

"Strange," she murmurs, brushing the fur on my shoulder blades as if she's trying to wipe something off.

"What?" I ask. "What's there?"

"Let me see," Anjali says.

I twist, keeping my eyes on Anjali. Her brow furrows.

"Tell me what it is!" I demand.

"You have markings on your fur," Anjali explains. "I thought it was just dirt when we were in the cave, but it's not coming off. And they're not random marks. It's like a drawing of a firewing bird with outstretched wings."

I crane my neck. I can see only the wingtips of the firewing on my shoulder blades, set in dark brown marks. I touch the fur there. It feels normal enough.

"That's not normal," Stick declares.

"It must have happened when the Great Firewing rested his head on you," Anjali concludes, observant as ever. "I don't remember seeing it before that."

The Great Firewing appeared right before we left Singara. He said I need to follow the path before me and find out who I am. He didn't say anything about bizarre marks on my fur.

"Maybe it will wear off?" I suggest.

Anjali studies my back and sniffs. "Not likely."

"That could be a problem for the Maguar," Stick warns.

"It might help," Zoya adds. "Don't they worship the Great Firewing?"

Stick scowls. "If you think they're going to worship

an enemy Singa with a cave painting on his back, you're as dumb as a bag of hammers."

"Stick has a point," Anjali concedes. "A Singa with a firewing mark could spook the Maguar. Best to be cautious for now. Stick, give Leo your torso cover."

"This is the only one I have!" Stick protests. "And it's too big for Leo."

"Do it, soldier!" Anjali orders. "The Singa-Kahn needs it. You can steal one from the enemy later."

Stick got his name for having the sticky hands of a thief.

"I bet the Maguar don't even wear clothes," Stick grouses as he removes his cover and hands it to me.

The torso cover is big, but it does the job.

Zoya raises a meaty arm and points. "Look."

Through a break in the tree line, perhaps five hundred meters away, we see the Great Wall of Singara rising like a mighty wave of stone. On the other side of the wall is our home and everything we hold dear.

Behind us, deeper in Maguar territory, the fur-raising roar sounds off again, like the blast of a giant horn. We whirl around to face a massive four-legged creature, barreling toward us from the woods.

"Back in the tunnel!" Anjali barks.

Stick slips down the hole before Anjali finishes speaking.

The beast's head is like a boulder. Two massive

horns jut out from its mouth, flanking a long thick nose that resembles a fifth leg. Its body is covered by a copper-colored hide. The eyes are pure white, staring at nothing. Directed by something beyond sight, it plows forward, swiftly closing the gap between us.

Zoya grabs my arm. "Come on, Leo!"

I'm mesmerized. The creature is unlike anything I've ever seen. It looks deranged and not fully in control of itself.

Anjali shoves me toward the hole. "Get down there now!"

We drop underground as the beast thunders overhead, dislodging earth onto our pelts.

Stick shudders. "What was that thing?"

"A Jin," I say, "a creature that came through fiction."

"So there are Spinners here, too?" Stick laments. "Powerful ones, like you. That's all we need."

"That Jin was different," I reflect. "It seemed sick."

"Sick or not, it's heading straight for Singara," Zoya notes.

"It won't get past the Great Wall," Anjali assures us. "Our soldiers have huge crossbows on the top of the wall designed to kill monsters like that."

Zoya cocks her head. "Really?"

"So the wall isn't only for keeping the Maguar out," Stick concludes, "but other creatures as well?"

"That's what Grandfather told me," I say.

Anjali nods. "Haven't you wondered why we need a wall that huge? The Maguar aren't the only threat around here. You three would have learned that if you had made it through your first year at the Royal Academy of War Science."

"Great," Stick grumbles. "Just great."

We climb out of the cave for the second time.

"What now, Captain?" Zoya asks.

"We head deeper into Maguar territory, avoid more sick Jin, and wait to be captured," Anjali says matter-of-factly.

Stick's tail lashes. "Wait to be captured?"

"It's unavoidable," I say. "The Maguar are probably watching us right now."

"When they choose to reveal themselves, and *if* we get the chance," Anjali says, getting nose to nose with Stick, "I will do the talking. You say nothing. Absolutely nothing. Is that clear?"

Stick shrugs. "Fine by me. I don't speak Maguar."

"And under no circumstances do we reveal that Leo is the prince—or, rather, the Singa-Kahn. And, Leo," Anjali adds, "we also won't mention anything about your mother. Not right away. If she is viewed negatively by the Maguar, it could make things worse in a hurry."

"Finding my mother is the whole point of coming here!" I argue, tail lashing. "That and stopping an unnecessary war."

"I know, Leo," Anjali replies curtly. "But we have to find out what we are dealing with here."

"Wouldn't your mother be on the lookout for us?" Stick says. "Her note sounded like she would meet you as soon as you arrived."

Last night Galil, Singara's chief scientist, shared a note from my mother instructing me to leave Singara before my thirteenth birthday.

"Galil didn't deliver the note on time," I remind him. "I was supposed to be here weeks ago. Now *we* have to find *her*."

"If we don't mention Leo's mother," Zoya asks Anjali, "what will you say when the Maguar ask what we are doing in their territory?"

"I will say we have an important message for their high command," Anjali reveals, "about the demon in the mountain."

Hasatamara is the fabled sea demon who was drawn onto land by the salty scent of blood spilled in a prehistoric war, long before the Age of Leos. He rose up with a mighty wave and flooded much of the earth. According to ancient legend, the demon was imprisoned in the Great Mountain of Singara by Alayah, the Maguar's god.

We learned all this last night from Shanti.

Shanti also told us that Hasatamara nearly gained enough strength from the blood shed during the Great War to escape his prison.

"We're not even going to try to stay hidden," Anjali says. "And remember, when the Maguar appear, I do the talking." Her eyebrows lift until we all nod our agreement. Satisfied, she points east. "Quadron formation."

We take our assigned quadron positions as a diamond: Anjali at the rear, Zoya and I just ahead to her left and right, Stick in the lead. We travel in silence for nearly an hour.

Just as I'm admiring Stick for keeping quiet this long, he pipes up. "Do you smell that?" We're in the center of a field surrounded by woods.

Anjali tastes the air. We've all witnessed Stick's superior senses often enough to know he might be on to something.

"Another demented Jin?" Zoya supposes.

Stick's fur fluffs up. "No. I thought I scented . . . *slaycon!*"

Anjali scans the clearing. "Where?"

"In front of us, maybe in those trees," Stick hisses. "When the breeze shifts a bit, you can— Wait! There it is again!"

"I smell it," Zoya rumbles.

"Me too," I say.

Slaycons are horrible creatures with razor-sharp claws, a venomous bite, and a clublike tail. They live to kill.

We all had to hunt a slaycon in one of the Border

Zones that lie near the Great Wall to prove ourselves worthy of training at the Royal Academy of War Science. It's a day we would prefer to forget, except maybe Anjali, who killed her slaycon in record time.

Anjali looks to her right. "Run for those trees across the clearing. Go!"

Stick takes off at full speed, forsaking our training that we stay together. On the other hand, he's forcing us to keep up, which is probably a good thing. If a wild slaycon attacks when we have no weapons, the best course is to scurry up a tree. Slaycons are vicious fighters, but they can't climb trees.

Stick slows to a trot, nose lifted, head shifting this way and that.

Anjali glides to his side. "What is it?"

"The scent. Now it's coming from the trees in front of us."

"It must have moved to head us off," I huff.

"Maybe, but the scent is still over there, too!"

"There are two of them?" I say.

"At least."

"Battle formation!" Anjali instructs. "Prepare to engage multiple attackers!"

CHAPTER 2

Sometimes courage roars; sometimes it whispers;
sometimes it says nothing at all.
— *Sayings of the Ancients*

E NGAGE WITH WHAT?" Stick yelps. "We don't
have blades!"

Shanti made us leave our weapons behind. That
way, the Maguar might allow us to live long enough to
explain what we are doing on their lands.

"Nature gave you claws," Anjali snaps. "Use them!"

We return to quadron formation, facing out, claws
unsheathed.

Waiting.

"Here's the plan," Anjali says evenly. "When the
first slaycon attacks, Zoya will cling to the tail and
anchor it in place. Stick, wrap your arms around its jaw
while I slash its throat. We'll have to work quickly and
be ready to attack the next one the same way. Don't
think about it. Don't flinch. Hesitate and we die."

The plan makes sense. A slaycon attempts to knock

opponents senseless with its tail before paralyzing them with one venomous bite. Then the beast eats you whole.

Or in pieces.

"You forgot about me," I grumble.

She wants to keep me out of the fight and out of danger. As usual.

"You have the most crucial job of all," Anjali says. "Stand watch. After we finish off one slaycon, you point out the next one closing in. Let's just hope they don't all attack at once."

The sickening scent of slaycon surrounds us like a rancid fog.

"I need to share something," Stick whines.

"Not now, Stick!" Anjali growls.

"It's important."

"Shut your front door and focus!"

"I didn't really kill the slaycon in my hunt," Stick continues. "It was really old. I was running away. It fell over and died."

I gawk at Stick, astonished. My slaycon hunt also ended accidentally. I poisoned the monster without knowing it.

"Lucky you," Anjali says. "Now you get to make up for it."

Zoya's throat rumbles. "I see one."

We follow the line of her gaze.

Sure enough, a slaycon has slithered out of the trees

and entered the field, head low, snout pointing at us. An icy chill climbs my spine. I hoped I would never have to face one of these monsters again.

Stick points left. "There's another one!" His arm swivels in a circle, stabbing at the air. "And another. And another! Four of them!"

"It's a pack," Anjali declares. "One for each of us."

"What's our plan now?" Stick moans. "Should we run? Split up? Fall down and play dead?"

At a time like this, Grandfather would tell me to keep my fear in check and to think like a Kahn.

"Definitely don't run," I say, channeling Grandfather's wisdom. "That will only excite them. Hold your arm out, tempting them to bite. When they move to strike, yank your arm in. Once they snap their jaws closed, they won't be able to open them for a few seconds. Use that time to jump over their heads, gouge out their eyes, and slash at their throats."

I tried something like this during my slaycon hunt. It didn't work very well, but I'm not going to mention that now.

We each extend an arm as the slaycons saunter closer.

Stick drops his hand. "I have a better idea. Do your Spinner thing, Leo! Call in the fiction army!"

Just a few hours ago, we were surrounded by hundreds of beings as I spoke their names, causing them to become visible and real, flesh and blood, just like anything else in this world. Some of them had been hanging around, invisible, for years, waiting to be called into action.

"I can't."

"Why not?"

"Because I sent them all back to the Haven!" I snarl.

Once they return to the Haven, I can't bring them back until their fiction possesses me again.

"Not *all*!" Stick counters.

He's right.

I ordered a draycon named Nagarjuna to guard the cave leading from Singara to the Maguar's realm. If I say his name, he might appear, but that would leave the cave unguarded. Tamir could explore the cave and discover where it leads.

Anjali must be thinking the same thing. "Don't do it, Leo! We need Nagarjuna where he is!"

"Tell a new fiction, then!" Stick shrieks. "Conjure up some other monster!"

"It doesn't work that way! I don't control it!"

The slaycons are less than ten meters away. Their flared nostrils draw in the delicious scent of our fear; their dark eyes sparkle with anticipation.

"Wait!" Stick says. "What's that thing wrapped around their necks and forelegs?"

We study the approaching beasts. Sure enough,

bands of leather hug their necks, shoulders, and front legs, each bearing a similar pattern and design.

"Those are harnesses!" Anjali gasps. "These slaycons have been trained, domesticated, like karkadanns."

"Impossible!" Stick says. "You'd have better luck training a tree stump!"

"Do you think they put their harnesses on by themselves?" Zoya retorts.

The monsters are only five meters away.

A sharp whistle sounds from the trees.

The slaycons do a full stop. We freeze as well.

"What was that?" Stick asks in a high, tight whisper.

"Someone who knows how to train slaycons, obviously," Anjali says. "Prepare to meet the enemy."

"There!" Zoya yelps. "I see one." The fur on her neck is up.

"There's another," Stick adds.

Not just one or two, but eight figures step out of the forest and into the clearing from every direction. They walk steadily and soundlessly. Each carries a raised spear or a bow with an arrow. At first, they are little more than shadows against the woods. As they draw closer, we see golden-brown pelts with dark stripes curling around their arms, legs, and faces. Like the Singa, they wear clothing made from deerskins, but their armor is made of hardened leather, adorned with shells and draycon horns. Bright firewing feathers are fastened to their arms or below their knees.

They are not as large as Wajid, the Maguar we met at the Academy. In fact, most of them seem underfed. Two of them are younglings.

Except for their style of dress, their choice of weaponry, and their pelts, they are exactly like us. They move gracefully, keeping their heads low and cocked to one side. Their strange scents, mingled with those of the slaycons, jam our nostrils.

"Steady," Anjali counsels. "No sudden movements. Don't look them in the eye. They will see it as a challenge. And remember"—she glares at Stick—"I do the talking."

The enemy encircle us.

The Maguars arrive at the sides of their slaycons. They are as fascinated by us as we are by them. For a few moments, we do nothing but stare at one another while the slaycons lick their venomous chops.

"*Halaylu,*" one Maguar growls. He must be their leader.

Anjali raises both hands, eyes downcast.

"*Halaylu!*" he repeats, more urgently, waiting for a response.

"We are unarmed," Anjali says. "We come . . . as friends." Her words might be as strange to him as his word is to us.

The Maguar rushes Anjali with astonishing speed. He guides his spear to the edge of Anjali's throat. The tip is made of sharpened flint. With one thrust, he could rip her life away.

The Maguar spits at her feet. His left hand darts about in the air in a series of complex movements. His companions observe and nod solemnly. Then he speaks, or rather the whole group speaks, each Maguar saying one word at a time until a complete sentence is formed:

"Why—" says the leader.

"Do—" says a second.

"Demonics—" follows a third.

"Walk—" adds another.

"These—" says a fifth.

"Lands?" the sixth concludes.

Demonics? Is that what they call us? At the Academy, Wajid called me *infidel*. Perhaps it means the same thing.

Our surprise at their peculiar way of speaking—one word at a time—is topped only by hearing our language roll from their tongues.

"We come in peace," Anjali tries again, "with an important message for your high command."

The leader makes more gestures with his hand. This time a different Maguar kicks off the response as each adult contributes a word:

"Demonics—"

"Are—"

"Liars—"

"And—"

"Deserve—"

"Only—"

"Death."

Anjali stays calm despite the mounting danger.

"First, we share our message with your leader," she says. "Then you may kill us."

Their leader scowls. He fires off another burst of hand signals at his companions.

"These—" he begins, and the others pick up the sentence:

"Slaycons—"

"Are—"

"Hungry."

The Maguars prepare to unleash their monsters.

"If you feed us to your slaycons," Anjali says, "our message will be lost, and everyone on both sides of the wall will die."

The leader holds up a hand.

Anjali dares to lock her eyes on his. "I have a deal for you. If one of you can defeat me in combat—no weapons, no claws—you can feed three of us to your slaycons, except him." She nods to me. "You will take him to your high command."

"If she wins," I hasten to add, "you take us all."

A few tense heartbeats pass.

The Maguar signals to his companions, who muzzle the slaycons. Stick, Zoya, and I are pulled to the edge of their circle, which has now become an arena for combat.

The leader drops his spear and removes several weapons from his body: two long daggers made from bone strapped to each leg, and a curved clublike weapon from his back.

Anjali waits in the circle, relaxed and ready. She's a talented soldier, and hopefully she learned enough about the Maguar's fighting style at the Academy to stay one step ahead of her opponent. What's more, she is fighting for our lives, while the Maguar fights only to feed his slaycons.

In the calculus of war, motivation matters.

The two face each other, one arm's length apart. The Maguar assumes a combat stance unknown to the Singa Science of War: the lead foot forward and the other foot twisted inward. He gestures for Anjali to do the same. She attempts to mirror his position.

Her opponent watches carefully, but not carefully enough.

As Anjali inches forward, struggling to get her feet to match the Maguar's position, she draws his attention away from her hands. With blinding swiftness, she fires a double strike: a blow beneath his ribs with her right fist and a simultaneous uppercut to his chin with her left. Then she sweeps one of his legs, sending the stunned Maguar sprawling to the ground. She pounces and drives a fist into his temple.

In less than three seconds, the Maguar is a heap of striped fur on the grass.

It's over. She won.

Anjali leaps away to observe her fallen opponent.

But the enemy refuses to grant victory. With a groan, he pulls himself to his feet. Blood oozes from his muzzle. Before he is fully upright, Anjali surges forward with a dizzying array of hand strikes, kicks, and attempted locks. Even in his battered state, her foe manages to block or evade every blow.

Anjali has the upper hand, having weakened her opponent at the outset. But the Maguar is furious. He's no longer fighting only to feed the slaycons.

Now he fights to preserve his dignity.

Anjali pauses to take a breath. The Maguar seizes the opportunity to unleash a storm of attacks of his own. Anjali takes a few hits and avoids others. His fighting style is strange: sometimes crouching, other times leaping, occasionally on all fours, while Anjali's movements are tight and straight, almost mathematical.

At last, Anjali finds a chance to counterstrike. She plows an elbow into the Maguar's chin and loops under his right arm to throw him down.

This time, the enemy is not so easily duped. Instead of being hurled to the ground, he rolls over Anjali, grabbing her arm and pitching her to the dirt. Luckily, she hops up before the finishing strike is delivered.

The battle has shifted to the Maguar's favor, and Anjali finds herself blocking and dodging attack after attack before the Maguar catches her on the shoulder with a double kick, knocking her off balance. Wasting no time, her opponent sweeps her legs. She crashes to the ground with a yowl. Knowing the danger she's in, Anjali rolls away, but not before the enemy drives a devastating kick to the side of her head.

Anjali flops to the ground and doesn't move.

She's as lifeless as a corpse.

CHAPTER 3

Your worst enemy cannot harm you as much as the
negative thoughts running wild in your mind.
— *Sayings of the Ancients*

COME ON, ANJALI," I plead. "Get up!"

"Stinking . . . sneaking . . . demonic!" the
Maguar rants, spitting blood.

He sends a foot into Anjali's stomach. She gives no
reaction, proving she's done and that he's the victor.

"That's enough!" I shout. I bound forward and push
the Maguar away. He wheels and smacks me across the
muzzle. For a brief moment, my head feels like it has
been separated from my body.

I fall.

Zoya hisses and comes to my side, ready to defend me.

But the warrior has lost interest in pummeling
demonics. Instead, he motions to his companions standing with the slaycons. They push us forward and prepare to unleash their monsters on us. Including me. So
much for Anjali's deal.

"Kaw!" cries another Maguar in warning.

Anjali springs up, tackles the leader (who is apparently named Kaw), and pins him to the ground. Whether Anjali's made a quick and miraculous recovery or was only pretending to be knocked out, she has caught her opponent off-guard. Anjali thrusts a fist at his head, pounding his muzzle into the earth. She follows up relentlessly, thumping Kaw again and again and again until he goes limp. She gives him two more good blows before backing away.

"Liar!" she says, nearly roaring. "You weren't going to keep your word!" Her speech is slurred. She's unsteady on her feet, struggling for breath, about to collapse.

Every eye is trained on the fallen Maguar, lying face-down on the ground. The closest slaycon whimpers and sniffs Kaw for signs of life.

"Kaw lost," a female Maguar announces to one and all. "Demonics live."

A silent argument erupts among our captors, spoken in furious hand gestures. Eventually the Maguar who pronounced Kaw's defeat roars and pounds the earth with the end of her spear. The others still their hands and dip their heads. She directs three of them to bind Kaw to a slaycon for transport.

"You will take us to your high command now," I declare. "That was the arrangement."

The Maguars say nothing. This brief encounter with the enemy has revealed two things. They boast some excellent fighters, and they prefer to speak as little as possible.

They bind our hands and tie us together.

"Can you walk?" I whisper to Anjali. One of her eyes is swollen shut. "You look horrible."

"I'll be fine as soon as the earth stops spinning," Anjali mumbles.

"We're alive, thanks to you," I say.

"For now. Let's hope Kaw is in a better mood when he wakes up."

We are marched out of the clearing, through the woods, and finally to an open space near a river.

"Smell that?" Stick murmurs behind me.

I part my jaws and taste the air. Interlaced with the aroma of water and mossy rocks is the strong and present scent of many more Maguars and slaycons. To our right is a stack of crudely made tools. To our left is a fishing net, abandoned on the riverbank. A dozen or so fish are laid out on a rock, drying in the sun. Farther off, there are two half-butchered deer carcasses and a slaycon chained to a tree, slurping down deer guts.

I nudge Anjali. She nods grimly.

"Don't look the enemy in the eye," she whispers, lips barely moving.

The lead Maguar mimics the cry of a firewing

bird. Maguars slide into view from every direction: from behind trees, shrubs, and boulders, even dropping soundlessly from branches overhead.

Some advance with arrows notched on a string. Others carry spears or hand weapons. Their cubs and younglings ride slaycons. They are every bit as fierce and battle-ready as the adults.

In a few heartbeats, at least fifty Maguars of various ages enfold us.

An elder approaches.

His face is withered with age. Bones jut out from a mangy pelt that has faded to a silvery gray. He wears a head covering made from the skull of a deer. His mane is a bird's nest of tangles. He brandishes a bone dagger, tail swaying over the ground.

Is this the high command of the Maguar?

The elder's free hand speaks to the warrior who led us into their camp. She bows and signals in return, dipping her head submissively. The elder gestures angrily at us, as if demanding an explanation. Our Maguar escort launches into a series of hand motions, punctuated by facial expressions and the occasional sway of her tail.

It's not hard to work out her message. She's describing the unexpected discovery of four young unarmed enemy demonics with an important message for the Maguar high command.

She recounts the fight between Kaw and Anjali,

announcing the outcome by pointing to Kaw, now lying on a bed of animal skins, still unconscious. The crowd regards Anjali with surprise and admiration, whistling and clucking their tongues. Several appear anxious for revenge.

The elder's face is like a mask, revealing nothing. He comes close to Anjali, who lowers her gaze.

"You . . . come . . . alone?"

The elder croaks the question as though he has not spoken for months. Maybe he wonders if we are only the tip of the spear of a full enemy invasion.

In a way, we are.

As soon as Tamir is ready, Singa soldiers will flood this place and slaughter every Maguar here—cubs, younglings, adults, and elders alike.

"Yes," says Anjali. "We come alone. We are outlaws, deserters, and we have important information for your Pride."

"Speak."

"It is for your high command only," Anjali declares.

Obviously, Anjali doesn't believe this withered and mangy Maguar is the enemy's highest leader. She's trying to buy time and preserve our lives.

The elder proudly lifts his chin. "This one . . ." he says, tapping his chest, "commander here. Speak." The elder raises his dagger and presses it against her throat. "Or never . . . speak . . . again."

I can't let him do this.

"The demon, Hasatamara, is stirring!" I blurt out.

Anjali scowls at me.

At the pronouncement of the demon's name, most of the enemy collapse and cover their ears, hissing, hacking, and gagging as though suddenly stricken by a violent illness.

"Do not . . . speak . . . *that* name!" the elder rages. He brings the blade to my neck. Anjali snarls and bends her knees, ready to pounce. That would be the end of her.

"Have you seen . . . the demon?" the elder demands.

"No," I say.

The elder is astounded. "You believe . . . what you . . . have not seen?"

This old Maguar has some insight into Singa society. Singas reject anything that cannot be seen, touched, measured, or put under a microscope. That's why he doubts we would believe in a gigantic monster no one has seen for eons.

"We come in peace," Anjali pleads, trying to reclaim the elder's attention, "risking our lives, to bring you this warning."

The elder frowns. "Demonics . . . are liars and cheats . . . deserving only death!"

The rest of the Maguars snarl and shake their spears, eager to make good on the elder's words.

"There is more to our message," I claim. "Much more. If you kill us, the demon will destroy everyone on both sides of the wall."

That quiets the crowd.

"The message is for your leader's ears only," Anjali repeats, glowering at me. Everything about her expression says *Shut your front door!*

That won't be hard. I don't know what the rest of our message might be. This ploy was her idea. And now the elder thinks I am the all-important messenger, which puts my friends' lives at greater risk.

The elder sheathes his blade and signals to the other Maguars. Anjali, Stick, and Zoya are untied. In the process, my hands are freed as well. The Maguars pull my three quadron-mates away and secure them to three trees, each about the same distance apart. The assembly of Maguars slinks away, leaving me with the elder.

A brawny Maguar, standing less than ten meters from Zoya, raises a bow with an arrow on the string and aims at her head. It would be an easy shot for a youngling. This brute looks as if he could split a tree from ten times as far.

The elder presses in until I can feel his breath on my whiskers. "Speak message. Or they die."

CHAPTER 4

Each life is a reflection of the whole universe.
Caring for one life is caring for the cosmos.
— *Sayings of the Ancients*

ZOYA SCOWLS AT THE ARCHER, daring him to get on with it.

Stick shudders, barely able to stay on his feet.

Anjali stares blankly ahead, resigned to her fate.

My mind scrambles for something to say, anything that might prevent or stall my friends' executions!

"Tamir . . . is . . . planning . . . I mean . . . he wants the demon . . ."

The elder is not persuaded by my ramblings. He gestures to the archer, who releases his arrow with a sharp twang of the string.

"No!" I cry, too late.

The arrow punctures Zoya's ear, pinning it to the tree. She winces but makes no complaint.

The archer reloads.

"Next arrow . . . here," the elder sneers, pointing to his forehead. "What is this . . . Tamir planning?"

At that moment, a Maguar-made firewing call fills our ears as a group of six Maguars lead a Singa soldier into the camp.

The gathered Maguars hiss and bristle as the lone golden-pelted captive is thrust forward. The soldier's weapons have been removed. He is beaten and bloody. Even so, Anjali recognizes him right away. A wild fire blazes in her eyes. She thrashes against her bindings with renewed energy. Whoever this Singa is, Anjali's not happy to see him.

Neither is the elder.

His hands erupt at the warriors who captured and brought the Singa soldier to the camp. The warriors meekly sign in return.

During this silent conversation, the Singa soldier lifts his face, and I recognize Mandar. No wonder Anjali is enraged. Mandar attempted to arrest us at the Border Caves and take us to Tamir. Fortunately, Nagarjuna, the Jin draycon, put a stop to that.

But how did Mandar get here? Has Nagarjuna been killed? What does Mandar want?

Mandar makes the mistake of looking the elder in the eye. With dizzying speed, the elder strikes Mandar in the face, raking his muzzle with extended claws. Mandar yowls and crumples to the ground. His captors take the trembling Mandar by the arms and drag him to the tree next to Anjali.

"Where's the rest of your quadron, Mandar?" Anjali is seething as they bind Mandar to the trunk. "Surely Tamir didn't send you over the wall alone?"

"That is a fact," Mandar mumbles.

Which means he is the lone survivor.

The elder is agitated. Who could blame him after five demonics show up on the same day?

"So you did *not* . . . come alone!" he exclaims. "You lied!"

"These four are very dangerous," Mandar says to the elder, keeping his eyes on the ground. "You would be wise to destroy them all and toss their bodies before the Great Wall as proof of your kill."

The elder turns to me.

"You will help the Singa by killing us," I argue. "These others followed us because we are outlaws. More will come. Many more. We must warn your leader!"

"Traitor!" Mandar blurts out. "You betray your own Pride!"

"*You* are the traitor, Mandar," I snarl, "for standing with Tamir!"

The elder cocks his head as this drama unfolds between his demonic captives. For a moment, I think the elder understands. Perhaps Mandar is proof that we are fugitives! Perhaps the elder will let us live.

But the elder only shrugs and motions to the archer.

The archer raises his bow, aiming for Zoya. Mandar grins.

Grandfather used to say there is a time for words and a time for action. This is *not* a time for words.

I charge the archer and knock him sideways. Another Maguar leaps forward and thumps me on the side of the head. That prompts an angry response from Anjali, who strains at her bindings.

I rise woozily, rip my torso cover off, and spread my arms to give the elder a clear view of the firewing mark emblazoned across my shoulder blades. The archer and the Maguar who knocked me over don't see the markings. One grabs me while the other raises his dagger, preparing to drive it into my chest.

The elder gives a sharp roar. The archer halts his weapon centimeters from my pelt. The old Maguar waves the two away. He stares at my back as though seeing the ocean for the first time.

"How . . . ?" he whispers.

In answer to his question, the feeling begins: a rushing wind between my ears, nausea in my stomach, as a lump of fiction drops onto my tongue in a mad dash to escape. I open my mouth and surrender to the invasion of words and images from another world.

There was a black tortoise called Lamasura who lived beside a magnificent lake.

Immediately the words conjure the scene of a black tortoise alongside a lake, as bright and vivid as anything else in this world, if not brighter.

Lamasura had slow legs but a quick mouth that moved all day. She talked and talked to anyone, whether they cared to listen or not.

The vision unfolds, like a painting from an invisible painter: the talkative tortoise, the lake, and the woodland creatures who are exasperated with her nonstop blabbering, doing almost anything to avoid her. Eventually we are swallowed up by this fiction.

One year, there was no rain. The lake was drying up, and all the animals left that place, all except Lamasura. She had much to say about the disappearing lake, but her short, slow legs made it hard for her to go elsewhere. Most creatures assumed Lamasura would soon die. Few complained, since Lamasura's death would make the world quiet and peaceful once more. Two swans, however, grew worried about the declining lake and the unhappy fate of Lamasura.

They came to the tortoise and said, "You will not survive much longer. All the water in the lake will soon dry up." They had to wait until Lamasura was eating, and therefore not talking, before they could get a word in.

"Lamasura, we are going to the other side of the mountain, where there is a beautiful lake and plenty of food. Won't you come with us?"

"But how can I get there?" said Lamasura. "My legs are short and slow, and I do not have the strength for such a journey. It seems I was born to die in this terrible wasteland and—"

"We can take you," one of the swans interrupted, "if you can only hold your tongue, close your mouth, and say nothing for one hour."

"Oh, that I can do," Lamasura boasted. "Some creatures think I cannot stop talking, but they have never given me the chance to prove myself. If I am given the proper reason to refrain from speaking, such as what you two have suggested, I can be perfectly silent. I will show you and the world that Lamasura has control over her tongue. I can be quieter than a mouse on moss. I can be as quiet as falling snow. I can be as quiet as a passing cloud. I can be as quiet as the dead in their graves. Why, I can be as quiet as—"

But the swans had already flown off, in search of a stick to assist them in transporting the talkative tortoise. When they returned minutes later, the tortoise was still chattering away, boasting about her ability to keep silent.

One of the swans inserted the middle of the stick into Lamasura's open mouth. "Dear friend," she said, "close your mouth around this stick and shut it tightly. Do not open your mouth until your feet touch land. If you speak, you will fall." The two swans took the ends of the stick in their beaks and flew high into the air.

Everything went fine for several kilometers, until the trio approached the edge of the mountain, where a herd of deer grazed in a lush green valley.

Seeing a tortoise carried by two swans, one of the deer called out, "Look at those swans carrying a tortoise by a stick! Have you ever seen anything so ridiculous?"

Lamasura became angry. "If my friends choose to carry me," she began to say, "what is that to you?"

Needless to say, Lamasura dropped the moment she opened her mouth, and the swans could do nothing to stop her from falling to the earth. Fortunately, Lamasura's strong tortoiseshell served her well. She landed on her back. Her sturdy shell did not crack, but the impact caused her to bite off her tongue. She remained in that place for centuries, still and silent as a stone.

The story ends.

The vision dissolves.

I'm breathless and glad to regain control of my mouth.

Every Maguar except the elder and the archer kneels before the wispy form of a giant black tortoise. Lamasura stands in the middle of the camp, taller than anyone here.

This is what happens. A character from the fiction always gets left behind. At first, they are ghostlike, transparent, not fully of this world. All I have to do to make the tortoise real and solid is speak her name.

The elder trembles with excitement. *"Damar ha shem."*

Others pick up his words from the Old Language: *"Damar ha shem!"*

The phrase washes around the camp, until every kneeling Maguar is chanting: *"Damar ha shem!"*

Grandfather taught me the meaning of those words.

He heard the Maguars chant *"Damar ha shem"* at the end of the Great War, as a powerful enemy Spinner brought forth an army of fearsome creatures, apparently from thin air.

Shanti said the same phrase before we left Singara, encouraging me to speak the name of the draycon Nagarjuna. According to Shanti, the words mean—

"Say the name!" the elder repeats in the common tongue while the Maguars keep chanting.

He knows how this works.

They all do.

Despite her unnatural size, the ghostlike tortoise is harmless enough. But there's no telling what will happen when I say her name. Will she hurt someone? Will the Maguars harm her?

"Say the name!" the elder barks.

I look to Anjali, who offers a slight nod. Stick does so more vigorously. One side of Zoya's mouth curves into a miniature smile.

Mandar is transfixed. And horrified. He never expected to see anything like this. Especially not from the exiled Singa-Kahn.

The elder gestures to the archer, who resumes his aim at Zoya's head.

I'm trying to talk. But my tongue is slow to obey.

The elder nods at the archer, who releases his arrow.

"Lamasura!" I shout.

The Black Tortoise's name is accompanied by a thundering boom, like having your head dunked under water. The air ripples outward from Lamasura. Everything becomes deathly still, frozen in time.

No, not quite frozen.

The Maguars, their younglings atop slaycons, and even the leaves on the trees continue their movements. Yet they move at a snail's pace.

Or at the pace of a tortoise.

Having said her name, Lamasura is no longer a phantom. She is solid, real, completely in this world. And she is glorious. Her black shell gleams in the sun. Her skin is as dark as her shell and as supple as soft leather. Obsidian eyes reflect ancient wisdom far beyond what she displayed in the story.

Lamasura blinks at me, then looks at the arrow lazily plowing through the air toward Zoya's head. Moving at my regular speed, I dash between the archer and Zoya and pluck the arrow from its path.

The boom sounds again, and things return to normal. It must seem as if I disappeared from where I was standing and reappeared here in a fraction of a heartbeat.

The archer and all the other Maguars are surprised by the sight of the littlest demonic holding the arrow that was just fired.

The elder drops to his knees, as does the archer. Lamasura lifts one leg and then another, gradually shifting her bulk to me. Soon her head is less than a meter from mine. The skin around her face and neck is a maze of cracks and wrinkles. She offers no words, but her deep, imploring eyes say it all.

She wants me to send her home.

These beings come from the Haven, a world beyond ours. They are brought here by the fiction, hoping to serve me in exchange for getting sent back. Their departure is as startling as their arrival.

The elder observes Lamasura's silent request, wondering what I will do. Maybe it's because most of the Maguars are on their knees, but for the first time since we came face to face with the enemy, I don't feel small and defenseless. I *will* send Lamasura back, and I will do it in plain view of everyone, including Mandar.

But not before my companions are free and safe.

"Release those three," I say, pointing to Stick, Zoya, and Anjali.

The elder directs the archer to do it. The archer drops his bow and unsheathes his dagger, the same weapon he almost drove into my chest. He goes to Anjali, Stick, and Zoya and slashes the ropes binding them to the trees. With a yank, he removes the arrow pinning Zoya's ear. Zoya doesn't flinch.

My companions dash to my side.

"What just happened?" Stick pants. "How'd you do that thing with the arrow? Or did the turtle do that?"

"Tortoise," Zoya corrects.

"Now they know what I am," I whisper. "Mandar, too."

"You did well, soldier," Anjali says.

It's the most we've said to each other since encountering the Maguar hunting party and their slaycons in the forest glade.

Lamasura paws at the ground. The elder and all the Maguars watch expectantly.

"Come," I say to the magnificent Black Tortoise. "I am willing."

Instantly a fluttering sensation fills my chest. A cavity of light blasts out from my ribs. The brightness swirls and expands until my upper body is replaced by a vision of the Haven, where countless beings orbit an unearthly light.

Anjali is enchanted. She's struggling to keep herself from leaping into the light ahead of the Black Tortoise. The Maguars, from the youngest to the eldest, lower their heads, shield their eyes, and purr.

Lamasura waddles closer and extends her neck. I assume she's going to touch my chest and return to the Haven. Instead, she rests her chin on my head, just as the Great Firewing did yesterday. Her sweet scent envelops me as a tingling sensation spreads over my back.

Lamasura backs away and locks her eyes with mine. In an instant she changes. She is no longer an ancient and massive tortoise. She has transformed into a tall leo with pitch-black fur bearing the pattern of a tortoise-shell.

Lamasura smiles and slowly, so very slowly, raises a hand, holding it before the vision twirling in my chest. Her hand creeps forward as though she has all the time in the world. Finally, with a great burst of light, Lamasura vanishes. The view of the Haven shrinks until it winks out.

Anjali exhales, disappointed.

The elder rushes to my side. His eyes scan my back, as do the eyes of Anjali, Stick, and Zoya.

"Not again," Stick mutters in disbelief.

"She marked me?" I ask.

Anjali flicks her tail as a silent yes.

The elder throws me a long, piercing look. At last he says, "You . . . are not . . . what you . . . appear to be."

CHAPTER 5

Silence speaks more powerfully than words.
Silence is the language of Alayah.
— *Sayings of the Ancients*

THE ELDER CONSULTS the female warrior who escorted us into the camp. They speak in their hand language, and she becomes increasingly upset. The elder slashes his finger with the dagger. He marks her muzzle, lips, ears, and cheeks with his blood and mumbles some words I can't make out. They lean forward and touch foreheads. Tears fall from her eyes, mingling with the blood on her face.

Whatever this means, she doesn't like it.

The elder strolls off as if nothing has happened. The bloodstained Maguar approaches. "Your executions are delayed," she announces. "For now."

She speaks awkwardly, as if embarrassed by the sounds she makes.

"We have questions. This one"—she taps herself on the chest—"will serve as Talker."

"Talker?" Stick asks.

"Our abba," she says, gesturing with her tail to the retreating elder, "used many, many words already, more words since you arrived than in the past three years. He is a sage and his mouth must be protected. This one will talk for him."

We stare at her, baffled, having no words of our own.

"Words have power," she clarifies, her eyes bouncing to me. "As you have demonstrated. But without silence, words mean nothing. That makes silence more powerful, and more noble, than speech. Silence is the language of Alayah, blessed be the name. That is why we use words sparingly. If possible, not at all."

That explains the Maguars' bizarre way of talking when we first encountered them—each uttering one word of a sentence, thereby sharing the burden of speech. This time, one Maguar has been marked with Abba's blood to carry that burden for everyone.

I dip my head to show respect. "We are grateful for your sacrifice."

"It is an honor," she replies, but I don't think she means it. "These words are for your benefit and for the benefit of the family."

"Family?" Stick exclaims. "You're all related?"

"We are four generations. This one," she says, indicating herself, "is third generation."

For the first time I notice how young she is, not much older than Anjali. "Abba is father and grandfather to us all."

Is this how the Maguar organize themselves? In little family tribes spread out across their territory?

"How come you speak our language?" Zoya asks.

The Talker's face hardens. "For hundreds of years, we were the slaves of demonics. You forced us to speak your language, and the Old Language was nearly lost. Now the Old Language is spoken only by the Shakyah and her Paladins. Most of our Pride only speak a few words and phrases."

The Maguar used to be slaves of the Singa? There's nothing about that in the Kahn's History. And now most Maguars know only a few fragments of the Old Language, things like *Halaylu* and *Damar ha shem*.

"So the Shakyah is the leader of your Pride?" Anjali asks. "Can you take us to her?"

"Save questions for Abba," says the Talker.

"At least tell us your name," I say.

She raises her chin as if making a grand announcement. "This one," she says, once again tapping her chest, "is called Li."

"Short names," Stick whispers to Zoya. "Kaw. Li."

"Less time talking that way," Zoya guesses.

I can't stop staring at Li's pelt.

We were taught to think of the Maguar as stained and blemished, ugly and disgraceful. But Li's golden-brown fur is wrapped in elegant stripes curling around her arms, legs, body, and head, like a living thing. The Maguar are beautiful.

"Follow," Li says.

She sprints, leaps onto the trunk of a tree, and climbs without breaking momentum. Around us, other Maguars skitter up different trees to a village of huts and shelters nestled in tree limbs connected by walkways.

"Wow," Zoya marvels. "How did we not see *that* before?"

"We were extremely busy trying not to die," Stick gripes.

"Let's check it out," Anjali suggests.

She extends her claws and leaps onto the same tree after Li. She's not as graceful a climber as Li, but you'd never know Anjali is still pretty roughed up from her battle with Kaw.

"What about Mandar?" I call after her.

The traitor is still bound to the tree, surrounded by four Maguars.

"He's not going anywhere," Anjali says.

"They might kill him," I say.

Anjali shrugs. "They'd be doing us a favor. Come on. Li said our executions are delayed. If we satisfy their questions, we might delay execution further or avoid it altogether."

We climb to a small shelter made of branches, bark, and animal skin. Li leads us along several walkways to the center of the tree village. A wide, circular platform, big enough to seat Abba's entire family, is supported by eight trees around the edges, with one massive tree rising through the middle. There's a hut built between one of the outer trees and another tree beyond.

Li strides across the platform to the hut. She pushes aside a flap of animal skin that serves as the hut's door and waves her tail for us to enter.

Our eyes adjust to the dim, dusty interior.

Abba sits against the tree trunk at the other end. The space is sparsely furnished with fur rugs and cushions. Something dead, gray, and furry is cradled in a basket to his right.

"Sit," Li invites, or rather commands.

We do, and Abba passes the basket.

It reaches Stick first. He extracts a squirrel and fails to hide his disgust. Singas do not eat rodents. Zoya and Anjali each select a squirrel, dipping their heads with appreciation. When the basket comes to me there is but one left. I lay the basket with the final squirrel at the elder's feet, offering it to him. Zoya bites the head and half the body from her squirrel and hands me the rest. I extend the claw of my forefinger, slice off the bushy tail, and gulp the rest down.

It isn't terrible. But I prefer the fresh meat of larger animals raised on the farms of Singara.

Abba grins.

Is this the same Maguar who nearly sent us to an early grave? The smile and squirrels are promising signs. He wouldn't waste food on four demonics only to feed us to their slaycons.

Would he?

Abba's hands dance in the air. Li translates.

"We have much to learn from each other. We begin with a time of silence. The Ancients say if you become quiet and still, you can hear the purr of creation."

Thirty minutes of silence drags on, during which Stick noisily picks his teeth with a squirrel's rib bone. So much for hearing the purr of creation.

Finally, as if awakening from a trance, Abba moves his hands, and again Li interprets.

"Demonics on our lands," she begins, "and the demon stirring. This can only mean war is coming."

"Yes," I say. "Soon."

The elder's face shows confusion. He signs again.

"You betray your Pride to warn us," Li says for him. "Why?"

"Our Pride has been taken over by a dangerous fool

named Tamir," I reply. "The soldier you captured is one of his followers. Tamir knows that violence and bloodshed give strength to the demon. He wants war because he wants the demon to escape. He thinks he can control it. Besides all that . . ." I pause before going on. "I'm not welcome among the Singa . . . because of what I am."

Abba's eyebrows lift.

"What are you?" Li says, speaking for Abba.

I look down, as if searching for the answer among the strands of the fur rug. "I'm . . . a Spinner."

Abba hisses, then stabs the air with hand motions.

"That is just another demonic lie!" Li snaps, matching her tone to the elder's fierce gestures. "You are a Truth Teller. You receive truths from Alayah, blessed be the name. But unlike other Truth Tellers, you bring powerful beings, Jin, from the Haven. Such a gift is very, very rare, only given to one Teller at a time . . . until now."

My head lifts. "What do you mean?"

"Truth Tellers like you are known as Shakyahs," Li says. "There is only one Shakyah at a time, all born from the same bloodline. That either makes you a very unusual demonic . . . or something else."

"Then the Shakyah is your leader," Anjali concludes. "Where does the Shakyah live?"

Abba's hands gyrate, and Li takes a deep breath, preparing for another long answer.

"She lives in the river city of Elyon in the Temple of the Shakyahs, guarded by the Paladins, who are the largest and wisest of our Pride. Because she is the Twelfth Shakyah in the twelfth cycle of Shakyahs, she is known as the Twelver."

Abba's hands rest in his lap. Li exhales and massages her jaw.

"Can you take us to her?" I ask.

Abba shakes his head.

"Impossible," Li states.

"Why?" I say.

A roar blasts from the ground beneath us, followed by a series of angry huffs and another quick roar.

Li's ears lift. "Kaw is awake. He wants the Ritual of Justice."

Abba rises stiffly and makes for the door.

"What's the Ritual of Justice?" Anjali asks.

"You will soon find out," Li answers.

"I bet he wants to fight you again," Stick speculates.

"You beat him once," Zoya says encouragingly. "You can do it again."

"Don't be too sure," Li cautions. "Kaw went easy on you the first time. The Ritual of Justice is a fight to the death."

CHAPTER 6

Those who believe it is better to be feared than to be loved have not learned that love is stronger than fear.
— *Sayings of the Ancients*

W E EXIT THE HUT and find Kaw glaring up at us. Abba signs to Kaw, who signs aggressively in reply.

"Abba wants him to wait until tomorrow," Li says, "but Kaw insists that the Ritual of Justice happen now. Abba cannot deny him."

I shiver.

Kaw is eager to restore his dignity. Anjali will have to kill him to save herself. That definitely won't help the Maguar feel better about us.

"Don't do it," I plead. "Your eye is still swollen shut."

"Not sure I have a choice." Anjali shrugs. "And he's pretty banged up too. I can see his busted lip from here."

We cross the gathering platform and descend the same tree we climbed earlier. The whole family, young and old, forms a ring for the Ritual of Justice. Kaw waits at the center, lashing his tail. Mandar is still alive and bound to his tree, watching everything with hungry eyes.

The crowd parts, and Anjali enters the ring. She observes Kaw's midsection. That's where we are trained to focus in the Science of Hand-to-Hand Combat. It's the best way to observe all of your opponent's moves at once.

Kaw signs to his kin. Li translates for us.

"If anyone believes this demonic is worthy to live, come take her place."

Kaw doesn't bother searching the gathering for any takers. Why would anyone switch places with a despised demonic in a battle to the death with their fiercest fighter?

Seeing no one step forward, Kaw grins, extends his claws, and settles into the fighting stance he struck at the beginning of his last bout with Anjali. Anjali reveals her claws and matches his stance, several meters away this time. Kaw scowls at his opponent, no doubt remembering the sneaky way Anjali scored the first blow before.

At first, the two warriors do nothing but growl, tails lashing. Finally, Kaw's legs twitch, and he bounds forward. Anjali dodges the attack by rolling under him.

Now they have traded places and begin circling each other.

Suddenly, a mighty roar explodes from the trees as a huge figure drops to the ground between Kaw and Anjali. The stranger crouches to absorb the impact of his landing. As he rises, the crowd cringes in fright.

I'm relieved the Ritual of Justice has been interrupted, but my ears go flat.

I've seen this overgrown Maguar before.

Stick nudges me. "Hey, is that . . . Wa—?" He can't get the name out.

The newcomer is powerfully built and two heads taller than everyone else. He wears nothing more than a piece of animal skin wrapped around his waist. Although his wide back is to me, there is no mistaking Wajid, the Maguar held captive in the Royal Academy of War Science since the days of the Great War.

We first encountered Wajid less than a week ago. On that occasion, there were iron bars separating me from him.

Not now.

"*Halaylu!*" Wajid bellows.

"*Halaylu Alayah,*" Kaw responds dully, claws still out. He's as alarmed by the arrival of Wajid as we are.

"*Shmi Wajid, eved Shakyah Daviyah!*" Wajid's big voice booms around the camp.

Whatever he just said gets everyone to drop to their

knees and dip their heads. Only the four dumbstruck demonics remain standing.

"Rise, children of Alayah," Wajid says at last, switching to the common tongue.

The Maguars climb to their feet, keeping their heads low. Kaw says something to Wajid in a rush of hand gestures.

"Friends? No! These demonics are not friends!" Wajid declares. "The demonics held Wajid prisoner for twenty-five years, locking Wajid in a cage like an animal. But this one"—he slaps his broad chest to indicate himself—"escaped and tracked them here."

Abba draws close to Wajid and stares him square in the face, the only Maguar bold enough to do so. Abba's eyes are watery as he says something to Wajid with his hands.

Wajid places two large hands on Abba's bony shoulders. "Yes, old friend. This one truly *is* Wajid, Paladin and servant of Shakyah Daviyah."

Abba keeps signing, hands moving in an excited blur.

"As you can see, Wajid is *not* dead as many believed," Wajid says in reply. "Although Wajid wished to die on many days during captivity among the demonics, for they are cruel taskmasters. But Alayah, blessed be the name, had other plans."

Abba addresses the whole camp with hand gestures.

Li translates for us: "While Wajid, the Lost Paladin, is here, he is our lord and master. Now we will feast and have the Ritual of Telling!"

Wajid and Abba drift away side by side, hands whirling in silent conversation.

Anjali returns to our group.

"I can't say I'm happy to see Wajid," I say to her, "but I'm glad he showed up when he did."

"Me too," Anjali agrees. "We might live to see tomorrow."

"So no one's worried about an invasion from the enemy?" Stick mutters under his breath. "They'd rather have a welcome party for 'Wajid the Lost Paladin,' instead of warning the Shakyah? They're as stupid as we thought!"

Zoya delivers a sharp elbow to Stick's gut. Li is only two meters away.

"This one's time of serving as Talker is about to end," Li informs us. She appears relieved, but I already miss the slow, thoughtful way she speaks.

"Why did Wajid speak instead of talking with his hands?" I ask before we lose her.

"Lord Wajid is a Paladin!" Li declares, as if that settles it. Then Li's tone softens, remembering we are ignorant demonics. "Those who dwell in the temple may use speech as they see fit."

"Why do you live out here," I inquire, "rather than in Elyon with the rest of your Pride?"

Li inhales, gathering enough air to make many more words. "Abba was a member of our high council. Twelve moons ago, he accused the Twelver of wickedness for hoarding Jin instead of returning them to the Haven, as is proper for a Shakyah to do. She did not appreciate the criticism. She exiled us from our homes in Elyon to live near the wall of the demonics."

Li edges closer. Now she is eager to talk, yet her voice sinks to a cautious whisper: "Abba was right to challenge her. If Jin are kept in this world too long, they become sick. Eventually they *shift* and become servants of the demon."

We are all in the tight grip of curiosity. I can't let her stop there.

"Servants how?" I ask.

"Shifters have one focus: to free the demon. They are drawn to Bad Mountain like moths to the flame. When they get there, they start digging. To be stopped, they must be destroyed."

"These Shifters," I venture, "do they have copper skin and creepy white eyes?"

Li's eyebrows lift. "You have seen a Shifter?"

"I think so," I say.

"Then you understand why Abba confronted the

Twelver. It is wrong, and very dangerous, to keep Jin in this world for too long."

My blood runs cold as Li ambles away.

I kept Jin in this world for years. And because I was inside the Great Wall, they were too. If any of them had become Shifters, there would have been no barrier to stop them. The result would have been devastating.

Unlike the Twelver, I didn't do it on purpose.

I ordered the Jin to disappear because they threatened to reveal my disease. But making them invisible is not the same as sending them back to the Haven. Though they can't be seen, the Jin are still present, waiting to be called into action and hoping to be sent home as their reward.

I didn't understand.

I didn't know I was putting them, and our world, at risk by keeping them here.

Anjali tugs at my arm. "Forget about Shifters. We have a bigger problem right now."

She points to the tree where Mandar had been tied up.

But he's not there now.

In all of the excitement around Wajid's arrival, Mandar has escaped.

CHAPTER 7

The greatest use of your life is to spend it on
something that will survive your death.
— *Sayings of the Ancients*

Y OUR PRISONER HAS FLED!" Anjali informs
Li. It's a strange thing to say, because we are prisoners too. "Find him before he reaches the wall!"

Li lashes her tail and signals three others. One
of them unties a slaycon. The beast sniffs and snorts
around the tree where Mandar was bound, then charges
away from the camp with the four Maguars in tow.

My quadron gathers in a tight huddle.

"This is terrible," I groan, reflecting on all Mandar
has learned about me and the Maguar. "Mandar has
seen this camp! He knows what I am! He'll report it all
to Tamir. Once Tamir knows that Leo Kahn is a Spinner, he can easily turn my own Pride against me!"

"That's right," Anjali says grimly. "So let's hope
they track him down."

"I hope they bring him alive, so I can rip that spine-
less hairball in half," Zoya growls.

"Not likely, Zoy," Anjali says.

"Why aren't they worried about *us* running off?" Stick ponders, making no attempt to hide his desire to follow Mandar's lead.

"They know we aren't welcome in Singara," Anjali explains. "We're exiles. Just like them."

"We have to convince them to leave here," I say. "Even if Mandar doesn't make it back to Singara, this camp will be wiped out first when Tamir attacks."

"What about us?" Zoya asks. "Where will we go?"

"Elyon, of course," I say. "We have to warn the Twelver about what's coming."

Stick folds his arms over his chest. "Please explain why we should warn the enemy before our Pride attacks them?!"

"Get a brain, Stick!" Anjali admonishes. "*Tamir* is the enemy. Not them."

"At least Tamir knows what side he is on!" Stick hisses. "Have you forgotten how many Singas the Maguar killed in the Great War? And they started it! We can't trust them."

"They didn't start the Great War to destroy us," I say. "Their eyes were on a much bigger prize: Hasata-mara, the demon in the mountain."

"Yeah," Zoya adds, "Tamir wants to free the demon. The Maguar want to destroy it. Any idiot can see who has the better idea."

Stick rolls his eyes. "There is no demon in the mountain! And anyway, we came here to find Leo's mother. Not to help the Maguar."

"Leo's mother isn't here," Anjali says. "But the Twelver might know where she is."

"Who's going to take us there?" Zoya asks. "Abba and his family are about as welcome in Elyon as we are in Singara. We won't get far without a guide."

"The perfect guide just arrived," I say.

Anjali nods.

Understanding dawns on Stick's face. "No way! You can't be serious, Leo."

I shrug. "He's our only chance."

"Question is," Zoya adds, "will he do it?"

The sun, having reached its highest point for the day, now begins its silent journey to the opposite horizon. Meanwhile, the family works in hushed harmony, butchering their kill and stacking hunks of meat into baskets. Others bring fish from the river. The baskets are lifted to the platform in the middle of the tree village by ropes connected to a carved wooden pulley.

A pulley!

I nudge Stick. "See that?"

"That's no big deal," he scoffs.

"It's an invention!" I argue.

"So what? A spear is an invention, and so is a fishing

net," Stick counters. "That doesn't mean they follow the scientific method."

Once the last basket of meat and fish has ascended, everyone climbs nearby trees and pours into the meeting place, abandoning us on the ground. We don't know what to do until the scowling face of Kaw appears at the edge of the platform, beckoning us to join them.

We climb and find the baskets of food placed before the central tree, while the Maguars sit around the platform.

Wajid squeezes through the little door of Abba's hut, doing his best not to bust the whole structure. The boards of the platform creak under his weight. He has exchanged the flimsy covering he wore around his waist for deerskin leggings and a chest plate made of hardened leather and decorated with shells, horns, and slaycon teeth. A dozen or so red-and-gold firewing feathers are woven into his mane and tied to his arms and legs.

Like all the Maguars, he is dressed and ready for battle, ready for the war that's coming. Yet they still find time to feast and celebrate. How unlike the Singa they are!

Wajid perches on a stool cushioned with deerskin, clearly the place of honor. Abba sits cross-legged to his right. Wajid leads a chant in the Old Language. Then Abba signals for the meat to be passed around, starting with Wajid. By the time the baskets reach us, there are only a few fish heads left. I'm all the more grateful for the half of a squirrel I devoured earlier in Abba's hut.

After feeding, Wajid's hands speak. For our benefit he announces, "Now we will have the Ritual of Telling!"

He beams with delight. Whatever the Ritual of Telling is, the Lost Paladin clearly missed it during his time of captivity.

"Truth Tellers, go to the tree," Wajid instructs.

Two Maguars approach the central tree and sit against the trunk.

"That includes you, young demonic!" Wajid says to me. Abba must have told him what I am.

I look at Anjali. "It's not a request, and we are in no position to argue," she says.

I creep to the central tree, aware of all the Maguar stares boring into my pelt.

A Maguar rises from the opposite side of the platform. He has a drum slung around his shoulder.

Wajid nods and the drummer strikes twice with a stick.

THUM-THUM!

The other Maguars, including Abba and Wajid, move their arms in tandem, scooping the air from their feet to their ears.

The drummer strikes again.

THUM-THUM!

It's followed by the same odd motions from Wajid and Abba's family. The drummer pounds the drum a third time.

THUM-THUM!

Anjali nods to Stick and Zoya. All three awkwardly join in on the beckoning arm movements.

The strikes of the drum are coming faster now. Soon they are roughly the speed of a heartbeat.

THUM-THUM!

And then a rapid heartbeat.

THUM-THUM! THUM-THUM!

Dozens of Maguar arms swing, along with those of the three Singas struggling to keep up. Over and over the drumbeat thrums, like the pulse of every living thing in the forest.

The two Tellers beside me jerk, sway, and heave as if they might throw up. Then my heart beats faster, keeping time with the drum. Soon a rushing wind fills my head. My stomach turns with nausea.

It's happening.

The drum and all this arm-swinging are pulling a fiction through me. This is what the Ritual of Telling is all about. If it's anything like what happened with Lamasura, they will be a very respectful audience, unlike the Singa.

A youngling led her father's herd of goats into a field.
One wandered away.

To my shock, the words do not come from my mouth but from the Truth Teller next to me. The bundle of fiction that nearly dropped onto my tongue dissolves, outpaced by the story of my neighbor. The drum stops, and the Maguars rest their arms.

The story-possessed Truth Teller continues:

The wayward goat happened to be the favorite of the youngling's father. The goat had long beautiful horns that gleamed in the sun.

A dim apparition of the fiction swirls around the tree, matching her words. The images are grainy, as though drawn in the dirt, but they do the job.

The youngling whistled and called, but the wandering goat paid no attention. The youngling refused to leave the herd to retrieve one disobedient goat, even the favorite.

At last the frustrated youngling threw a stone at the goat. The stone hit the goat's horn, breaking it in two. Only then did the horrified youngling run out to meet the goat. She begged the goat not to tell her

father. The goat replied, "You are a foolish youngling.
My broken horn will speak even if I am silent."

The fiction passes, and the Teller collapses, panting and exhausted. The vision dwindles like smoke, and everything returns to normal—as normal as things can be when you are sitting with a bunch of battle-ready enemy fighters in the middle of a tree village.

But no Jin appear. And no one seems to expect a Jin to appear.

"Praise Alayah for this gift of wisdom!" Wajid proclaims. He signals the drummer, who resumes his beat.

THUM-THUM!

As before, the beat starts slowly. In time, the pounding quickens to a rapid heartbeat. My quadronmates join the Maguars in their swooping arm motions. The beat locks onto my heart, forcing it to keep time with the drummer.

Once again, I sway and heave.

Soon a wind howls in my head. My stomach rolls with nausea. A hot lump of fiction drops onto my tongue and expands. There's no use holding it in.

My mouth pops open, and the words take over.

In the days of the Ancients, when leos were new to the earth, there was a youngling named Ursus.

The story vision bursts into view, blotting out everything: the trees and the gathering of Maguars. Wajid's mouth drops open. Abba glances at Wajid, then at me, flashing his broken-toothed smile.

Ursus's parents were farmers who grew their own vegetables and raised animals for food. Like his brothers and sister, Ursus worked hard tending the farm and caring for their animals. There was so much to do on the farm, they toiled from sunup to sundown.

And yet the family had barely enough to feed themselves and almost nothing to spare for others in their village.

Ursus and his siblings were forbidden to enter the woods lest they be devoured by wild beasts and never seen again. As Ursus worked in the pastures each day, his mind was drawn to the unknown regions of the woods that lay beyond the farm.

One day, while repairing the fence at the edge of their lands, Ursus heard a twig snap in the woods. The breeze carried a wild new scent. He looked up and saw something large and brown dash between the trees and melt into the forest. Ursus was both frightened and curious, but he did not dare leave the safety of the field to investigate. He returned home and said nothing to his family.

One week later, Ursus again found himself at the edge of the pasture and smelled the same strange scent. This time he saw a large fierce creature staring back at him from the edge of the woods. The beast was covered in thick shaggy hair, with powerful shoulders and huge clawed paws. She walked on all fours, yet her eyes were intelligent and noble. Ursus did not know that he was in the presence of a mighty grizbear, the ruler of the forest.

"Who are you?" Ursus asked.

"Come and see," the beast replied.

"My parents say those who enter the woods never return."

"As long as you are with me, no harm will come to you. You will be home before the sun dips below the trees."

Because the sun was already beginning to sink, and his family was nowhere in view, Ursus leaped over the fence and dashed into the woods.

"Climb upon my back, and I will show you the wonders of the forest," the beast said.

Ursus did as he was instructed, and the beast carried him away, introducing him to the various trees, animals, rivers, and caves of the woods. She taught him to fish and to hunt, and where to find the juiciest wild berries.

"There is so much food here!" Ursus declared. "And you don't have to work for any of it!"

"Alayah provides in abundance," the beast said.

When Ursus returned home, he could not stop thinking about the things he had seen and tasted. He found he was no longer hungry after eating in the forest. The next day and every day that followed, one hour before the sun dropped below the trees, Ursus would meet his new friend and enjoy the bounty of the forest. His family wondered how Ursus grew strong and robust after he had stopped eating their food. After several weeks, it was obvious that Ursus was changing. His fur became longer and darker. His body grew large and powerful. His hands, feet, and claws got bigger. He was becoming a creature of the forest. Ursus's family was alarmed, and Ursus had to confess.

"I have been visiting the forest every evening for the past moon," he admitted. "A friend has taught me to hunt and fish, and where to find the ripest berries. There is plenty to eat and no need for toil and labor. Come! Let me show you!"

But his family would not accept his offer. Ursus knew he could no longer live happily on the farm, so they allowed him to return to the forest.

That afternoon, Ursus met his friend and said through many tears, "I want to stay here with you. Forever."

The beast licked Ursus's tears. As she did so, Ursus completed his transformation into a creature like her. Together they vanished into the forest.

The words halt, and the vision scatters on the afternoon breeze. My tongue returns to my command.

"*Damar ha shem,*" Wajid says in a husky whisper.

"*Damar ha shem,*" Abba echoes.

I follow the angle of their gawking faces.

There, behind the central tree, is the colossal grizbear known as Ursus. He is faded and wispy, not yet fully in this world. All I have to do to make him real is *damar ha shem*—say his name.

"*Damar ha shem . . . damar ha shem . . .*" every Maguar chants in one voice.

Ursus balances on his hind legs, making him three times the height of Wajid. He bares his teeth and roars. I don't know why the Maguars want me to bring this terrifying creature into our world.

I regard my quadron-mates. They, too, are fixated on Ursus.

Ursus lowers to all fours, and the Maguars scamper away. His head is less than a meter from mine.

"Say my name, Lord," Ursus murmurs beneath the chanting Maguars. "Have no fear."

There is something about his way of speaking that reminds me of Oreyon the hunter and Rukan the giant wolf. Noble and direct. Strong yet kind.

"Damar ha shem!" the Maguars thrum, punching each syllable with greater intensity. *"Damar ha shem!"*

Well, everyone is agreed.

"Ursus!" I cry out.

At once, the great grizbear becomes flesh and blood, as real as anything else in this world. His fur is dark brown. Long claws gleam like metal in his paws. Alert eyes shine as though lit from behind. He roars to make it completely clear that he is fully here and not to be trifled with.

Ursus's roar is replaced by the creaking and snapping of wood. If the platform was at risk of collapse before Ursus arrived, it is now beyond hope. With an ear-piercing crack, half the floor drops away, breaking off a whisker's length from where I'm sitting. The Maguars sitting on that side plummet to the ground with Ursus, surrounded by a storm of debris.

Although the Maguar differ from the Singa in some obvious ways, they are just as skilled at landing on their feet.

Ursus, however, is sprawled out like a big bulging

carpet, covered with pieces of the busted platform. The Maguars who did not fall hurry to the ground to assist the others.

Wajid and Abba remain with us.

"Ursus!" I call. "Are you all right?"

Ursus shakes rubble from his shaggy pelt. He rolls onto all fours and then hoists his bulk onto his hind legs. His chin is level with what's left of the platform.

"Not my best arrival, Lord," he mutters. "How may I be of service to you?"

Abba's face reflects curiosity and concern about what I might ask Ursus to do.

That gives Stick an idea. "Could you destroy every Maguar in this camp if he asked you to?"

"I respond only to the master's orders," Ursus replies coolly. "But if that is his wish, I could finish the task in a few minutes' time." He extends his claws and glares at Wajid and Abba. "Shall I begin with these two, Lord?"

CHAPTER 8

Life is a mystery to explore, not a problem to solve.
— *Sayings of the Ancients*

ABBA AND WAJID are alarmed. The fur on their backs rises up.

"No!" I instruct Ursus, scowling at Stick. "Don't hurt anyone in this camp. I will let you know if I need your help. Or would you like to return now?" I say, ready to open the door to the Haven.

Abba's and Wajid's alarm switches to surprise. Stick's whiskers droop.

"Very kind of you, Lord. However, I would prefer to stay until you have an important task for me. That is why I have come."

"You could repair this platform."

Ursus snorts. "My paws are not made for that sort of work. Perhaps a mission more suited to my skills will soon be revealed."

Ursus lowers himself to the ground and saunters

off to the river for a drink. The slaycons tied to trees keep as far away as their chains will allow.

"Young demonic," Wajid utters. "Abba says you have been marked by two of the Four Guardians. Do you know what that means?"

"How can I?" I say. "I don't even know what a Guardian is."

"The Four Guardians are the most powerful of the Jin," Wajid shares. "They are called the *Shijin* in the Old Language."

"And the Great Firewing and the Black Tortoise are both Guardians," I conclude.

Wajid winces. Abba swats his ears, as if trying to knock something out. Was it something I said?

"Only Alayah is *great*," Wajid explains. "It is offensive to our ears to call anything else 'great,' even one of the Shijin. You have been marked by the *Red* Firewing and the Black Tortoise. The other two Guardians are the Green Draycon and the White Tiger."

"What's a tiger?" Stick inquires.

"Demonics," Wajid murmurs, astounded at our ignorance.

"It's an ancient four-legged creature," Anjali explains, in an effort to make us look slightly less dumb. "One of our prehistoric ancestors from eons ago."

"What's so special about the Four Guardians?" Zoya asks.

"More special is a Shakyah who is marked by the Four Guardians. When all four mark a Shakyah," Wajid explains, "the time has come for the destruction of the demon. The demon is the cause of the separation of the Prides. When the demon dies, the two Prides will become one, as we were in the days of the Ancients."

"How many Guardian marks does the Twelver have?" I ask.

Abba holds up three fingers.

"According to Abba, she waits for the Red Fire-wing," Wajid reports, anticipating our next question.

Abba's hands jab and stir the air.

"Abba wants to know why you opened the door to the Haven for the Black Tortoise," Wajid translates.

"The Haven is her home," I say. "Who am I to keep her here?"

The two elder Maguars exchange a look of astonishment.

"The Singa will attack soon," I say, hoping to bring this conversation back to the perils developing here on planet earth. "Abba's family should leave as soon as possible."

Abba responds with a defiant gesture.

"They will not go," Wajid says. "They will stay and kill any demonics who enter these lands."

"That is not a logical choice," Anjali protests. "They will overtake you, killing everyone, even your cubs."

Abba's determined expression is unchanged.

"And you, Wajid?" I probe. "What will you do?"

"Wajid longs to complete his mission," he says.

"What mission?" Anjali asks.

Wajid closes his eyes and inhales, collecting memories, assembling words. "Wajid was at Shakyah Daviyah's side during the Last Campaign, what demonics foolishly call the 'Great War.' Shakyah Daviyah had collected hundreds of Jin to fight with us. With their help, we nearly defeated the demonics. Nevertheless, all the blood spilled gave strength to the demon, nearly enough to free himself from his mountain prison, which caused a massive earthquake. In that moment of distraction and alarm, Shakyah Daviyah was killed. With Daviyah's death, all his Jin returned to the Haven. Daviyah's son, however, only a cub at the time, was left on the field of battle."

"Wait, Daviyah took his cub into a war?" Stick interjects. "That was stupid."

Wajid glowers at Stick as Zoya elbows him.

"Shakyah Daviyah wanted his son to witness the defeat of the demonics and the death of the demon," Wajid says. "Daviyah was so certain of victory, he did not see any risk to his son or to himself. He was very wrong. Fortunately, Daviyah's mate was already pregnant with their second cub."

"The Twelver," Anjali says.

Wajid nods. "Verily."

"But you still haven't told us your mission," Anjali reminds him.

"Wajid was just coming to that," Wajid grumbles, making no attempt to hide his irritation at the rudeness and impatience of demonics. "After the campaign, Wajid was sent to Singara to find the missing cub of Shakyah Daviyah. It was an impossible mission, punishment for failing to protect him during the campaign. Wajid was captured, but the mission remains, unfulfilled and incomplete."

"What makes you think Daviyah's son survived?" I say.

"After twenty-five years in captivity, Wajid lost hope that this was so. That changed only a week ago, when Alpha brought three new cadets to my cage."

"Us!" Stick exclaims.

Wajid levels his dark eyes on me. "One of them has the scent of a Shakyah." His words slow to a trickle. "One of them so resembles Daviyah's son, Wajid thinks he is seeing a ghost."

My breath stops.

"Oh, Leo." Anjali sighs.

"Oh no," Stick groans.

"Whoa . . ." Zoya says.

"You mean—" My voice cracks.

Wajid lifts his chin. "You are the son of Daviyah's son!"

"The son of Daviyah's son . . ." I repeat, heart racing. "That means Daviyah is my . . ." I can't get the word out.

"Your abba," Wajid says. "Or, as demonics say, your grandfather."

My grandfather. My *other* grandfather. On my father's side.

I recall the moment I first met Daviyah, on the beach of the Haven, right after Storm bit me. He was shifting back and forth between the Red Firewing and a leo like us. The Red Firewing came several times after that, and each time it was Daviyah's voice I heard because Daviyah's spirit lives on in the Red Firewing, like all the Shakyahs before him.

"Wait, you said Daviyah's son vanished in the Great War!" Stick counters.

"Someone must have found him after the battle," Wajid surmises, "kept him hidden, kept him safe, and eventually introduced him to your demonic mother."

The image of a wise old Singa fills my mind. I once had a dream of the same Singa, as a younger soldier in the moments after the Great War. He discovered a little Maguar on the field of battle, no more than seven years old.

"Shanti," I whisper.

"That old shepherd?" Stick exclaims. "He protected your father?"

"This Shanti," Wajid says, "is the instrument of Alayah, blessed be the name. These things cannot be a coincidence. Daviyah's son was *meant* to be among the demonics. Wajid was *meant* to be captured. Wajid was *meant* to encounter you. Wajid was *meant* to escape and find you here."

It all adds up to an even more startling conclusion. If my mother is a Singa and my father is a Maguar, then —

"Leo is half Maguar?" Stick blares. I can't tell if he is impressed or disgusted. "That explains why your mother gave you a Maguar name, Eliyah."

Anjali waves her tail, urging silence.

"A *Shakyah* name," Wajid says admiringly. "But your other name, Leo, is your destiny and ours. You are what we once were, and must become again, as one Pride of leos."

"*Damar ha shem,*" I gasp, quivering. "Say his name, my father's name."

"Makayah," Abba says, startling us all by using his voice.

"Makayah." I roll the name over my tongue. "Where is he now?"

Abba shrugs.

"According to Abba, Makayah has not been seen for years," Wajid responds. "Only the Twelver knows where he is."

"You have no reason to help us, Wajid," I say, "after all our Pride has done to you. But we need to see the Twelver. And we need someone who knows the way to Elyon, someone with connections to the temple."

Wajid considers my request. "Wajid is not known to the Twelver, and there would be many dangers along the way."

"More dangerous than today?" Stick snorts. "Not sure *that's* possible."

The truth is, we would put Wajid in danger as well. It won't be easy to explain why he's traveling to Elyon with four demonics, one of whom has marks from two Guardians.

"You're our only hope, Wajid," I plead.

At that moment, Li and her companions enter the camp, wearily dragging their tails after the pursuit of Mandar. Li looks at the broken platform and then to Abba sitting with us.

Abba signs to Li, who dismally shakes her head.

We don't have to know their sign language to understand.

Mandar got away.

Wajid studies my face, a face that resembles my father's. "Rest in Abba's hut while Wajid prepares," he declares at last. "We leave for Elyon in two hours."

CHAPTER 9

The best way to earn someone's trust is to trust them.
— *Sayings of the Ancients*

I DREAM OF ELYON and the Twelver.

Hundreds of Jin crowd a huge subterranean chamber. Some are gigantic figures; others are small and dainty. They howl and roar and screech as a single Maguar observes them from a high balcony. She wears an ornate headpiece. Rows of multicolored beads and feathers adorn her torso, arms, and legs. Her striped pelt is draped with a long green cloak. Her face is shrouded in shadow.

The Twelver steps away from the balcony and from the unruly Jin. She climbs a curling flight of stairs and enters a room furnished with a broad table, where twelve Maguar elders are seated.

One of them is Abba.

Abba is better groomed than in exile. Like the other elders around the table, he is dressed in fine clothing. The elders bow to the Twelver, as do twenty massive Maguars draped in white robes, standing at the sides of the room like pillars. They are Paladins, like Wajid, the servants and protectors of the Shakyah. The Twelver takes a seat at the head of the table while everyone else chants something in the Old Language.

A discussion follows between the Twelver and the Council of Elders, spoken in their silent hand language. The Paladins look on, offering neither words nor gestures. I have no idea what is being said, but the conversation grows heated, with hands flying, tempers rising, and tails lashing. One by one, the elders bow and give up.

Not Abba.

He presses on with his argument, eventually leaping to his feet.

"Let them go!" he roars. He must mean the hundreds of Jin held captive in the cavern.

The Twelver pounds the table with both fists. "Take him away!" she thunders.

The white-clad servants of the Shakyah rush forward and seize Abba.

"Now receive these words," the Twelver snarls. "Mu and his entire family are no longer welcome among the Pride. They are banished to live by the wall of the demonics, grateful for the Shakyah's mercy in sparing their lives."

I awake in a nest of pillows and fur blankets inside Abba's hut.

Anjali is up, watching me.

I wonder if she went to sleep. I'm not sure she *ever* sleeps.

"You okay?" she asks.

Midafternoon light peeks through cracks in the hut's walls. I stretch and rub my eyes.

"Weird dream, that's all."

Zoya stirs and rolls over, accidentally whacking her brother in the head. Stick grunts, only mildly annoyed given how often that happens when they are both awake.

"Someone brought food," Anjali says, pointing with her snout to a basket filled with dead squirrels and mushy, half-rotten apples along with a skin of river water waiting by the door.

"I thought I smelled dead rodent," Stick mumbles sleepily.

I toss a squirrel to each of my quadron-mates. "Might as well have some. Who knows when we will eat again."

Stick stretches and yawns. "Kind of like yesterday."

Was it only yesterday I saw Grandfather's body lying stiff and cold in his den? Was it only this morning that we left Shanti at daybreak and went under the

Great Wall to Maguar territory? So much has happened, this day feels more like a week.

We sit in silence, munching on squirrel and apples and drinking from the skin.

"I have to make water," Stick announces, wiping his mouth.

He crawls to the door, opens the flap, and yowls as if he's staring death in the face.

Anjali pulls him back and peers outside.

"Don't be such a 'fraidy cub." She chuckles. "It's only Ursus."

Ursus! I nearly forgot about the giant grizbear. I can't blame Stick for his reaction. Ursus *is* frightful.

I push the flap aside and there is Ursus, hind feet on the ground, chin resting on the edge of the broken platform. His dark twitching nose is only a meter or two away. He brightens at the sight of me.

"Good morning, Master Eliyah!" Ursus says cheerily. "Have you decided how I may be of service to you?"

"You can join us on our journey to Elyon and to the Twelver," I say. "We might need your strength and claws."

"If that is your wish."

I exit the hut and come closer to the mighty grizbear. "Ursus, can you become invisible, like the others?"

"Of course."

"And you will return when I call you by name?"

"That is how it works, Lord."

Anjali, Stick, and Zoya gather behind me.

"Ursus, I command you to disappear."

As soon as the words leave my mouth, Ursus dwindles from view.

"Where'd he go?" Stick asks, gaping.

"He's still hanging around," I say. "He is both there and not there. Watch." I take a breath. "Ursus!"

I expect the great grizbear to rematerialize in the same position. He doesn't.

"Ursus?" I repeat, feeling foolish.

"Right here, Lord," the familiar voice rumbles.

We whirl around and find Ursus clinging to the tree supporting Abba's hut, only a meter or two above the little dwelling.

"I am not very good with trees," Ursus says, struggling to hold on. "If you command me to disappear now and say my name later, preferably when your feet are firmly on the ground, I can avoid the climb down."

"Vanish!" I say, trying a new word.

"Many thanks to you, Lord." Ursus exhales as he melts from our sight.

A chorus of angry growls draws our attention to the ground.

"Looks like trouble," Zoya observes.

A small group of Maguars, led by Kaw and Li, encircle Wajid, weapons drawn. It's a sudden reversal from yesterday, when the Paladin was treated like royalty. Their slaycons are still tied to trees at the edges of the camp, but a few younglings stand by, ready for the signal to unleash them on Wajid if needed.

Wajid remains as tall and proud as ever, just as he did when we first met him in Alpha's fortress at the Academy. It appears he was packing weapons and supplies for our journey when Kaw, Li, and the others made their move. He could easily pick up one of the spears or daggers at his feet and defend himself, but he's greatly outnumbered. Whatever happens, our journey is at risk. If Wajid is not permitted to take us to Elyon, we have no chance of getting there on our own.

Abba pushes through his family and stands beside the Paladin. A storm of hand talk breaks out between Abba and Kaw. The argument continues as we make our way down the tree.

"We might need Ursus sooner than we thought," Anjali whispers.

I hope it doesn't come to that. Grandfather taught me to use weapons only when words have lost their punch. Then, he would say, attack with ferocity and without hesitation.

"*Halaylu*," I say, repeating the Maguar greeting we heard earlier.

"*Halaylu Alayah*, young Shakyah," Wajid replies.

"What's going on here?"

"That one," Wajid says, pointing to Kaw, "does not trust Paladins, because it is the Paladins who exiled their family from the Pride."

"They were only following orders from the Twelver," I argue.

Kaw responds with furious hand speech.

Wajid translates. "That is his point. The Paladins must follow the orders of the Shakyah without question. He believes Wajid will be unable to protect you from the Twelver. He believes Wajid will betray you. He says you should go to your homeland and allow Wajid, and Wajid alone, to warn the Twelver of the demonics' invasion."

Kaw gives a quick flick of his tail to show agreement.

"Sounds good to me!" Stick whispers.

"Much has changed in the years since Wajid left Elyon," Wajid laments. "It appears that under the Twelver, the Paladins no longer have the trust and respect of the Pride."

"Why is Kaw suddenly so concerned about our safety?" Anjali asks warily. She has good reason to ask. Kaw nearly turned us into slaycon food and hoped to kill Anjali in the Ritual of Justice.

Kaw signs and Wajid translates. "He cares nothing for your safety. He only wants to help his Pride by sharing the demonics' plans. He believes your presence in

Elyon might get us all killed, and your message would die with us."

"Kaw has a fair point," I say. "Can you protect us, Wajid?"

"Wajid does not know the Twelver, and the Twelver does not know Wajid," the Paladin says. "However, Wajid is the Lost Paladin, the missing and loyal servant of her father, Shakyah Daviyah. That is a powerful advantage."

Kaw slashes the air with more hand signals.

Wajid bares his teeth at Kaw. "He says Wajid failed to find Makayah, the Twelver's older brother. Because of that, he says, Wajid should not expect a warm welcome."

"Even so, Makayah survived," I say.

"Thanks to a Singa!" Stick adds.

Wajid directs his next words to Kaw. "You could be correct, brother. The Twelver might not receive Wajid. But these four have risked their lives to come here. Such courage must be honored."

"And why waste time fighting among yourselves when our Pride is preparing to attack yours?" I claim. "If you are not willing to leave, you need to be ready. The soldier who escaped will lead them here first."

"The young Shakyah speaks truly."

Kaw and Li lower their weapons.

Abba faces Wajid and me. "There . . . must be . . . trust . . . among those who . . . walk together." With the same age-defying speed Abba exhibited when we entered the camp, the elder clutches my wrist. Wajid extends his large hand until it is side by side with mine.

Anjali and Zoya growl a warning.

Abba removes the bone dagger strapped to his chest. Before I know what has happened, Abba swipes my hand and then Wajid's hand. He mutters something in the Old Language while pressing my stinging palm into Wajid's. The Paladin interlaces his thick fingers around mine. Blood streams along our palms and forearms.

"Blood is life, and life is blood," Wajid says. "That is what the Ancients teach. Our blood and our lives are bonded now. Wajid takes you as master, and you receive Wajid as your servant until death separates us."

Wajid releases my hand.

Kaw's throat rumbles. He doesn't trust Wajid any further than he could throw him. Kaw counts our entire mission as lost before it has even begun.

"Wajid knows it will take more than words and blood for you to trust Wajid. Demonics require, what is the word . . . evidence? Evidence of Wajid's loyalty will come soon."

CHAPTER 10

Challenges do not make heroes. Challenges reveal heroes.
— *Sayings of the Ancients*

THE MAGUARS ASSEMBLE on the riverbank, chanting in the Old Language. The rising voices stir birds from the trees, including one firewing. The brightly colored bird does not escape Wajid's notice.

"That is a good sign," Wajid declares from the river's edge.

There is a raft floating on the surface of the water, bound to the riverbank by a crudely made rope. Wajid unties the rope and, to our surprise, marches directly into the river. He guides the raft into deeper water and holds it against the swift current. A Maguar on the riverbank uses a thick branch to make a bridge from the land to the raft. He grins, welcoming us onboard.

Zoya groans.

We Singas are happy to wash with water, but we hate to be dunked in the stuff. Floating on water is only one wrong step from being submerged. There are no rafts or floating vessels in Singara. We prefer to travel by karkadanns, and the sea near our lands is far too rough and rocky for safe passage.

"I'm not getting on that thing," Stick declares. "I'll walk to Elyon and meet you there."

"Great idea," Anjali says wryly. "Paint a big target on your chest while you're at it."

She nimbly crosses the tree limb to the raft. The platform dips under her weight. Startled, she digs in with her toe claws and drops to all fours.

Wajid stifles a laugh.

Anjali waves her tail. "No problem. You next, Leo."

I extend my claws and cross on all fours like our ancestors from ages and eons ago. The Maguars keep on with their chanting while sharing a smirk or two at the water-wary demonics. Zoya and Stick creep onboard after me. Because we are all crouching on one side, the raft tips.

"Spread out!" Anjali cries. We scramble to different corners until the raft stabilizes. Wajid climbs on, and the current pulls us downstream. He holds a staff connected to a flat board trailing in the water to steer us along. The voices of the Maguars fade as the river bears us away.

"Are rafts like this common among your Pride?" Anjali inquires.

"When Wajid left our Pride to search for Makayah,"

he says wistfully, "there were many rafts and boats in Elyon, much larger than this."

We struggle to keep our tails dry and the fur on our backs flat, but not Wajid. He is as comfortable and sure-footed on the raft as on land.

"This river is called the Tigra," Wajid says. "It merges with two other rivers at Elyon, the heart of our Pride. If we stay on the Tigra, we will arrive in three days."

"Once we get to Elyon, how will you explain your escape from Singara," Anjali says, "and bringing four Singas with you?"

"Leave that to Wajid" is all the Paladin reveals. "We will enjoy silence now. Like Abba, Wajid has spoken many, many words today."

An hour later, the sun slips beneath the tree line. The wind blows harder. The river runs faster.

Stick perks up and gazes downriver. "That looks bad."

Ahead, water gushes and foams up around sharp boulders rising from the surface of the river like teeth. Wajid guides the raft to the center of the river, straight for the rapids.

"What are you doing?" Stick shrieks. "We should head for land!"

"That is what those slaycons want," Wajid replies.

Sure enough, half a dozen slaycons match our progress on each riverbank, hissing and screeching.

"Those are not trained slaycons, like at Abba's camp," Wajid explains. "They are wild, which is why the river is the safest means of travel."

"And that's why Abba's family sleeps in the trees," Anjali says.

Slaycons are deadly hunters but not gifted climbers.

Wajid keeps the raft floating down the middle of the river. Water sloshes onboard. "You will find weapons in those bundles," he says, nodding at the two packs. "Start with arrows."

Anjali wastes no time unraveling the bundles and passing a bow and a bunch of arrows to each of us.

"In our Pride, it is forbidden for a Shakyah to touch weapons," Wajid grumbles as I arrange my arrows. "A Shakyah *is* a weapon."

I shrug. "I've been handling weapons my whole life."

Anjali fires off three arrows before the rest of us notch one to the string.

Her first and second arrows find two slaycons behind their forelegs, penetrating their hearts and killing them instantly. The third arrow skims a tree trunk and wobbles harmlessly away. The slaycons on the left side of the river scatter and take cover among the trees.

"Target those on the right," Anjali commands.

Arrows from Stick and Zoya each hit a monster.

My arrow barely crosses the river.

Despite my confident words about handling weapons, I don't have the strength to pull the string far enough. Meanwhile, the other slaycons melt into the forest. Wajid keeps his eyes on the river, expertly guiding us around boulders and fallen branches. The rapids accelerate our journey and douse us with cold water until we're drenched and shivering.

"Are they gone?" Stick asks hopefully.

"Not likely," Anjali says. "Slaycons are relentless."

"Keep an arrow on the string," Wajid counsels.

"Look!" Anjali cries.

Downstream, three slaycons take cautious steps onto boulders scattered throughout the river, leaping from one to another. Two on the opposite riverbank make the same move. They're positioning themselves on the river rocks to attack from both sides as we pass.

"Give them everything you've got!" Anjali barks.

She, Stick, and Zoya unleash a blizzard of arrows. But slaycons are clever creatures. They tuck their legs and lower their heads to shield their eyes. Most of the arrows bounce off their hides, but one or two, fired from Anjali or Zoya, hit their mark, prompting hideous howls.

Wajid hurls three spears with such force, the skewered slaycons are knocked off their feet.

Anjali regards Wajid with admiration. Stick considers the Paladin with fright.

"You two!" Wajid directs Stick and Zoya. "Take up blades and leave the arrows to her!"

Zoya drops her bow and uncovers a stash of Singa-made blades.

"Where did you get those?" I ask.

"From dead demonic soldiers," Wajid replies. He means from Mandar's quadron. We came without weapons. They might have fared better if they had done the same.

I take a short blade and hand a long blade to Wajid. He waves it away, disgusted.

"Our Pride is forbidden to touch metal that comes from the mountain," he explains, drawing the club-like weapon from his back. "That metal was placed by Alayah, blessed be the name, to hold the demon."

I select a dagger as Stick and Zoya put a blade to each hand.

Anjali continues the assault with her bow. Her face is a picture of stony concentration, but her arms flow nonstop—picking up one arrow, aiming, releasing, and grabbing the next. Her aim and power improve as the rapids draw us closer to the slaycons, who wait on the rocks scattered along the middle of the river.

One beast, punctured with three arrows, floats

away in water tinted with its own blood. A second soon suffers the same fate. That leaves two slaycons ahead to our left, one to the right, and several more running along the riverbanks. Another beast leaps into the river by the same series of rocks that brought the first batch.

We're less than fifteen meters from them.

Now ten.

Anjali drops her bow and extends a hand. "Leo, give me the aero-blades."

Aero-blades are ringlike weapons that soldiers wear on their backs. There are four here from Mandar's quadron. Anjali sends each one flying as soon as I transfer them to her waiting hand. She brings down three slaycons and badly wounds a fourth.

"Impressive," Wajid says.

Anjali grabs a long blade and a short blade. "Remember your training!" she says over the rushing water. "Strike at their underside as they leap. Mind their teeth and tails."

When we were farther away, the slaycons seemed to be bunched up together. Now it is clear they have spaced themselves apart on a number of rocks and boulders downriver for a series of attacks as the current carries us along. If the raft tips or gets stuck, we are done for.

"Come to Wajid, Eliyah!" Wajid commands. He has the steering stick in one hand and his weapon in the other. "Wajid will protect you."

"I want to fight!" I protest.

"You may get your chance if Wajid fails. Kneel beneath Wajid now!"

"Do it, Leo!" Anjali hollers without taking her eyes from the monsters.

Frustrated, I scramble on all fours to Wajid.

The nearest slaycon quivers with excitement, preparing to leap. We are close enough to see gooey tendrils of venom hanging from its mouth. If slaycon teeth break through your hide, their venom will paralyze you in seconds.

The monster leaps.

Zoya roars and eagerly rams her blade into the brute's chest. A second slaycon spins and swats at Anjali and Stick with its tail. Anjali bends to avoid the blow and simultaneously slices the underside of its tail with her blade. Stick's face is sprayed with slaycon blood. His cry of complaint is drowned out by the wail of the wounded beast. It spins for a bite at Wajid as we roll by, but Wajid swings his weapon and chops off the slaycon's lower jaw.

That beast won't bite anything ever again. It will starve, if it doesn't bleed to death first.

More slaycons have made their way onto the rocks. They are everywhere, waiting for their chance.

Two attack, from both sides. Anjali chops at one, while Stick and Zoya deflect the other. The next slaycon nearly boards the raft, but Zoya manages to shove it into the water while jabbing a dagger into its eye, narrowly avoiding the snapping jaws.

The determined one-eyed beast clings to the raft with its foreclaw and attempts to scramble onboard, made easier by the raft tipping dangerously toward it. I shoot forward and hack at its arm until there is nothing left.

Killing them won't always be possible, or necessary, given our rate of travel. All we need to do is stay afloat, keep moving, and prevent them from boarding the raft or injuring us. The river will do the rest.

But there are so many! We risk getting worn out and sliding off the raft from pure exhaustion.

"Call him!" Wajid yells to me as he bashes the snout of another slaycon. *"Damar ha shem!"*

"Who?"

"Ursus! Say the name!"

I nearly forgot about the grizbear. Just as I have forgotten so many others after making them disappear.

"URSUS!"

Instantly the colossal grizbear appears in the river,

towering over us on his hind legs and shaking the trees with his roar. Given the obvious danger, Ursus needs no instructions from me. He takes two slaycons by their tails, dashes their heads on nearby rocks, and flings their lifeless bodies onto the riverbank. He slashes with his claws and greets others with bone-crushing kicks.

Then something happens that makes my heart stop.

Startled and enthralled by the arrival of Ursus, Stick fails to notice the slaycon to his left.

"Stick!" Anjali shouts in warning.

Too late!

The slaycon lunges and sinks its teeth into Stick's thigh. Stick yelps with terror and pain. Anjali swings upward and separates the slaycon's head from its body, but it's still attached to Stick. Anjali drops her blades, kneels, and pries the beast's mouth open. Stick's leg is a bloody sight, and he is already going rigid from the venom.

Suddenly, the raft gets wedged between two rocks and comes to a full stop. The abrupt halt causes Anjali and Zoya to lose their balance, while Stick's stiff body tumbles into the river. Two slaycons on the riverbank take notice and trot alongside the water, keeping up with Stick as the current carries him away.

Meanwhile, Ursus has killed two more slaycons and then another.

Zoya looks as if she wants to jump in after her brother. Who could blame her?

"Keep fighting! Stay focused! We'll find him later!" Anjali shouts. She grabs a blade and impales a slaycon that nearly latched on to Wajid's arm.

"Ursus!" I yell.

Ursus angles his head to me while ripping a slaycon in half.

I point downriver to Stick. "Save him!"

Ursus plunges ahead, swatting and clawing every slaycon in his path. Wajid, Zoya, and Anjali form a protective circle around me as slaycons come at us from all sides. Water gushes up at the rear of the raft. The wood creaks, threatening to snap. Through the mayhem of battle, I see Ursus pull Stick from the water and head to shore. Once on land, he lays Stick in the sheltering arms of a nearby tree.

During this rescue mission, Ursus's claws have not been available for fighting, causing him to receive multiple bites from the slaycons swarming at his feet. Forepaws now free, Ursus swipes left and right until he is surrounded by corpses.

Ursus's movements become sluggish as the slaycon venom does its work. He lumbers dizzily up the riverbank, doing his best to assist us in the fight. He seizes two attacking slaycons by their tails and pitches them into the trees. The motion throws the great grizbear off balance. He wobbles and tips over backwards, head smacking the riverbank.

His body is sprawled out in the river.

Blood darkens the water.

CHAPTER 11

A friend who dies to save a friend has honor, but one
who dies to save an enemy has the light of Alayah within.
— *Sayings of the Ancients*

NJALI AND WAJID finish off the last slaycons as I leap into the river. Were it not for Ursus's rigid body serving as a blockade, I would be swept away like Stick. I cling to his shaggy, soaked fur and make my way to his head. The grizbear's eyes are half-open. His breathing is shallow.

Zoya trails me while Wajid and Anjali drop into the river. With their combined strength, the two warriors get the raft over the rocks and guide it to the shore.

Zoya and I hover over the battle-weary face of Ursus.

"Did I serve you well, Lord?" he rasps.

"You were very brave," I say.

Anjali and Wajid join us.

Ursus exhales with relief. "May I return now?"

"He has more than earned his way to the Haven," Wajid says.

That much is clear. But how?

On the two occasions I have sent Jin to their Haven home, they have always walked into me as though I were a door. Given Ursus's injured and paralyzed condition, he won't be doing that. Perhaps if he can extend an arm . . .

"I am willing!" I say. "You may return."

Immediately there is a fluttering sensation inside me like the beating of a thousand wings. A golden beam pokes through my chest and expands into a brilliant shaft of light. Soon, the space between my waist and neck reveal the now-familiar scene of a bright light in a blue sky, surrounded by countless winged beings. Zoya shields her eyes while Wajid bows his head and chants something in the Old Language. Anjali gapes at the Haven, transfixed. Ursus's ears lift, and a faint smile lands on his muzzle.

"I don't know what do to," I say.

Wajid stops chanting. "Embrace him."

"What?"

"Fall on him."

I extend my arms and lean forward. As soon as my chest touches Ursus's fur, he vanishes, sucked into me with a great blast of light. Without him there to break my fall, I splash into the river—dripping, shivering, miserable, but grateful Ursus is home and no longer suffering.

My body is back to normal. The scene of the Haven is gone. The door is closed.

Wajid nods approvingly.

All that remains of Ursus is the blue-black patch of blood sliding downriver.

"He will be all right, won't he?" I ask no one in particular.

"He is more than all right now," Wajid says. "It will take time, but he will heal. All things are made new in the presence of Alayah, blessed be the name." He turns to Anjali and Zoya. "You fought bravely."

"Our elders tell of the strength and ferocity of the Maguar," Anjali replies. "They spoke truthfully."

"You honor Wajid and our Pride," the Paladin says. "The Ancients teach, 'A friend who dies to save a friend has honor, but one who dies to save an enemy has the light of Alayah within.'"

"Maybe the Ancients were wrong," I say. "Maybe one who is willing to die to save an enemy proves they are no longer enemies, but friends."

Wajid's eyebrows lift. "You have deep wisdom, Eliyah."

"I prefer to be called Leo. She's Zoya. Our captain here is Anjali."

Wajid cocks his head. "An*jali*?" He says her name in an unfamiliar way, accenting the second syllable instead of the first. "Anjali is . . . a very, very powerful name."

He studies her closely and sniffs. "When did you first meet Leo, Anjali?" he queries.

"It's *An*jali," Anjali repeats, correcting his pronunciation. "I met Leo when we were cubs."

That's curious. I don't remember meeting her before she started serving in the castle.

"And in case you're wondering," Anjali continues, "our friend in the tree goes by—"

"Stick!" Zoya cries. She nearly flies down the riverbank to where Ursus left him.

"We have to get him down!"

"Let him climb down himself when the venom wears off," Wajid calls after her. "Tonight we will join him. This swarm of slaycons is defeated, but there are many more."

"We should be safe here on the ground," Anjali says. "Living slaycons avoid their own dead."

"Safer aboveground," Wajid insists. "If An*jali*," he says, still pronouncing her name the wrong way, "would assist in hoisting a slaycon tail into that tree, we will feed together."

Zoya is already in the tree, checking on her brother. I climb up after her. Stick's body is rigid, but he is still breathing. The venom affects only skeletal muscles, not internal organs.

"Do you think he can hear us?" Zoya asks, stroking her brother's stiff hand.

"Can't hurt to try," I say, studying the nasty wound on Stick's leg.

Zoya bends to Stick's ear. "Stick, you're going to be okay. Leo and I are right here with you." Her eyes beg me to say something.

"That's right, Stick," I say. "You're fine. We wiped out half of the slaycons, and Ursus took care of the other half. He saved your life."

"Leo saved your life," Zoya corrects. "The grizbear was following his orders."

"We all owe Ursus our thanks."

Zoya's whiskers tremble. I wonder if she might shed a few tears. Never seen that before.

"He's the older one." She's looking at Stick but talking to me. "By a few minutes. When we were cubs, he was always there to protect me. Whenever my temper landed me in trouble, he would figure a way to get me out."

"He'll recover in an hour or so," I assure her. "Slaycon bites stun but don't kill."

Anjali and Wajid settle in the branches around us. Together, they haul up a severed slaycon tail with two ropes. Anjali gets to work carving it up.

Wajid rummages through a sack slung over his shoulder. He finds a small pouch and pours the dusty contents into one hand. He spits several times and mixes it until a jelly-like lump forms in his palm. Then he spreads the stuff over Stick's wound, pressing deep into his torn fur and flesh. It's a good thing Stick can't feel anything.

"I wish I could call the healer from the Haven," I say. "She fixed Zoya's broken leg yesterday."

"Vishna has appeared to you?" Wajid says, impressed. "She is a good Jin to know."

"But I sent her back," I say. "I sent them all back."

Wajid nods his approval. "That is the right thing to do," he says, "after they complete their service."

His words are both an affirmation of me and a criticism of the Twelver. The problem is, once Jin go back to the Haven, I can't get them to return without their fiction coming to me again. And that is beyond my control.

"Jin are not meant to stay in this world," he continues. "The longer they stay, the weaker they become, until they shift and become servants of the demon. At that point, they must be killed."

"So the Jin can die," I say.

Wajid cocks his head and furrows his brow.

"I'm new to all this," I remind him. "Growing up Singa didn't come with a great education on Jin."

"Once a Shakyah says the name of a Jin, it is flesh and blood like all creatures in this world," Wajid instructs. "When its earthly body is destroyed, or when the Shakyah who brought it dies, the Jin returns to the Haven."

"Then Ursus would have returned to the Haven when he died of his wounds, even if I hadn't sent him back," I conclude.

"It was a kindness to end his suffering."

"What happens to a Jin when a Shakyah tells it to disappear?" Zoya asks.

"That is more difficult to explain," Wajid admits. "They linger about the Shakyah, invisible, waiting to hear their name. In that state, they lose their solidity and become more like spirits, able to move through walls."

"Does the Shakyah command the Four Guardians like other Jin?" Zoya asks.

Wajid's eyes drift to Anjali carving up the slaycon tail.

"No," Wajid says. "Like other Jin, the Shakyah is the Guardians' anchor to this world. Unlike other Jin, the Guardians come and go as they please. However, the Four are so powerful, so glorious, if they arrived all together, their combined energy would kill the Shakyah who brought them and cause disaster all around. That is why Alayah gave the Axis to the Ancients. The Shakyah who has marks from all Four Guardians *and* holds the Axis can bring the Four to the earth without risk."

"What's the Axis?" I question.

"It is a bridge between this world and the Haven,"

Wajid replies. "To your eyes, it would look like a staff or a pole, but alive and glowing with intense power."

Anjali takes a break from carving the slaycon tail. "So one Shakyah plus the Four Guardians' marks plus the Axis of the Ancients equals the ability to destroy the demon and unite the Prides," she summarizes, as though this is a formula from the Science of Numbers. "Is that right?"

"Verily," Wajid concurs.

"That must mean Daviyah was marked by all Four Guardians," I say. "Otherwise he would not have attacked the Singa."

"Not so," Wajid despairs. "Three of the Four Guardians marked Daviyah. The Red Firewing held back. Daviyah grew impatient waiting. He had collected hundreds of Jin and attacked the demonics, taking the Axis of the Ancients with him into the battle. He knew the blood of war would allow the demon to escape, but he believed the Red Firewing would mark him in time to summon all the Guardians, who would then destroy the demon. He was wrong. Very wrong. The war ended with Daviyah's death, before the demon had enough strength to escape."

"And now Daviyah's spirit is in the Red Firewing," I say.

"Like all the Shakyahs before him," Wajid states solemnly.

"So the Red Firewing held back from Daviyah, just like Daviyah, who is *in* the Red Firewing now, holds back from the Twelver," Anjali ponders, wiping slaycon blood from her blade.

Zoya wearily rubs her forehead. She's having a hard time keeping up with all the Shakyah family drama.

"Obviously," Anjali says, looking at me, "all the Shakyahs who dwell in the Red Firewing, from Daviyah back to the very first, were waiting for someone else."

Wajid grunts his agreement. "And the Red Firewing was the *first* to mark Eliyah. The wait is over. The time has come."

"Why me?" I protest. "I don't know anything about any of this—the Guardians, the Axis, killing an ancient demon—none of it makes any sense!"

"You don't have to know," Wajid says, nearly purring. "You only have to be willing."

We sit in silence for a time, contemplating these mysteries.

"Is the Red Firewing the most powerful of the Guardians?" I ask.

"The Red Firewing is the messenger of Alayah and leader of the Shijin," Wajid reveals, "but he is not the most powerful. The most powerful is the one who can bend time."

"Lamasura," I say. "The Black Tortoise. If she is the

most powerful, why did she wait for me to open the door to the Haven?"

The corners of Wajid's mouth rise. "Lamasura was testing you, testing the quality of your heart. It is a high honor for a Guardian to *choose* to return to the Haven through a Shakyah."

Anjali delivers a healthy portion of slaycon tail to each of us. Zoya is too focused on Stick to take her piece.

"You should eat, Zoy," Anjali advises. "I'll put some aside for Stick. I have a feeling he'll be hungry when the venom wears off."

"Verily," Wajid confirms. "Slaycon venom makes the victim ravenous when he recovers."

Anjali doubles Stick's portion.

Wajid raises his hunk of meat and mumbles something in the Old Language. We wait until he's done before tucking in to our portions. We feast until there is nothing left of the slaycon's tail but skin and bone.

"If the Twelver only has three marks," I say, picking up the last thread of our conversation, "she isn't ready to use the Axis to summon all Four Guardians any more than Daviyah was."

Wajid nods glumly. "And there is another problem. Abba tells me the Axis of the Ancients was stolen a year ago, right around the time Alayah stopped sending Jin to the Twelver. The Twelver is searching frantically for the Axis, but without success."

"That couldn't have been easy to steal," Zoya says, "considering how important it is. Whoever did it must be a master thief."

Without warning Stick begins to twitch.

"The venom must be wearing off!" Zoya cries.

"Hold him," Wajid advises, "lest he fall."

Zoya wraps a thick arm around her brother's chest. Stick's eyelids flutter. He gasps for air as if rising from deep water.

"Stay calm," Zoya cautions.

"Wha . . . happ'n . . . ?" His words are slurred and muffled, like his mouth is stuffed with food.

"You got bit by a slaycon," Zoya explains. "Thanks to Anjali, it won't bite anything ever again."

Stick strains to lift his head and check his wounded leg. "Whath tha gunk?"

"Medicine from Wajid," Zoya says.

Stick scowls. "You twust tha Magwa?" He hasn't seen Wajid resting against the dark tree trunk, cloaked in evening shadows. "He led usth into a twap. Almosth got usth kilt."

"Shut it, venom brain!" Zoya snaps. "We owe Wajid our lives."

"Ah don owe any Magwa anyth—"

"Stick," I interrupt, "did you see or hear anything

between when the slaycon bit you and now?" I want to know if he went to the Haven, like I did after a slaycon bit me.

"Jus dahkness, like deep shleep. Ah tell y'wha tho, ahm s'hungry ah could eash a whole shlaycon tail by myshelf."

Anjali hands Zoya the cuts of meat she saved for Stick. "This should keep your mouth busy for a while," Anjali says, already tired of Stick's slurred yammering.

Zoya puts the meat between Stick's teeth so he can tear a piece off.

"And there's plenty more on the ground."

"We will not leave this tree until morning," Wajid says.

Stick stops chewing. His eyes inflate with dread upon hearing Wajid's voice.

Wajid isn't bothered by Stick's harsh words. He's too busy being helpful. He reaches into his pack again and extracts three large nets. At first, I think he's prepping to do some fishing in the morning. Instead, Wajid stretches the nets and ties two in the limbs above us.

"For sleeping," he explains.

The Paladin lifts Stick as if he were only a cub and rolls him into a hammock. Stick grumbles until Zoya joins him. Wajid signals for Anjali and me to take the second net as he climbs higher with a hammock of his own. The net reminds me of the few nights I spent in

113

the bunkhouse at the Academy, surrounded by snoozing cadets cocooned in their hammocks.

Anjali squeezes into the net with me. Our bodies press together, faces so close our whiskers interlace. Her muzzle and face are peppered with drops of slaycon blood. I have a sudden urge to lick her face clean. Our eyes meet. I look down, embarrassed.

"Relax, Leo," Anjali says, grinning and displaying rows of pointed teeth. "I'm not going to bite you."

She rolls over. My chest is nestled against her back. We lie like that for a time, listening to the encroaching sounds of night.

"You trust Wajid, don't you, Anjali?" I whisper.

She twists around, pinching my tail in the process. "I'll trust him until I have a reason not to. He reminds me a bit of Kaydan—tough, loyal, attentive, smart."

"I think he's more like Shanti—wise but definitely not someone to mess with."

"A mix of the two," she agrees. She rolls away, pinching my tail a second time.

"Leo wishes he has his own hammock," I say, imitating the slow, thoughtful Maguar way of speaking and avoiding the use of "I."

"Whath goin' ahn over dare?" Stick asks.

"Nothfin, Shtick," I say, prompting a snort of laughter from his sister. "Tahm fo' shleep."

The screech of a slaycon shuts us all up. Suddenly

I'm grateful to be this close to Anjali and for the safety of this hammock.

A large raven is perched in the highest branches of the tree, barely visible against an indigo sky dotted with pinpricks of light. Our eyes meet, and something tells me today's slaycon attack wasn't the only hardship we will face before reaching the Twelver.

And then what?

What will happen when she finds four demonics with Wajid, one who has two Guardian marks?

Grandfather's struggles with Tamir taught me how much rulers dislike rivals, even from their own kind. I can't imagine any of us getting a warm welcome from the Twelver when she discovers a rival Shakyah among the demonics.

Grandfather would tell me not to let emotion cloud my judgment. Likewise, Kaydan would instruct me to put fear aside and stay focused on my mission.

And my mother? What would she say?

Where in this vast, terrifying world is she?

Will I live long enough to meet her and my father?

Or will Tamir's war and the demon destroy everything, including my one chance to find them?

CHAPTER 12

Fighting is impossible when you walk
shoulder to shoulder with your enemy.
— *Sayings of the Ancients*

IN SLEEP, I see Tamir.

He's in the royal courtroom of the castle. I'm relieved he's not sitting on the throne. Not out of respect for Grandfather, but simply because of the painful wound on his backside where Kaydan removed his tail.

Tamir is not alone. His daughter, Amara, is with him. The color of Amara's armor reveals that she has been promoted to the level of general. Anger burns in my gut. Tamir has appointed her to replace Kaydan, who would not surrender to Tamir's treachery.

Father and daughter listen to a soldier speaking hurriedly. Tamir's ears are alert to every word, his expression swinging from disbelief to delight. Amara, for her part, is agitated by the soldier's report.

The soldier is wounded, haggard, and without weapons. His eyes are bloodshot. His hands shake.

The soldier is Mandar.

"So, Prince Leo is a Spinner?!" Tamir crows with disgust and delight. "And he has been captured by the enemy."

"Not just any Spinner, Lord Regent," Mandar gushes. "He spun a terrorizing vision. I can't get it out of my mind! Then a monstrous tortoise appeared, which turned into a leo as black as night. She touched the prince's chest and vanished with a terrible burst of light. While it happened, the enemy kneeled before the prince as though he were a god. But I tell you, Lord Regent, he is a demon!"

"So he is," Tamir says thoughtfully. "You have done well, Mandar. This is far more than I hoped to learn from your quadron's expedition into enemy territory. Have you shared this with anyone else?"

"No one, Lord," Mandar stammers. "I saved these facts for your ears and yours alone."

Tamir glances at Amara.

"Your ears and General Amara's ears, I mean," he corrects sheepishly. He's barely holding himself together.

"Your behavior indicates that you are severely traumatized by exposure to fiction," Tamir determines.

"I just need time to rest, Lord," Mandar pleads, already sensing what's coming.

"Rest will be yours," Tamir says. "We thank you for

your service, Mandar. You are relieved of duty. Permanently."

In a blink, Amara draws a blade and strikes the unarmed Mandar. It happens so quickly I wonder if I am mistaken. Mandar removes all doubt by crumpling to the floor.

Dead.

Tamir steps over Mandar's fallen body. Amara sheaths her blade and follows.

"We can't have him blathering that all over Singara," Tamir says. "We don't want to dampen the spirits of the army before the invasion begins or confuse their loyalties by announcing that the prince is among the enemy."

"However," Amara proposes, "the fact that Leo is a Spinner is a very useful piece of information."

"I share your assessment," Tamir agrees. "That is the one part of Mandar's report that we will share with the Pride. The fact that Leo abandoned his Pride because of the fiction affliction will counter the idea that Leo left because his life was in danger. I don't know why I didn't think of it sooner."

"Reason suggests Leo is the cause of the draycon at the Border Caves," Amara muses, "as well as the wolf who appeared at the Academy. There is no other logical explanation."

"It is a solid hypothesis, Daughter."

"I am preparing a legion of soldiers to kill the dray-con," Amara boasts.

"Don't bother," Tamir says. "You might succeed, but it will cost you many fine soldiers. When our new weapons are ready, you can kill the beast without shedding one drop of Singa blood."

"And what about the great power in the mountain?" Amara asks. She isn't talking about the explosive powder found in the deepest part of the mountain. She means the demon itself. "When will you tell me what it is? And how you plan to use it to wipe out the Maguar?"

"That will be revealed in time," Tamir says. "You will have to see it to believe it."

. . .

I awake to the soft light of morning, with Tamir's words lingering in my mind.

Anjali is gone. So is Wajid.

Stick and Zoya are still curled up in their hammock as one lump of fur. Zoya's nose whistles in that familiar way.

The raven that was perched in the highest branches last night has flown away, replaced, or maybe chased away, by a firewing bird now roosting in the same spot. It's just a common firewing, but the sight of it reminds me of Daviyah.

I roll over. Anjali and Wajid are knee-deep in the river below. They secure the raft with fresh ropes, clean bloodstained weapons, and assemble our gear. The area is littered with slaycon corpses from yesterday's battle, mostly slain by Ursus.

Anjali looks up and flicks her tail. "Wake them. We're moving out."

I crawl out of my hammock and shake the one cradling Zoya and Stick.

"So hungry," Stick moans. His tongue is better at least.

"Plenty of food on the ground," I say.

I descend the tree to Anjali's side. Wajid repacks our stock of weapons.

"I dreamed of Tamir and Amara," I whisper to her. "Mandar told them everything. Then Amara killed him!"

"Maybe it was just a dream," she offers.

"My dreams are different," I say. "They let me see things that have happened, or things that will happen."

"If they killed Mandar," Anjali reflects, "it's because they don't want what he knows spreading around Singara. But it won't stop Tamir from saying you have sided with the enemy to gain more support for himself."

I'm sure she's right. I wish there was something we could do to—

Anjali reads my face. "There's nothing we can do about that, Leo. We must stick to our mission: warn the

Twelver and find your parents. Who knows? Maybe your parents are the key to stopping Tamir and the demon."

Wajid walks by, bearing the bundle of weapons.

"More slaycons on the river today?" I ask.

Wajid shakes his head. "Few places for slaycons to attack downriver."

Anjali hands me a Maguar dagger. The blade is made of bone. "Get some breakfast."

The dagger gleams in the morning sun. It's as sharp, strong, and well-crafted as any Singa weapon. The leather handle welcomes my grip like an old friend.

The nearest slaycon tail has already been partially eaten by Anjali and Wajid. I carve out three portions, devour one, and toss the two others to Zoya and Stick as they approach. Stick uses Zoya as a crutch because of his wounded leg. Otherwise he appears to be back to his old self.

Wajid sloshes through the water and crouches to observe Stick's wound. He sniffs and grunts with satisfaction. Stick recoils at having the Maguar so close.

Wajid offers some twine to Zoya. "Wrap his leg in slaycon hide."

"Will that help it heal?" Stick asks.

"No, but it will prevent slaycons from smelling your blood," Wajid says. "We don't want to tempt them."

"In that case, make it two layers," Stick requests.

Zoya sets Stick on a boulder and wanders off to a

dead slaycon with Wajid's bone dagger. She returns with a few sheets of slaycon hide and wraps them around her brother's leg. Stick winces as she secures them with twine. Then Zoya lifts her brother, wades into the water, and lays him on the raft next to our supplies. Anjali and I follow. Wajid pushes the raft into deeper water, hoists himself onboard, and claims the steering pole.

We travel downriver in silence, which is how Wajid likes it. There is nothing to hear except the warble of water around the raft and a gentle wind in our ears.

Hours pass until the sun is directly overhead. The river widens and hugs the base of a steep hill. Wajid guides the raft to the shore.

"What are you doing?" Anjali snaps. "Why are we stopping?"

"There is something important beneath that hill," Wajid says mysteriously. "Something every Shakyah must see."

Anjali's eyes narrow. "More important than getting to the Twelver as quickly as possible?"

"Stopping here will get us to the Twelver faster," Wajid assures us. "Trust, Anjali."

We drift to a large shelf of rock jutting into the water, a natural dock. Zoya helps Stick to his feet as Anjali and I leap to the rock and onto dry land. Wajid ties the raft to a tree and hands Anjali an unlit torch.

"Come," he says, marching down an overgrown path that snakes along the riverbank and out of sight.

Anjali glances at the raft with its bundles of weapons. "We are leaving everything behind."

"You need your arms free for gathering kindling," Wajid says over his shoulder. "Grab every twig and fallen branch you find along the way."

"I don't see how this is going to get us to the Twelver any faster," Anjali calls, but the Paladin has already gone around a bend.

"What if it's another trap?" Stick warns.

"There was no trap before!" Zoya counters.

"If you'd rather stay here, Stick," Anjali says, hastily strapping a Singa short blade to her hip, "or go back to Singara, I won't stop you."

By the time we catch up with Wajid, Anjali and I each have an armload of branches. For what, we don't know. Zoya carries some too, as best she can manage while lending an arm to her grumbling brother.

Wajid rips vines and brush away from the side of the hill, uncovering a huge stone door built into the steep ground.

"What you are about to see is known only to the Shakyahs and Paladins," he says.

He fits his feet into two slots at the bottom of the door and inserts his hands into two identical slots closer to the top. Only someone as big as Wajid could manage this. His arms and legs shake as he presses down with his toes and fingers. At last, there is a loud clack from behind the door, and the whole thing grinds inward. Daylight drenches the dusty interior, revealing a set of crude stone steps leading down.

The door stops and Wajid hops off.

"Torch," he says to Anjali.

She finds the torch at the bottom of her stack of kindling. Wajid takes two flint rocks from a pouch attached to his belt. He strikes the rocks until a spark jumps and ignites the torch.

"No amount of demonic science can prepare you for what you are about to see." He grabs the blazing torch and strides through the door and down the steps.

We stare at one another, astonished, uncertain, and extremely curious.

"What are we waiting for? Let's go!" Stick exclaims from atop Zoya's stooped back, slapping her shoulder as if she's a karkadann.

My eyes narrow. "You're not worried about a trap anymore?"

"He wants to know if there is anything to steal down there," Zoya comments, stepping gingerly on the stairs after Wajid. "Hidden Maguar treasure or something."

Wajid and his torch are only a blob of light twenty

meters away. The stairs randomly angle this way and that. Down, down, down.

"How many steps so far?" I ask Anjali after a time.

"That's 247 . . . 248 . . . 249 . . . 250 . . . 251 . . ."

"Okay, we get it," Stick interrupts. "You can count."

Suddenly the space changes from the muffled, musty dampness of the stairway to the airy and echoing feel of a much larger area.

Wajid crosses a floor of smooth rock as we reach the bottom and gape around. The only light we have is Wajid's torch, but it's enough for our night vision to make out the dimensions of a vast underground cavern. It's nearly as high as the castle of Singara and twice as wide.

"On second thought, this place gives me the creeps," Stick whispers.

"Me too," Anjali admits, tilting her face to the shadows of the cave's ceiling. "I get the feeling something up there is watching us."

"Cave leeches?" I ask, shuddering at the memory of our last experience with those overgrown, sharp-toothed slugs.

"I don't think so," Stick says, sniffing the air.

"Bring the wood here!" Wajid calls from across the chamber.

"This is a holy place," he says as we huddle around

him. "For thousands of years, our ancestors have come here to confirm and appoint the next Shakyah. It is called the Ritual of Illumination."

"Doesn't your Pride already have a Shakyah?" Stick asks.

"There are fire pits—there, there, there, and there," Wajid says, ignoring Stick and pointing at four different spots on the floor around us. "Divide the branches equally among them."

Wajid brings an armload of thick logs from the far side of the cavern and arranges them on our piles of brush and branches. Someone has already stocked this cavern with wood for burning, but not recently. The wood is well-aged and dry.

"I don't see how this will get us to the Twelver any faster," Anjali protests, her tail waving anxiously over the floor.

"And besides that," Stick says, "if we light these fires, we will all die from the smoke. That would make this the Ritual of Suffocation."

"There is a crack in the center of the ceiling for the smoke to escape," Wajid reveals. "The draft from the door at the top of the stairs drives it out."

He touches the torch to each fire pit. Soon four flaming pillars illuminate the cavern. The fires are set in a square, roughly eight meters apart.

Wajid lifts his face to the ceiling. "Behold."

"Wow," Stick gasps as we gaze upward.

There is a sprawling painting on the cavern's ceiling, with thousands of winged figures reflecting the light of the fires. There are images of leos, like us, and many other creatures, some known, some unknown and beyond imagining. In the center, four majestic creatures, larger and more powerful than the others, are pictured around a blazing sphere of light.

"What is all this?" Stick asks.

"It's the Haven," I state. "Or a painting of it."

"It's so beautiful," Anjali gushes, mesmerized.

It is beautiful, but it's not nearly as stunning as the original. Not even close.

"There are so many," Zoya says.

"The Jin are infinite, like the stars," Wajid says reverently. "They are also infinite in size, shape, and kind. The four in the center, around the light of Alayah, blessed be the name, are the Shijin, the Four Guardians: the Red Firewing, the Black Tortoise, the Green Draycon, and—"

"The White Tiger," Anjali finishes for him.

Wajid nods. "That is correct, Anjali, the White Tiger."

"Who made this?" I ask.

It couldn't have been an easy job. The painter or painters would have had to build a vast network of scaffolding, high enough to reach the ceiling.

"The Ancients," Wajid croons.

"There must be more to the Ritual of Illumination than this," I say. I don't think Wajid brought us here to admire ancient art.

"Better to show than tell," Wajid says. "Lie down here, young one."

He points to a place at the center of the four fires, near our feet. A life-size figure of a Maguar is painted on the floor, arms and legs stretched out. Leather straps are bolted to the stone floor at the wrists and ankles.

Anjali snaps out of her trance, notes the bindings, and snarls a warning to Wajid. "Leo's not getting strapped to the floor. No way."

"To show you what this cave is designed to do," the Paladin says, "he needs to lie there."

"Is this some kind of sick sacrifice to your make-believe god?" Stick says accusingly.

Wajid frowns. "Alayah does not require sacrifices like that. No harm will be done. Wajid has sworn in blood to protect Eliyah."

"You are right about no harm coming to him," Stick says, lifting both of Wajid's daggers. He tosses one to Zoya and keeps the other for himself.

"Nice work, Stick," Anjali says, drawing her own blade.

Wajid's hands instinctively travel to where those

same daggers were attached to his body only minutes ago, one on his chest and the other on his leg.

"Sneaky demonic," Wajid grumbles. "Violence is unnecessary." He looks to me. "What do you say, Eli-yah?"

"I'll do it," I agree quickly, anxious to avoid a fight.

Stick has evened the score if Wajid has something sinister in mind, so why not? I lie down, matching my body to the figure painted on the floor.

"Your companions may apply the straps to your arms and legs," Wajid offers. "Wajid will stand apart and do nothing."

Stick and Zoya fasten the straps. The stone floor is cold, and I shiver despite the fires. The countless glow-ing figures painted on the ceiling are like constellations in an open night sky.

Stick turns to Wajid. "What now?"

"On the far wall is a drum. Strike the drum, slowly at first," Wajid says. "Then gradually make the beat faster and faster."

He's trying to get a fiction to come out of me. He wants to open the door to the Haven.

"Like at the Ritual of Telling yesterday," Stick says, "but why the straps?"

"For his protection. Do it now."

At the mention of protection, Anjali crouches at

my side, blade ready. "I won't let anything happen to you."

"I know," I say. "You're completely obsessed with that."

Stick limps to the edge of the cavern and finds the drum attached to the wall. He pounds out a steady beat. Not bad for his first time making music.

"Breathe deeply, young Shakyah," Wajid counsels me. "Empty your head of thought. Let breath sweep mind."

I inhale and exhale, abandoning thoughts and fears.

Stick's pace increases, and my heartbeat quickens, keeping time with the drum. Soon the familiar feeling begins: stomach turning, a rushing wind between my ears. At the moment when the story usually drops onto my tongue in a mad dash to get free, something different happens. The firelit figures on the ceiling begin to move, stiffly at first, as if waking from sleep.

Then they are no longer crude paintings, but radiant living beings. The light in the center pulses with unearthly power. The creatures drift and swirl like a massive pinwheel revolving on a blazing hub. It's a spectacular and hypnotizing sight.

Stick's head jerks up. "Whoa . . ." His drumbeat slows.

"Don't stop!" Wajid bellows.

Stick refocuses on his task, keeping his head down to avoid distraction.

The lively scene of Jin whirls overhead, arcing and dancing and spinning around the light. One by one, Jin detach from the assembly on the ceiling and dive at me. A few I recognize, like Rukan the wolf; most I don't. Many of them are stranger than anything I could have imagined. Every time one plummets for my head, I startle and attempt to roll away. Now the purpose of the straps is clear.

Fortunately, each Jin stops just before impact and gets yanked back to the swirling assembly on the ceiling, as if attached to an elastic cord.

Anjali stands over me, snarling and swinging at the descending characters with her blade and her claws. Her hands flow right through them like smoke, and the bright figures take no notice of her attacks.

"There is nothing to fear," Wajid calls. "This is only a reflection of what happens in the Haven when a story is about to come through a Shakyah. Only Alayah, blessed be the name, decides which story, and which of the Jin, arrives. Soon, one is chosen."

Anjali studies the vast cloud of orbiting figures. "Some of them aren't moving like the others. They're just paintings on the ceiling."

"Those are the Jin who are already in this world,"

Wajid says, drawing closer. "Most of them came through the Twelver, who refuses to let them return, putting them and our world at grave risk."

At that moment, a glowing squirrel-like creature descends. Instead of getting snatched up to the ceiling like the other Jin, the squirrel plunges into my mouth. Instantly the glowing figures return to their original positions as stationary paintings on the ceiling.

Alayah has chosen.

CHAPTER 13

Love is the only thing that increases when you give it away.
— *Sayings of the Ancients*

MY MOUTH SWELLS as the fiction and its visitor prepare to break into our world. I don't try to hold it in. I part my jaws, and the fiction vision flies out.

> *Once upon a time, there was a mother and her youngling. The youngling did not have a name and was known only as No Name.*
>
> *No Name and his mother were very poor. Each day, No Name would take his bow and some arrows and go into the woods to hunt for food.*
>
> *"Good luck, my son," the mother would say as No Name set out.*

Bright, lifelike images pour off my tongue and fill the cavern. Soon the cave walls slip away, and we are all inside the world of the fiction. The glowing paintings of the Jin twinkle like constellations in the story's after-noon sky.

One day, as No Name hunted the forest for a rabbit or a deer, he was surprised to hear a small crea-ture crying. He looked up and found a silver squirrel sitting on a branch of the tree above his head. The squirrel wept inconsolably. No Name took the squir-rel in his arms, stroked her fur, and assured her that all would be well.

When at last the squirrel's tears stopped flow-ing, No Name learned that she was called Latha, and that this part of the forest was her home. No Name explained how he came to the forest each day in search of food.

"I have seen you many times before," said Latha. "Do you eat squirrels as well as other ani-mals?"

No Name's whiskers drooped, ashamed to admit that this was true.

Latha said, "You have been very kind to me today. Instead of seeing me as food, you have com-forted me, so I am going to help you in return."

The little squirrel jumped out of No Name's hands and said, "Follow me!"

The youngling followed Latha through the for-est, struggling to keep up, for the squirrel moved with surprising speed. After several hours, they reached a cliff overlooking a beautiful green valley.

"Climb down this cliff," said the squirrel. "At the bottom you will find the Goose Queen. She will ask you three questions. If you answer them correctly, she will reward you."

Latha climbed onto No Name's shoulder and whispered the answers to the Goose Queen's questions. Then Latha scampered away.

No Name made a rope out of vines and lowered himself over the cliff. As soon as No Name's feet touched the ground, the Goose Queen was there to meet him.

"I have three questions for you!" she honked. "If you answer correctly, you will be handsomely rewarded. If you do not, I will turn you into one of the animals you hunt! The predator will become prey!"

No Name shuddered at the thought, but he agreed. The Goose Queen looked at a nearby cherry tree.

"How many cherries are growing on this tree?" she asked.

No Name closed his eyes and recited the answer he had been given. "There are as many cherries on that tree as there are feathers on your back."

The Goose Queen honked approvingly and then asked, "Where is the middle of the earth?"

"You are standing on the middle of the earth," said No Name, with a bit more confidence. "Because every place is the middle of the earth."

Using her beak, the Goose Queen pointed to two walnuts on the ground. "Which of these two walnuts is the heaviest?"

No Name tossed both nuts into a nearby stream. One floated on the surface of the water, while the other sank.

"The one that sank is the heavier of the two, Your Majesty."

The queen could not deny that No Name had answered all three questions correctly. She honked and gave No Name a chest full of treasure as his prize. He and his mother would never be poor or hungry again.

No Name climbed up the cliff face, with the treasure strapped to his back. He ran into the forest to thank Latha for her kindness. When No Name found the little squirrel, she was crying once again. Her head rested on her front paws as tears dampened the ground.

"Why are you sad?" asked No Name.

"I used to be a princess until the Goose Queen turned me into a squirrel for failing to answer her questions correctly. The only thing that will set me free is a drop of Emerald Water from the lake in the draycon's cave at the top of the mountain."

No Name was so grateful to Latha for saving him and his mother from a life of poverty, he pledged to bring a drop of the magic water to his new friend right away. No Name used some of the treasure to buy armor and the sharpest and strongest blade from the blacksmith. Then he climbed the mountain where the feared draycon made its home.

As he reached the cave, No Name was attacked by two giant serpents guarding the entrance. The fight was fierce, but No Name defeated the serpents and threw their hissing bodies over the edge of the mountain.

Deep inside the cave, the draycon stirred, awakened by the sound of the battle and of his dying guards. He slithered out of the cave to learn what had happened. Meanwhile, No Name slipped inside, found the underground lake, and filled his canteen with the Emerald Water. Then he ran from the lair and scurried down the mountain to find Latha.

"I have the Emerald Water!" he told his friend, raising the canteen triumphantly. No Name poured some of the water into his open palm. Latha hurried down from the tree and drank eagerly from No Name's hand.

An explosion of light illuminated the shady forest. Latha the squirrel was no more. Now a warrior princess stood before No Name, dressed in pearl-like clothing and armor.

"Thank you! Thank you!" said Latha. No Name bowed to the princess and escorted her to the palace. When the Kahn saw his beautiful long-lost daughter, he was overjoyed.

"You are a brave youngling!" the Kahn said to No Name. "How may I reward you? Whatever you ask will be yours!"

"I do not need anything, Your Majesty," No Name replied humbly. "Seeing you and Latha so happy is all the reward I need."

"I know how you can reward him, Father," Latha said. "You can give him a name."

The Kahn clapped his hands. "An excellent idea! From this day forward, you shall no longer be known as No Name. You will be called Eesak, which means 'laughter' in the Old Language, because you have turned our tears into joy!"

The lively fiction vision fades until we are all in the dim cavern again. In fact, we never left. The fires have dwindled to a few flames dancing over clumps of hot coals. I'm gasping for breath as I regain control of my mouth and vocal cords.

"And now, young Shakyah," Wajid purrs, "we await the arrival of the mighty Jin who will escort and protect us for the remainder of our voyage to Elyon."

Anjali hurries to undo the straps binding me to the floor. Wajid's eyes dart about the cave, searching for the Jin.

Will it be Eesak? The draycon? The serpent guards or . . .

"Over here," a tiny voice squeaks.

I peer into the damp shadows behind me. The wispy figure of a silver squirrel approaches, no bigger than my foot. It is Latha. She is in the halfway state, not fully in this world.

"This is the 'mighty Jin' who will protect us?" Stick jeers. "We're doomed."

"Welcome, Latha," I say.

At the sound of her name, the little squirrel becomes as real and solid as the rest of us.

Latha shakes her tail and offers a bow. "It is my pleasure to serve you, Eliyah. May I have your hand?"

I reach out. Latha leaps into my palm and climbs to my shoulders. She perches there, fuzzy tail wrapped around my neck like a scarf. She smells of flowers and dew-kissed grass.

Wajid extinguishes three of the fires by separating the embers with his blade. The once-bright paintings on the cavern's ceiling fade to a glimmer. Wajid leaves one fire burning and adds a fresh log.

"We're leaving," Anjali asserts. "Why not put them all out?"

Wajid settles onto the floor near the remaining fire. "We will stay a bit longer."

"We've been here long enough!" Anjali protests. "Every minute we waste down here gives Tamir more time to prepare for war."

"We will wait for one or more Paladins to come," Wajid says, "most likely with a team of warriors and some of the Twelver's Jin. They will take us to Elyon faster and safer than we could travel on our own."

Anjali is aghast. "Paladins!"

"Of course," Wajid replies. "The smoke rising from these fires is visible in Elyon. As Wajid said before, this cave and these fires are only used to confirm a new Shakyah. Paladins will come to investigate."

"You tricked us!" Anjali fumes. "We are not in a strong defensive position down here! We need more weapons! We need to take cover!" She draws her blade and bounds to the stairs.

"Listen to Wajid, Anjali!" Wajid calls. "It is better to remain here. In daylight, they will clearly see that you are demonics and kill you without a second thought. They might even kill this young Shakyah if they do not see the Guardian markings first. Down here, where the light is dim, your identity will be hidden, and Wajid will have a chance to explain why you walk our lands."

Anjali pauses at the foot of the stairs. "Is that really the best way?" she huffs.

"It is not only the best way. It is the only way," he continues. "Wajid is a stranger to the Twelver. Walking into Elyon with demonics and without escorts known to her will bring a swift death to all of us. Kaw was not wrong about that."

"From now on, you need to tell us what you are doing," Anjali admonishes, "before you do it. No more surprises. Is that clear?"

Wajid keeps silent.

"Is that clear?!" Anjali repeats, more forcefully.

"You are worthy of the highest respect, Anjali, but you are not in Singara anymore," the Paladin says coldly. "There is much you do not know about our ways. Wajid is doing what is best to protect you and, especially, the young Shakyah among us."

Anjali does not sheathe her blade as she wanders back to the fire and stares down at the Paladin. Big as Wajid is, she is only a head or two taller than he is while sitting.

"I don't need *your* protection," she asserts. "And I was assigned to protect him long before you."

"Both points are true," Wajid affirms. "And because our missions are the same, we should not quarrel."

"Wajid speaks the truth, Anjali," Latha says, pronouncing her name like Wajid does.

Anjali relaxes a bit. "Then let's start working as a team," she says, "and be open and honest with each other."

"In that case, there is something you should know before our escorts from Elyon arrive," Wajid says, poking the fire with his dagger to quicken the flames. "We are not the Maguar."

CHAPTER 14

The most dangerous enemy is the idea that we have enemies.
— *Sayings of the Ancients*

OUR EARS RING with Wajid's announcement.
Did we hear that right?

They are not the Maguar?

Who are they, then?

And where are the Maguar?

Wajid is not blind to our stupefied expressions.

"We are the *Panthera*," he explains. "Demonics are Panthera also. At least you were in the days of the Ancients. Then, six hundred years ago, you rejected Alayah, blessed be the name, and split away from the Pride, calling yourselves the Singa."

"Then who are the Maguar?" Stick demands. Zoya rolls her eyes.

"Maguar"—Wajid spits the word out like a piece of rotten meat—"is a name invented by the demonics to describe a race of less intelligent, bloodthirsty savages. Yet, except for the markings on our fur, we are the

same. It would be best if you never say that name again, not to the Paladins who will soon arrive, not to anyone in Elyon, and most especially not in the hearing of the Twelver."

"Forgive us for insulting you and your Pride," I say. "Yet everyone in your Pride calls us 'demonics.' That's not a compliment."

"Demonics is the right name for those who live beside the mountain where the demon is trapped, who deny Alayah, and who see themselves as the superior race. Creating division and hostility between the Prides is the demon's doing and part of his plan to get free. Calling you 'demonics' is not an insult. It is . . . as you like to say . . . a fact."

"I don't get what you have against facts," Stick states. "Facts are truth. Fiction is just . . . fiction!"

Latha gasps.

"No offense to the squirrel," Stick adds.

"That is stinking demonic thinking," Wajid counters. "There is more truth in fiction than in facts. There is more power in faith than in knowledge."

Stick holds up his hands as if blocking these ideas from entering his brain. "You can stop right there. We're not real big on the faith thing."

"Spoken like a true demonic," Wajid chortles. "Yet faith is the most basic thing there is. Faith is the crying of a cub for its mother. Faith is one candle in overwhelming darkness. Faith is the light of Alayah in every living thing. Every breath, and every step we take, is an act of faith. Faith is life itself. That is what the Ancients teach."

Latha leaps from my shoulder to the floor. "They are almost here!" she says, tail quivering.

Stick angles his ears forward. "I don't hear anything."

"Jin never lie, and you won't hear them at all," Wajid says. "How many, Latha?"

Latha becomes deathly still, ears erect. "Eight. And three large Jin."

Wajid stands and sheathes his blade. "Sit there, between the fire and Wajid. With the fire behind you, you will be little more than shadows. With any luck, the smoke will mask your scents. Wajid will do the talking. You will say nothing."

"We understand," Anjali says.

"And remove your blade, Anjali," Wajid advises. "They will not hesitate to kill an armed demonic."

Anjali looks as if she'd rather pluck out her claws than surrender her blade.

"Keep it nearby, but do not touch it. Latha is all the protection we need."

Stick snorts at that. Anjali considers the little Jin on the cavern floor before untying the blade at her hip.

Wajid removes his weapons, then searches the bag slung over his shoulder and tosses Stick's torso cover to me.

"Put it on," he says.

I wiggle into the garment.

"When they come, Wajid will seem different," Wajid intones. "Trust that whatever Wajid says and does, it is for your protection."

"Why are we trusting him?" Stick murmurs as we huddle together on the cavern's floor. "What if he's using us? What if he's going to hand us over to the Twelver as a gift to make his arrival smoother? As in, 'Look, Twelver, I didn't save your brother, but here are four demonics instead! All good?'"

I won't admit it out loud, but part of me has been wondering the same thing.

Without warning, the scent of the enemy gathers in my nostrils.

Latha climbs to my shoulder. "They are here," she whispers.

Silent black shapes drift like shadows before Wajid. They weave between one another, making it impossible to know how many are down here. Suddenly, a torch blazes up and gets thrown to the floor at Wajid's feet.

Wajid holds his ground.

The torch illuminates a single Panthera, even larger and taller than Wajid. He wears a head covering made of animal bones. Armor adorned with draycon horns, slay-con teeth, and firewing feathers covers his shoulders and chest. A broad belt shields his stomach and supports several weapons. His right hand clutches a large curved club, similar to Wajid's. His left hand bears a bone dagger. More draycon horns of various sizes are strapped to his arms, knees, and feet.

He is, in a word, terrifying.

His throat rumbles a warning.

Where the others have disappeared to, I can't say. They must be somewhere down here, lurking in the darkness, waiting.

"Do not be afraid," Latha whispers, no doubt smelling my fear scent rising like steam. "I will protect you."

It's a kind thing to say, but not much comfort coming from one as small as Latha.

"*Halaylu.*" The Paladin's voice is like thunder, echoing around the cavern.

"*Halaylu Alayah,*" Wajid replies calmly.

"This is a holy place," the Paladin says. "Trespassers deserve death."

"It is not trespassing for a Paladin," Wajid counters, tapping his chest.

The big Paladin cocks his head and studies Wajid. "*Ma shimkha.*"

"*Shmi Wajid, eved Shakyah Daviyah!*" Wajid announces with pride.

"Liar!" the big Paladin accuses. "Wajid was captured by the demonics twenty-five years ago."

Wajid lifts his chin. "The Lost Paladin has returned."

I don't know how much more evidence this overgrown Paladin needs. Wajid is nearly the same size. He speaks the Old Language. He knows how to open the door to this sacred cavern. These two should be fast friends.

The Paladin sniffs the air and points his weapon at us, clustered together behind Wajid. "A true Paladin would not desecrate the Cavern of the Ancients with demonics!"

"They helped Wajid escape. They have an important message for the Twelver," Wajid argues.

"More lies!" the Paladin rages. "We will kill you and burn your bodies to purify this sacred place."

His arms fan out, and six fighters emerge, three to his left and three to his right. They were concealed behind the massive Paladin, waiting for this signal. Each bears a weapon or two. In this light, they are little more than shadows. They crouch low, ready to pounce when the order comes.

"One of these demonics is a Shakyah," Wajid asserts. "It is forbidden to harm a Shakyah, or for one Paladin to kill another."

"There are no Shakyahs among the demonics!" the big Paladin bellows, enraged by the idea.

"With Alayah, all things are possible," Wajid says.

"If there *is* a Shakyah in this sacred chamber, there must be some Jin here as well," the Paladin responds. "Those Jin should come forth now."

I don't have *some* Jin. I have only one. And a very small one at that.

"That's my cue," Latha breathes into my ear.

Latha crawls down my back beneath the torso cover. She skitters unnoticed around the five of us and stares up at the towering Paladin.

"There are no Jin here. And you are not Wajid, the Lost Paladin," the Paladin sneers with satisfaction. "Abdu will cleanse this holy place."

Abdu raises his clublike weapon, preparing to strike Wajid across the face.

Will Wajid allow himself, and all of us, to be slaughtered by this thug?

"Look more closely, Abdu," Latha squeaks at his feet.

Abdu pauses, searching for the source of this warning. Finding none, he snarls and swings at Wajid.

"No!" I yell, despite Wajid's order to stay quiet.

In that moment, an unknown silver-pelted leo rises up from the floor, dressed in pearl-like armor and radiant clothing. From what I can tell, she has no weapons. Her moves are unnaturally quick, flashes of silver and white in the dim firelight. She grabs Abdu's attacking arm and redirects his motion until he is off balance. In a blink, she steps behind the big Paladin and sweeps his legs, sending him crashing to the floor.

The other Pantheras are spooked to see their leader taken down by this stranger who has appeared seemingly from nowhere. The silver warrior vanishes, and Latha the squirrel is in her place. She scrambles up one of the other Panthera warriors. Suddenly the silver leo is on his shoulders, causing him to collapse under her weight.

Latha switches back and forth, from squirrel to leo, with dizzying speed. As the next Panthera swings a long dagger, Latha changes into a squirrel in mid-pounce. The enemy's blade slices nothing but air. Latha reappears as a leo and scores a rapid double hand strike to her opponent's ribs and chin. He falls, and she finishes off the other attackers in the same way, morphing in the blink of an eye, too fast for her opponents to defend. As the final Panthera is defeated, Abdu sits up, rubbing his head.

The entire battle is over in less than ten seconds.

Wajid has not moved.

"Surely you have heard of the Jin called Latha," he says to the jumble of groaning bodies, "from the days of Shakyah Daviyah."

Abdu and his fighters kneel before Latha, who has resumed her squirrel form. They bow until their foreheads touch the floor. One topples over from exhaustion.

"May Alayah forgive us, Latha," Abdu says graciously, "for not seeing you sooner."

"You are forgiven, noble Paladin," Latha says in her high-pitched squeal. "It is good to be reminded how to move in this world."

Abdu's troops struggle to their feet, winded and woozy.

"You came through one of these demonics?" Abdu inquires.

"Verily," Latha confirms.

"It is impossible, and yet it must be so," Abdu concedes. "Jin never lie."

Abdu dips his head to Wajid. "Abdu was only a cub during the Last Campaign, but the stories about Wajid, the Lost Paladin, are well known. The Twelver might welcome you, but she cannot easily accept four demonics on our lands, or a rival Shakyah who is also a demonic. The very idea is outrageous."

"It will be less outrageous than you imagine, my brother," Wajid responds, "when the whole truth is revealed."

CHAPTER 15

No one is more dangerous to others
than one who has lost self-respect.
— *Sayings of the Ancients*

ABDU SPEAKS to the Panthera warriors with his hands. Following the Paladin's directions, they extinguish the fire, studying us with fascination and disgust. I suppose we should get used to that. If Singa soldiers brought a group of Pantheras into Singara, the enemy would be met with hostility. The entire Pride would have their backs up for days. No doubt Tamir would treat them terribly.

Will anything less happen when we arrive in Elyon?

We climb the long, winding flight of stone steps. Wajid and Abdu take the lead. My quadron trails behind, Stick once again leaning on Zoya to take some weight off his damaged leg. Six growling Panthera warriors are at our tails. Soon the stairs brighten with daylight, and new fur-raising scents fill the narrow passageway.

"Draycon," Stick whispers, his voice tight with

terror. "That's a scent I won't ever forget. And something more. Two other scents I don't recognize."

"Me neither," I say. Their scents are mingled with traces of honey-sweetness, the signature smell of Jin.

Latha leaps to Stick's shoulder. "More Jin who are servants, and prisoners, of the Twelver."

Abdu and Wajid speak in a combination of words and hand language, perhaps to keep their conversation hidden from us. Wajid has a new spring in his step, despite the fact that Abdu nearly bashed his brains out a few minutes ago.

Outside, the air is warm, and the sun feels especially bright compared to the damp darkness of the cavern. Instead of going down the path to the river, where our raft and stash of weapons await, we follow a different trail that winds up the hill. Anjali glances over her shoulder, hating to leave all those weapons behind.

The scent of Jin is overwhelming. My blood turns icy in my veins.

The hilltop reveals a draycon. No surprise there. With a horned head on a serpentine neck, powerful body wrapped in scaly armorlike skin, long tail covered in spikes, this enormous lizard is nearly identical to Nagarjuna, the draycon who came through one of my fictions at the Border Caves in Singara. Nagarjuna was under my command. This one came through the Twelver. There's no way to know what the monster's orders are.

The other two creatures become visible as we crest the hill.

One stands on four legs as thick as trees. Its wide forehead is like a boulder. Two curved horns extend from the mouth, and there is a long nose like a fifth leg that nearly reaches the ground. It is the same kind of creature that came to us as a Shifter when we first arrived in the realm of the Panthera.

The third Jin is smaller than the other two: a graceful reptilian creature about twice the size of a slaycon but not nearly as ugly.

The first two beasts have seating platforms strapped on their backs. The smaller one is fitted with a saddle for one rider. None of them shows much interest in us.

Latha hops to my shoulder. "It is Nimshook, Kaitan, and Tula!"

"You know them?" Anjali says.

"I know all the Jin, Anjali."

"Are they friendly?" Stick asks.

"Friendly or fierce," Latha replies. "Depending on the will and needs of the Twelver."

The draycon's ears slant our way. The terrible horn-covered head glides to within centimeters of my face. I tremble and try not to scream.

"Hello, old friend," Latha says, leaping to the beast's snout.

"Latha," the draycon moans. "Dear Latha. You are a welcome sight to these weary eyes."

"They seem so sad," I say.

"She has been in this world too long," Latha answers bitterly. "Tula, too. They are homesick, weak, and sulky. If they don't return to the light of Alayah soon, they will become Shifters. Shifters stop at nothing until they reach Hasatamara's prison and attempt to free him."

A new Panthera appears from the other side of the draycon, bringing the enemy total to eight, just as Latha predicted.

Abdu addresses his team in their hand speech. They break into two groups. One group takes me and Stick to the draycon, while the other leads Zoya, Anjali, and Wajid to Kaitan, the big boxy creature with the boulder-like forehead and long nose. Anjali growls and shows her claws at being separated from me.

"I'll be okay," I assure her. "They're taking us to the Twelver. That means they don't plan on killing us. Yet."

"Prepare to receive passengers," Abdu says to both beasts. Nimshook rests her horned head on the ground. Wajid flicks his tail, indicating we should climb her neck to the riding platform.

"Go on," Latha urges. "Nimshook is kindhearted. She will not harm you."

I turn to Stick. "Think you can make it with your bad leg?"

I place a foot on a horn jutting out from above Nimshook's mouth like an exterior tooth and use it as a step. I gaze into her unhappy eyes for a moment, eyes that are bigger than my entire body, then scamper on all fours up the long, thick neck to the platform. There are six seats here, with ropes to fasten the riders.

From this height, I can peer far into the distance, where a sloping tower reaches up from the horizon. That must be Elyon and the Temple of the Shakyahs.

Stick and four of the Panthera warriors join me on the platform. Stick slumps into a seat, grateful to rest his injured leg. Abdu climbs onto the smaller reptile-like Jin. He takes the lead and lets out a quick roar. The three Jin saunter down the hill. There are no reins on these creatures, perhaps because it would be impossible to steer them, big and brawny as they are. Or perhaps they are simply following orders from the Twelver to obey Abdu.

Abdu's Jin takes the lead and sets a brisk pace. For an hour or more, we bound over streams, zigzag between forest trees, and barrel through fields at high speed. In addition to tying the ropes around my waist, I hold on to my seat to keep from flopping around.

Stick throws up.

Twice.

The Pantheras with us are disgusted. Fortunately, Stick has the sense to hang his head over the side of the seating platform. Otherwise, they would gladly pitch him off without a second thought. From this height and at this speed, that would be the end of Stick.

For most of this harrowing trip, the Shakyah temple is hidden behind trees and rolling hills. The final mount offers a stunning view of the entire river city of Elyon, built on the high cliff banks of two rivers merging and flowing into the sea. The Temple of the Shakyahs is nestled on a rocky chip of land where the rivers meet. The curved temple tower rises up like a single claw scratching the sky. The city can't be more than a kilometer away.

I don't see anything resembling a wall or any other structures designed for defense. If Tamir and the Royal Army of Singara were able to advance this far into enemy territory, Elyon would be easy to conquer. That being the case, why wasn't it overthrown centuries ago? And how did our two races become separated long before that?

Abdu descends his Jin and hops onto Nimshook's head.

"Lift me, Nimshook."

The Jin draycon extends her neck to the limit. Abdu takes a piece of polished metal from his belt and uses it to send flashes toward Elyon. Moments later, beams blink from the peak of the temple in reply.

"Brother!" Wajid calls to Abdu. "You have signaled that the Lost Paladin will return to Elyon tonight!"

Nimshook lowers Abdu to the ground as Wajid climbs down Kaitan.

"Brother Wajid should receive a proper welcome," Abdu says cheerily. "Abdu did not, however, say anything about demonics among us. That is why we will wait until night before entering Elyon. With the cloak of darkness, Abdu can get them as far as the temple. After that, their protection cannot be guaranteed."

"Their destiny is in the hands of Alayah," Wajid says, "blessed be the name."

My quadron dismounts from the two Jin and assembles on the ground. The Panthera fighters gather around, weapons drawn.

Anjali's pelt bristles.

"You don't need to guard us," she snaps. "We aren't going anywhere."

Abdu's hands give a silent command to the warriors. Three immediately back off. The one Anjali spoke to doesn't give up so easily. Anjali stares him down until they are both hissing at each other.

Her opponent's hands stab the air with a series of gestures before he storms away.

"What did he say, Latha?" I ask.

"Foolish demonics," Latha translates. "The Twelver

sees everything. She knows you are coming. You are nothing but bait to her."

Without warning, the Jin who served as Abdu's mount screeches and shakes uncontrollably before tumbling to the ground. He thrashes about, churning up the earth.

"Get back! Hurry!" Wajid directs.

"May Alayah have mercy!" Latha says.

"What's happening to him?" I exclaim. "Can we help?" The poor Jin is suffering horribly. His gray skin takes on a copper glow. His eyes roll into his head until they show only white.

"Tula is shifting!" Latha explains. "He must be destroyed before the transformation is complete."

"Nimshook and Kaitan!" Abdu commands. "Kill Tula!"

We bound away as Nimshook and Kaitan roar and pounce on their fellow Jin. The battle is brutal and swift. Given his tortured state and smaller size, Tula is easily defeated. Kaitan finishes Tula off by stomping on his skull with a sickening crunch of bone.

Kaitan and Nimshook dip their heads before Tula's corpse and wail. They calm themselves only when Tula's broken body fades to a ghostly version of itself before disappearing altogether.

"Ordinarily, Jin will not harm one another," Latha informs us. "That changes when they shift. Though it breaks our hearts, it must be done. Tula is in the light of Alayah now. He is free."

Anger boils up within me. "How many of the Twelver's Jin are this close to becoming Shifters?" I ask.

"It is hard to say, but I imagine dozens are only days away from the same fate," Latha reveals. "Tula was fortunate to be destroyed. The Twelver keeps a number of Shifters locked up beneath the temple, not far from where she keeps her Jin."

"Why?"

"I shudder to think of what purpose she might have in mind," Latha says, "but I can tell you this, Eliyah: no good will come of it."

CHAPTER 16

Forgiveness is the most powerful weapon of all. It
disarms opponents and replaces hostility with hope.
— *Sayings of the Ancients*

"REST NOW," WAJID ADVISES. "While you have
the chance."

"Sounds good to me," Stick says, yawning, already a
mound of fur in the tall grass.

Zoya lies next to him, contemplating the clouds
passing like giant white beasts on a silent journey.

Latha clings to my shoulder.

"Should I open the door for you, Latha? Do you
want to go home?"

"I will speak the truth," she says, "as the truth is
the only thing I can speak: My heart yearns for the light
of Alayah more than Wajid yearns to be in Elyon. But
my service to you is not yet complete. I will tell you
when the time comes. And you need not worry about
me becoming a Shifter. That point will not come for
years."

"These other Jin, Nimshook and Kaitan, is there a

way to get them back to the Haven? Could . . . another Shakyah . . . help them?"

"Your heart is kind," Latha affirms, "but only the Shakyah who brings a Jin can send that Jin home. The Twelver is their master. They must obey her until she decides to free them."

Or until they become Shifters and make a beeline for Hasatamara.

I glance at Nimshook and Kaitan. The draycon's metallic scales and horns glow and shimmer in the setting sun. Kaitan's huge bony head hovers over the ground. His long nose rips up the grass that covers this hilltop, and stuffs it into his mouth.

"What she's doing to these Jin is cruel," I say, anger flaring up in me once again.

"And that is why Alayah has not sent her any more Jin for over a year," Latha says.

"If Alayah is so powerful and so good," I ask, "couldn't Alayah free the Jin?"

"Alayah could do that in an instant!" Latha exclaims. "But you must understand, despite the Twelver's faults, Alayah loves her as much as any creature. Alayah wants the Twelver to decide to send the Jin home for herself."

"If she hasn't by now, what would change her mind?"

"You are not the first to wonder about that," Latha

says. "Rest your mind, Eliyah, and sleep. We have a long night ahead of us."

. . .

I wake to a foot nudging my ribs.

Abdu hovers over me like a dark statue against the evening sky. The retreating sun paints bright orange clouds along the horizon.

Wajid reclines on the hillside, gazing at the lights of Elyon winking at us like stars clustered along the high river cliffs.

"Come!" Abdu calls behind us. "It is time."

Latha returns to my shoulder. We mount the two Jin in the same arrangement as before. This time Abdu rides with us. Stick has a hard time motivating himself to return to Nimshook's back. It's not just his damaged leg that causes him to hesitate. His first ride on a draycon's back didn't agree with his stomach.

"It's not far," Zoya coaxes. "And since you already puked your guts out, there's probably nothing left."

"Thanks, Zoy," Stick grouses. "Nice to know you care."

Before the Jin venture down the hill toward Elyon, Abdu addresses our group. "On Abdu's signal, demonics will lie flat on the riding platform, so that we may pass into Elyon without causing a disturbance. Let us hope the wind stays calm, to keep the demonics' stench away from the keen noses of our Pride."

Nimshook and Kaitan descend the hill side by side as they make for the river city. The land flattens, and most of Elyon drops below the horizon. Only the Temple of the Shakyahs, that grand tower arching to the sky, remains visible.

When we are a quarter of a kilometer from Elyon, Abdu signals and we lie down, hidden from view by the sideboards of the riding platform. Stick and I lie shoulder to shoulder. We slipped out of Singara in much the same way.

That time we were covered with trash.

This time, according to our escorts, we *are* the stinking trash.

I nudge Stick. "You okay?"

He nods, although his fur is standing up and his fear scent blankets us both.

"Don't worry," I say. "We have Latha on our side."

"One unarmed changeling squirrel against thousands of Maguars?" he scoffs. "Sure, why worry?"

"Ease up, Stick. We've made it this far. And don't call them Maguars, at least not out loud."

"They will always be Maguars to me!" Stick snaps. "Just like we will always be demonics to them. Don't get too cozy with them, Leo. They are the enemy. They hate us. They might skin us alive and eat us to celebrate Wajid's return. Did you ever think of that?"

"Don't be silly," I reply. "They would never *eat* us."
Stick's frosty stare makes me question my own words.
"Would they, Latha?"

She does not reply.

"Latha?"

"I can only speak the truth," she says meekly, "and
the truth is they have eaten your kind . . . once or
twice . . . long, long ago."

"Not surprised!" Stick says smugly. "Your fiction
visions are the only reason we are still alive, Leo. Which
means *you* don't have anything to worry about. You are
the grandson of the great Shakyah Daviyah. You share
their blood. You are a Shakyah!"

"We are a quadron," I remind him. "We live or die
together."

"Good luck explaining that to them," Stick says,
rolling away from me. "Mark my words, Leo, they will
kill Zoya, Anjali, and me as soon as they realize we are
just average demonics."

I peek between the sideboards of the riding platform. We are passing through a village of simple earthen
huts spaced out along a quilt of farm fields. Slaycons
with harnesses prowl the fields, perhaps keeping watch
for deer, rabbit, or other animals that might snack on
their crops.

"Look!" I say to Stick. "The crops feed their Pride

in two ways. They produce vegetables, and they attract prey to be killed by slaycons. They probably also keep the wild slaycons away. Smart!"

Stick refuses to look.

Nimshook descends a steep trail zigzagging to the river. Innumerable boxlike dwellings are tightly packed and stacked on the sloping cliffs of each river. The dwellings, more elaborate than they appeared from the hilltop, are connected by a network of ladders, walkways, and leaping platforms. Here and there, I see water collecting in pools from streams and waterfalls that tumble down the cliffs to the rivers below.

But there is no one in sight.

The city is empty, deserted.

Halfway down, the uninhabited city is explained. Below the city dwellings, a long, wide road hugs the river. The road is crammed with thousands of eager faces waiting to see Wajid, the Lost Paladin. They watch in perfect stillness and silence, eyes gleaming like coins in firelight, as our procession follows the switchback trail all the way down to the river road. Wajid kneels on Kaitan's broad head, savoring the sights, sounds, and smells of home.

The ancient temple is built on a massive mount of rock where the rivers merge. The thick walls of the temple are lined with figures dressed in white robes. I recognize them from my dream as the Paladins, the brawny Panthera who serve as protectors and servants of the Shakyah. Unlike Wajid and Abdu, none of them are dressed for battle. Perhaps they wear armor and carry weapons only outside the temple grounds.

As we near the river, the Paladins launch into a series of roars and huffs, mixed with words from the Old Language. Their song is strong and rhythmic, bouncing around the river canyon like the pounding drum in the Cavern of the Ancients.

My heart begins to race in time with the beat.

Soon everyone in the river city joins the chant, from the tiniest cub to the most withered elder, until the whole chasm is shaking with sound. Wajid takes it all in, tears staining his muzzle.

Meanwhile, I'm struggling to keep my heart rate in check, to prevent a story from barreling out of my mouth and giving us all away.

Stick, wise to what's happening, says, "Not now, Leo!"

The crowd moves in harmony with the rhythm, swaying their arms, legs, and tails in the most fascinating ways. Even Abdu and the Panthera warriors riding with us join in. I have read about dancing in the ancient books in Galil's secret reading room, but I never imagined seeing it for myself.

The only thing more bizarre than the dancing is how relaxed everyone is in the presence of Kaitan and

Nimshook. Even the littlest cubs show no signs of fear. I've spent my entire life running from Jin who came to me, terrified they would expose my disease, horrified of the harm they would cause if I said their names and made them real. But in Elyon, the sight of Jin is as normal and everyday as the steady presence of the rivers.

Here and there among the crowd, fiction visions swirl into the air, released by Truth Tellers caught up in the spell of the Pride's music. Soon dozens of fictions are playing out over the crowd. The visions are dim and smoky, but they add to the festive atmosphere.

Latha clings to my head and whispers words from the Old Language in my ears. Immediately, my heart slows, and whatever fiction was about to push through retreats.

The grand bridge to the temple is lined with more white-robed Paladins, all feverishly dancing and chanting as we pass over the river. The tower isn't the only structure on the temple grounds. There is an imposing square building around the tower like a wall, and a stout castle-like building at the tower's base.

We enter the temple grounds through a high arch. Nimshook has to hunch down and waddle her way through. Wajid and Abdu dismount as the warriors bow and walk backwards out of the temple and across the bridge. If regular Panthera troops aren't permitted in the main section of the temple and can't turn tail on the temple as they leave, the Paladins will be horrified to discover demonics here.

We enter the outer structure, where Wajid and Abdu shed their battle garb, along with their weapons, and place them in cabinets by the wall.

Wearing only skins around their waists, Abdu and Wajid slip into white robes waiting on hooks. We move inward, toward the tower, arriving in a courtyard with a sunken garden adorned with fragrant flowers and medicinal plants. All at once, the deafening chants halt, and fifty or so white-robed Paladins parade like ghosts into the temple garden.

Wajid kneels in the center of the garden and weeps. His fellow Paladins encircle him, purring and stroking him with their tails. Some of them are not much older than we are, while others claim many more years than Wajid.

Wajid bows until his forehead touches the ground. His fingers dig into the homeland.

From our hidden roost on Nimshook's back, Wajid looks like the center of a flower surrounded by rings of white petals. After several minutes, he rises to his feet.

"The Lost Paladin has returned," an elder Paladin

purrs. "Welcome home, Brother Wajid. As the Ancients say, 'There is no homecoming like the return of a brother who is lost and counted as dead.'"

"Brother Jakobah," Abdu says to the elder, "out of respect for your welcome, there is something you must know. The Lost Paladin was not alone when we found him."

My pelt bristles. He's warming up to reveal us, right here in the heart of enemy territory!

Jakobah regards Abdu with mild interest, waiting for more.

Abdu takes a breath. He straightens his back and widens his stance as if bracing himself for impact. "Wajid was found in the Cavern of the Ancients . . . with four young . . . demonics."

The other Paladins step back in shock, hissing and scratching the air with their claws at the mere mention of demonics on their lands and in one of their most sacred places.

Jakobah alone remains calm. "That is unexpected and troubling news. Certainly these demonics are now dead by your own claws, Brother Abdu, and the sacred cavern has been purified."

"No, Brother Jakobah," Abdu says cautiously. "They live."

Tension swells in the courtyard. Tails that comforted Wajid moments ago now lash with fury.

Jakobah's jaw tightens. His lips curl into a snarl. "Where are these demonics now?!" The question is delivered like a slap to the face.

To everyone's horror, Abdu motions to the Jin lingering on the far side of the courtyard.

"Show yourselves!" Abdu instructs.

Stick and I rise on trembling legs from Nimshook's riding platform, while Anjali and Zoya do the same from the back of Kaitan. We bow our heads, avoiding eye contact with the Paladins, all of whom growl and lash their tails. It's a good thing we're not down there right now. We'd be ripped to shreds.

No doubt, this was part of Abdu's plan to buy us a little time.

"Be at peace, kindred," Wajid begins. "Allow Wajid to explain." He weaves through the ruffled mass of Paladins and positions himself in front of Kaitan and Nimshook. "These demonics are outlaws. They fled their Pride to bring a message to the Twelver, a message that must be heard."

"You have been among demonics too long, Brother!" Jakobah spits through gritted teeth. "You forget they are controlled by the demon in Bad Mountain and could infect all of us. They are no better than Shifters. And like Shifters, they must be destroyed at once!"

Several Paladins take this as a direct order and rush forward to pluck us off Kaitan and Nimshook. The two Jin are not going to make that easy to accomplish. Nimshook lowers her head, and her throat rumbles a warning. Kaitan swings his head, horns, and long nose, ready to sweep the advancing Paladins away. The two of them could turn the temple garden into a Paladin burial ground in a few heartbeats.

A booming roar echoes from the top of the grand steps leading into the temple tower. "Enough!"

The speaker wears a bejeweled green cloak and a tall horned headdress.

"Kaitan, Nimshook! Stop this insolence at once!"

The mighty Jin cower like scolded cubs. They shuffle away, taking us with them.

"The demonics will come down!" the figure on the steps announces.

I watch Anjali, perched on Kaitan's back. She shrugs. I suppose we have no choice. Knowing Anjali, she would rather be by my side on the ground than separated on different Jin.

Something is off about Anjali. It isn't just her submissive attitude. Her head is slumped. Her eyes lack their usual sparkle and quickness. Her body looks deflated. Maybe the ride made her nauseous, like it did Stick.

Anjali and Zoya use a rope to climb down Kaitan, while Stick and I make our way to the ground via Nimshook's long, serpentine neck.

I place a hand on Nimshook's nose, the way Latha did, and silently mouth the words *Thank you*. The draycon's sad eyes brighten, but only for a moment.

"Kaitan and Nimshook, leave us! Return to the holding chamber."

Nimshook huffs a steamy breath and trudges off with Kaitan to a yawning cavelike opening at the rear of the courtyard. A strong gate closes behind them. If the Jin obey the one at the top of the steps, that must mean she is—

"Come closer, demonics. Let the Twelver have a look at you."

CHAPTER 17

Those who use others for power have lost the path of Alayah.
Those who use power for others walk with Alayah in all they do.
— *Sayings of the Ancients*

TENSION CRACKLES around the temple garden.

The Twelver, however, placidly descends the steps. I still can't see her face beneath that ornate head-dress.

She comes to Wajid first. "So you are Wajid, the Lost Paladin. The Twelver was only a newborn cub when Wajid went to find my older brother among the demonics . . . after failing to protect him in the Last Campaign."

Wajid kneels. "Wajid deserves only death at your hand, Lord Shakyah."

"This one agrees with you," she replies curtly, tapping her chest, "especially when you return *with* four demonics and *without* my brother."

"These demonics are a gift to you," Wajid replies. Stick nudges me. It appears his suspicions about Wajid are true, unless this is a ploy to gain the Twelver's favor.

"They are outlaws who have betrayed their Pride to bring us an important message."

"Wajid is a slow learner," the Twelver says, chuckling darkly. "Demonics are all liars, cheats, and thieves. You, above anyone, should know not to trust what demonics say."

Zoya and I share an uneasy glance. This isn't going well.

"All the same, we will treat them better than they treated Wajid," the Twelver continues, igniting a tiny spark of hope in my heart. "We will kill them, as Jakobah said."

She sashays up the steps, long green cloak trailing behind. The back of the cloak is open to reveal her Guardian marks. The images of a draycon, a tiger, and a tortoise are clearly visible in the stripes of her fur. Just as Wajid learned from Abba, three of the Four Guardians have marked her.

The Red Firewing has not.

"Remember," the Twelver says without bothering to turn around, "no blood can be spilled on this holy ground. Drown them in the river. Feed their bodies to our slaycons. Burn whatever is left." She pauses. "You do it, Wajid. You and Abdu."

Wajid bows. "As you wish, Lord."

I can't believe this!

Wajid brought us all this way only to drown us like

rats in the river and serve us as slaycon food? We trusted him for nothing!

Anjali slips in front of me.

Zoya comes to my side, growling.

The Paladins circle us. Wajid and Abdu enter the ring. Abdu carries a coil of rope. Wajid's face is a mask of determination. Then he winks at me, an almost invisible gesture.

Anjali extends her claws. "We will not go peacefully. You might not want to spill our blood in this place, but we will gladly spill yours." Strong words, but she appears winded and battle-weary, as though she has already fought ten of them.

The Paladins step forward in unison, preparing to hold us so Wajid and Abdu can bind us with the rope. Before Anjali and Zoya attack, a silver streak zips between my feet.

Latha rises up in leo form and throws a surprised Paladin away. She does the same to one after another, throwing, flipping, knocking them to the ground. She shifts between her squirrel and leo forms, moving at blinding speed as she did against our opponents in the Cavern of the Ancients.

In seconds, eight Paladins are sprawled out on the grass, gasping and confused. The others think better of following their example.

"Apologies," Wajid says. "Wajid forgot to mention that one of these demonics is a Shakyah."

The Paladins who are still on their feet drop to their knees and bow their heads to Latha. The Twelver, who was serenely climbing the temple steps, stops.

"A Shakyah among the demonics," she declares. "What will Alayah come up with next?"

Unlike the Paladins, the Twelver is neither startled nor impressed by the presence of Latha standing in the courtyard, her silver pelt and armor gleaming in the moonlight. The Twelver tips her headdress, revealing dark eyes and a face marbled with elegant stripes. She descends the steps a second time and comes nose to nose with Latha.

"Welcome back, Latha," the Twelver says. "You served my father, Daviyah, when he was the Shakyah. You fought by his side against the demonics in the Last Campaign. However, in all likelihood, you did not mention that to *these* demonics."

Latha doesn't flinch. "As with all Jin, I serve the Shakyah who calls me until the Shakyah does what is right and sends me home."

The Twelver ignores Latha's verbal jab. "Perhaps you would like to share how many demonics you killed in the Last Campaign. You even killed one of the Kahn's own sons. Yet you failed to protect Shakyah Daviyah."

Latha's whiskers quiver.

"She did what she was commanded to do," I say.

The Paladins growl at my brashness. The Twelver levels her steely gaze on me, gray eyes flecked with green. One corner of her mouth arches into a half smile.

"If your message is so important," she says, creeping closer. Her scent fills my nostrils and mouth. "Why did the demonics send those who are little more than cubs?"

"We were not sent," I correct. "We escaped."

"It's you, isn't it?" she says. "You are Latha's master. Let's make it clear for all the Paladins."

She lifts a hand and extends gleaming claws, preparing to strike me. Anjali crouches, ready to pounce. In a flash, Latha drops into squirrel form, darts through the Twelver's legs, and appears in her leo form, serving as a shield between me and the Twelver. Anjali is relieved. She doesn't have any fight left in her.

The Twelver grins and retracts her claws. "Thank you, Latha, but we were expecting one of the Guardians." The Twelver glides past Latha and rips the torso cover away from my shoulders. She stares at my upper back, taking in the Guardian markings.

"We risked our lives to come here," Anjali groans meekly, trying to draw the Twelver's searing attention away from me, "to tell you that both of our Prides are in great danger."

The Twelver shows no interest in Anjali's warning, preferring to run a hand over my shoulder blades. "If the Red Firewing and the Black Tortoise have marked you, you must know their names."

She's testing me.

"The spirit of Shakyah Daviyah now dwells in the Red Firewing," I say. "The Black Tortoise is called Lamasura."

"And Latha is the only Jin who walks with you now. Isn't that right?"

"I sent the others back."

The Twelver shakes her head in disdain. "Perhaps you regret that now, alone as you are in the realm of the enemy, with nothing more than a changeling squirrel to protect you. My Jin, however, are never far from my side or from my command."

Without taking her eyes from mine, the Twelver whispers: "Laylin, Akelah, Mizu, Kartik, Yohan, Sunjay, Timereth, Naraka, Bazer, Dalami, Kumar, Zuman!"

As the names cross her lips, huge and fearsome Jin pop into view, forming a ring behind the Paladins. The Paladins recede as the Jin advance.

"It is a shame no one taught you how to control Jin," the Twelver says. "They can be so very useful. Allow me to demonstrate. Yohan! Prepare to execute these three."

A giant with two heads, four legs, and four arms,

each bearing a blade as tall as Zoya, thumps forward and towers over my friends. He rests the tips of his blades on their necks, ready to skewer them all upon the Twelver's order.

"Wait!" Stick squeaks. "Didn't you say no blood can be spilled here?"

The Twelver glowers at Stick. He's called her bluff. She brought these Jin to impress and threaten, but not to kill.

"Your message isn't the only reason you have come," the Twelver says to Anjali. "After all, Wajid could have brought your message for you."

"The Twelver is very wise," Anjali admits, stepping away from Yohan's enormous blade. "We know there is another Singa on your lands, one who arrived here many years ago. We have come to bring her home."

"Ah," the Twelver says thoughtfully. "So there is the true reason for your journey to our lands. You seek Mira, the demonic mate of my brother."

My heart nearly leaps out of my chest.

"Is she . . . here?" I ask, unable to stop myself.

The Twelver faces Abdu. "Take him to the Hall of the Guardians. We will see what he knows." She returns to the temple steps.

Anjali snarls as we are separated. But she doesn't put up any resistance. Her movements are sluggish. Something is seriously wrong with her.

"And my friends," I say to the Twelver, "they will not be harmed."

"They are safe," the Twelver assures me, "as long as you cooperate."

CHAPTER 18

Those who are not satisfied with what they have will never be satisfied with what they want. Those who are satisfied with what they have are not persuaded by their wants.

— *Sayings of the Ancients*

ARE YOU COMFORTABLE?" the Twelver asks. I nod uncomfortably.

We sit opposite each other on a woven carpet at one end of a torch-lit room. Each wall is painted with a magnificent sprawling picture of one of the Four Guardians: the Red Firewing, the Black Tortoise, the Green Draycon, and the White Tiger. We are closest to the painting of the Green Draycon.

The corners of the room are furnished with shelves reaching from floor to ceiling, packed with hundreds of books. This library dwarfs Galil's collection hidden deep in the castle of Singara.

All of our books except those on science and the Kahn's History were gathered and burned hundreds of years ago to protect our Pride from fiction and other dangerous ideas. Only a few were saved, preserved to this day in Galil's secret reading room. Could Galil's books be copies of some of the books in this chamber?

In the middle of the room, which might be the very center of the temple, is an ornate and ancient rack obviously designed to display something important, something that is no longer there.

Except for the books, the wall paintings, the rack, and Latha—still curled around my neck—the Twelver and I are alone in this room.

The Twelver has removed her headdress and green cloak. She wears a jeweled garment made from thin strips of animal hide, draping her shoulders, tucked under the wide belt around her hips, and flowing about her folded legs like tentacles. More of her pelt is visible now, golden orange laced with dark stripes common to all her Pride. Bright firewing feathers adorn her wrists, neck, and ankles.

She carries no weapons. As Wajid said earlier, she *is* a weapon.

"Goram!"

A smiling, round two-legged Jin materializes at her side. He sports a tall hat, tunic, and foot coverings with bells.

"Bring some hot herb brew," the Twelver demands.

Goram bows and trots out of the room, bells chiming merrily as he goes. He reenters moments later with two steaming mugs on a tray. He sets them before us and awaits further instructions.

"You may disappear, Goram," the Twelver says without even looking at him, "and reappear in the holding chamber with the others."

Goram bows as he fades away. Even though Alayah stopped sending Jin to the Twelver, she still has the power to command Jin who are already here.

She lifts her mug and takes a sip, staring at me over the edge of her tipped cup. "The Twelver has waited many moons, many years to meet you . . . *Eliyah*."

My mouth hangs open.

Her eyes sparkle. "Yes, the Twelver knows who you are. You are the son of the Twelver's brother and his demonic mate. How could a Shakyah be born among the demonics otherwise? Besides that, you resemble Makayah. The only surprise is that you would come to our realm and make your way to Elyon. Mira must have lured you here. Why else would you take the risk of venturing unarmed, beyond the demonics' ridiculous wall, into enemy territory? Nevertheless, your arrival is very fortunate for us. The Twelver owes Mira a debt of thanks."

I struggle to keep my fur flat. I'm dying to ask her more about my mother. And I wonder if she knows the Singa are about to attack.

"The Twelver knows the demonics are prepar..
for war," she continues, "led by your fool-headed cousin
Tamir, after the death of your grandfather only a few
nights ago. That is your message for us, is it not?"

"H-how . . ." I stammer, "how do you know these
things?"

"She knows less than she thinks!" Latha exclaims.

"There are hundreds of Jin under the Twelver's
command," the Twelver boasts, ignoring Latha. "For ten
years a flock of Jin ravens has flown over the demonics'
wall each week and reported what they see. Through
them, the Twelver keeps up with everything among the
demonics, including you: when you did your ritual hunt;
how you killed your slaycon; which Jin came to you and
when you foolishly sent them back; how your heart was
broken by your grandfather's death; how you came to
our lands; when you were captured by Abba's family.
The Twelver knew you were coming with Wajid, the
Lost Paladin, and that you were the prince and are now
the Kahn of Singara, and that, most of all, you hope to
find your mother, Mira."

"Is Mira here?" I blurt out. "In Elyon?"

"No," she says bitterly. "You will not find her in
Elyon."

"Then . . . where?"

The Twelver notes the rising tide of tears in my
eyes. She keeps me in suspense by taking an extra-long

She puts her cup down and leans forward,
gh for me to feel her breath on my whiskers.

r Eliyah," she purrs, "the Twelver understands
feel. It is hard to have never met one of your
parents. The Twelver never met her own father."

"I know," I say, confidence returning to my voice.
"Daviyah died in the Great War—I mean the Last
Campaign—right before you were born. And now his
soul dwells in the Red Firewing, like all the Shakyahs
before him."

"That's right," she admits. "The loss of parents is
something we share. And so, we should help each other!"

"What do you mean?"

"The Twelver will help you find your mother *and*
your father. In exchange, you will bring Daviyah here
and help find something very important to our Pride."

"The Axis of the Ancients?" I venture.

The Twelver sits up straighter. "What has Wajid
told you about the Axis?"

"He says only a Shakyah who has been marked by
the Four Guardians *and* holds the Axis can summon all
Four Guardians at once."

"Verily," she agrees, "and when the *Twelver* is
marked by the Red Firewing *and* has the Axis of the
Ancients, the demon in Bad Mountain will be destroyed.
We can end the feud between our Prides, if we work
together!"

"But I don't know where the Axis is," I protest, "and I don't control the Red Firewing."

"You have much to learn about the Shijin," she says. "The Red Firewing was the first of the Guardians to come to you. That means he is your protector, as the Green Draycon is for the Twelver. If we want the Red Firewing to appear, we have only to give him a good reason."

Latha paces on my shoulders, her tail twitching. "What you call 'a good reason' is not good at all," she chitters. "It is forbidden!"

The Twelver brushes Latha's words aside with a wave of her hand. "When a Guardian is in the presence of a Shakyah whom the Guardian has not marked, that Guardian longs to mark the Shakyah. Isn't that right, Latha?"

"It is true," Latha admits. "That is what the Guardians were made to do."

"And so, when Daviyah arrives," the Twelver says with an air of triumph, "he will be compelled to mark the Twelver at last. The time for the demon's destruction has come!"

I'm still not sure what the Twelver is getting at, and there's something she might not understand either.

"If you know so much about what's happening in Singara," I say, "you must know Tamir is making new powerful weapons. He will be able to slaughter your warriors from twenty meters away. He wants to shed as much blood as possible to free the demon. He thinks he can control the demon and use it to destroy your Pride completely and rule the world."

For a split second, the Twelver's whiskers droop. Tamir's weapons and hopes to unleash the demon are new information. Clearly, those ravens didn't observe everything.

"All the more reason to summon the Red Firewing and find the Axis as soon as possible," she asserts. "Nothing is more powerful than the Four Guardians. When I am marked by the Four and hold the Axis, victory is assured."

We are interrupted by vibrations in the floor and walls, as purring interlaced with deep humming fills the hall.

"Time for evening prayer," the Twelver announces. "You will join us."

She springs to her feet and walks briskly to a door set at the White Tiger's mouth. She opens the door, and the humming booms through like the White Tiger's own roar.

We enter a high-ceilinged chamber where dozens of robed Paladins kneel in rows. Wajid must be here, but he's not easy to pick out.

The purring voices become more complex, with groups of Paladins breaking off into variations of the same tune. The Twelver takes her place on a cushion at the head of the room and directs me to sit on the stone floor to her right.

The music grows louder and includes words from the Old Language, and the Twelver joins in. Her voice is strong and clear, riding atop the voices of the Paladins like a raft over the sea. The effect is hypnotic and deeply moving, even though I don't know the language. After a time, the words hush and then fade like the last breath of the dying. The room is submerged in silence.

A half hour creeps by. My muscles ache from the effort of keeping still. The Paladins are completely relaxed. The Twelver, by contrast, appears bored and impatient.

At last the Twelver speaks. "As you know, dear Paladins, three of the Four Guardians have marked the Twelver: the Green Draycon, the White Tiger, and the Black Tortoise. Today, four demonics came to the temple, one of whom is a Shakyah, marked by the Red Firewing and the Black Tortoise. He is the son of the Twelver's brother and his demonic mate."

The Paladins do not twitch even a whisker. This is not news to them.

"Wajid serves the Twelver well by bringing these demonics," she goes on. "Tomorrow, this youngling will bring the Red Firewing and lead us to the Axis. Then we begin our invasion of the demonics, with all Four Guardians fighting with us. Soon the demon will die!"

The Paladins grunt their approval, but it's not the most enthusiastic response I've ever heard. Perhaps, like me, the Paladins doubt the Twelver can pull it off. Even if the Red Firewing appears, what makes her think I can find the Axis?

"Take the demonic to the holding chamber," she commands.

Abdu rises and grabs my arm, wincing as he touches demonic fur. He leads me out of the room, with the Twelver at his tail. We enter the Hall of the Guardians and proceed to a door positioned in the mouth of the Green Draycon on the opposite wall. This door opens to a large room furnished with a broad oval table.

It's the same room I saw in my dream, when Abba demanded that the Twelver release her Jin to the Haven.

We arc around the table and enter a dim passageway. After descending a few steps, we come to a balcony. The cool air carries the sweet scent of many Jin.

My vision adjusts to the scarce light. The balcony overlooks a massive subterranean cavern. Outlines of numerous creatures, large and small, crowd the gloomy space. A banging noise issues from the far side of the chamber, accompanied by muted screeches and roars.

"So many," I say.

"Nearly eight hundred," the Twelver says smugly.

"All prisoners!" Latha cries.

"No, Latha," the Twelver retorts. "They willingly serve the Twelver. Perhaps you will learn something from them about respect and obedience." She leans over the balcony. "Tikun!"

A winged creature, with arms and legs bearing long talons, flaps to the balcony and perches on the rail. Its smooth leathery skin gleams even in this dim light, but its eyes are as sad as those of all the Twelver's Jin.

"Take him down," she says, turning to leave.

The Jin grabs me in its talons and beats its wings furiously. I hook one foot onto the balcony railing.

"Wait!" I call after the Twelver. "Where are my friends?"

But she has already gone up the stairs.

The Jin struggles to stay airborne with its resistant cargo. I'm dangling over the cavern and at risk of causing us both to crash to the stone floor, or into the waiting jaws of some dreadful beast below.

"Don't struggle!" Latha squeals. Her little claws dig into my shoulder. "Let go!"

I release my foot and swing into the air beneath thumping wings. The Jin swoops to an empty patch of floor and drops me the remaining distance.

Otherworldly beings bunch up around us, some towering, some tiny. A few are leos; many are not. As

Wajid said, Jin are infinite in their shapes and variety. Each presses forward to get a better view of the new-comers. Those behind me whisper excitedly to one another. I whirl around, drawing more cries of astonishment as the rest of the Jin get an eyeful of my back.

"He has marks from two Guardians!" some exclaim.

"He is a Shakyah!" says another. "He's the one we saw in the courtyard!"

"But he is a Singa," another chimes in. This Jin has the head and upper torso of a Panthera warrior and the lower body and legs of something like a karkadann. "There are no Shakyahs among the Singa."

"Don't we have a Shakyah already?" a draycon asks.

Latha scrambles to the top of my head to address the assembly.

A fox Jin with eyes like black marbles is the first to notice her. "Latha! Is that you?"

"It is, Kumar. I am honored to present Shakyah Eli-yah," Latha says grandly. "He is the grandson of Shakyah Daviyah, whose spirit now dwells in the Red Firewing!"

"If he is the grandson of Shakyah Daviyah," bellows Yohan, the giant with two heads, four arms, and four legs who threatened to kill Anjali, Stick, and Zoya in the temple garden, "perhaps he can send us home!" His fur-covered arms are folded in two layers across a broad chest like a shield.

"Most of us have been held here for years on end!"

says Yohan's other head. "Too many of us have become Shifters!"

"You know he can't open the door to the Haven for you, Yohan," Latha says. "Only the Twelver can do that."

"There is another way," adds a serpent Jin, who is as thick and sturdy as an old oak tree. "If we are killed in battle or if she is killed, then we can be released!"

"That is bound to happen when war begins, Mudra!" a Jin chimes in, hanging upside down from the horn of a draycon. He is the same sort of creature as Tikun, the flying beast that brought me down here. "The sooner the better, I say!"

"If only someone had the courage to kill her first!" Yohan declares. Hundreds of Jin roar, squawk, and stomp the floor in agreement.

"That is not the way!" Latha protests. "You know it is forbidden to harm a Shakyah."

"Easy for you to say, Latha. You have been sent here through this young Shakyah," the serpent called Mudra argues. "He could send you home right now if he wanted to. The rest of us are stuck here until we die, or until we become Shifters, or until Hasatamara is destroyed—and perhaps not even then!"

I suddenly feel very alone among this crowd of grumbling Jin. And that continuous banging noise at the far end of the cavern, whatever it is, only adds to the tension. The Twelver sent me here to learn something.

Mostly, I'm learning how much I miss the company of my friends.

"Anjali!" I call out. "Are you here?"

The crowd of Jin falls silent.

"He's calling on Anjali!" Kumar exclaims. The fox Jin says Anjali's name like Wajid and Latha do, emphasizing the second syllable instead of the first.

"Anjali is here? Can it be?" says another Jin.

"Stick! Zoya!" I cry.

"Back here! We can't get through!" Zoya's voice is muffled and distant.

"Make way for Anjali!" Latha says grandly. "Make way for Anjali!"

The Jin shuffle aside, creating a long alley to three Singas huddled at the edge of the cavern.

Anjali prods Stick with an elbow. "Come on. They're not going to eat you."

Stick doesn't look too sure about that.

Zoya takes Stick's arm and nearly drags him through the Jin to my side. Anjali follows, lumbering along as if she's fighting an illness. Her bright green eyes have lost some of their color. Her scent is off too. Most peculiar of all, the Jin bow and dip their heads to Anjali as she ambles unsteadily down the aisle.

"Are you all right?"

"I think so," she mumbles. For Anjali, who is always

strong and vigorous, "I think so" might as well be admitting a deadly condition.

"The Paladins brought us here right after you went with the Twelver," Zoya says. "But these Jin haven't done us any harm."

"The Twelver will not ask much of us until it is time to attack the Singa," says one of Yohan's heads.

"When will that be?" Zoya asks.

"Soon," I say. "She knows Tamir's planning to attack, and she's confident the demon can be destroyed. She wants me to bring Daviyah here and help her find the Axis of the Ancients."

"What makes her think you can do all that?" Stick asks.

"I wish I knew!" I reply.

"She would like nothing more than to have the Axis and the Four Guardians fighting with her," a small voice puts in. It's Goram, the Jin who served us in the Hall of the Guardians. "But she has a plan to destroy the demon without the Guardians if she must."

"How?" I ponder. "Daviyah tried that and failed. He didn't even get close to Bad Mountain."

"She has another way," Goram says, lowering his voice. "She will use . . . the Shifters." He stares anxiously at a soaring metal door at the far side of the cavern. The rest of the Jin gawk in the same direction. Now I know where that nonstop banging is coming from. There are Shifters on the other side of that door, trapped in a cell of their own.

"How many Shifters are in there, Goram?" I ask.

"Sixteen," Goram replies. "A new one is added every few weeks. Often they cannot be rounded up into their cell and must be destroyed."

"Then the Twelver can't control the Shifters?" I ask.

"No one can control Shifters," Yohan answers. "However, the Twelver doesn't have to control them. Shifters will find the easiest path into the mountain and start digging until Hasatamara is free or until they die trying. And since the Singa have removed much of the metal that surrounds Hasatamara, it will be easy for them to accomplish their goal. The Twelver thinks she can use the Shifters to uncover enough of the demon for us to move in for the kill, but not enough for the demon to escape. That is her plan."

"Sounds risky," Zoya concludes, "like poking holes in a beehive and not expecting to get stung."

"And the Singa Royal Army won't let her get that close," I say. "At least not without spilling a lot of blood, which might give Hasatamara enough strength to escape on his own. That's what almost happened last time."

"She has a way to avoid that as well," Goram adds.

"Ships!" squawks a raven perched on Kaitan's head. "Big ships!"

"What's a ship?" Stick queries.

"A ship is a large boat that can carry many passengers over the sea," Latha explains. "Even over the rough seas that border the territory of the Singa."

Stick shivers at the thought. "Who would be crazy enough to make something like that?"

"I did," a new voice says.

The speaker is the most bizarre and ugly two-legged Jin I have ever seen. He is no taller than I am and lean. He has fur on top of his head and around his chin. It's not quite a mane, but it's enough to cover his mouth and neck. He lacks claws and a tail. He has puny flat teeth, and only a smattering of hair around his body.

"It's a humana!" Stick exclaims. "I recognize his kind from Shanti's story!"

"That I am," the humana says with a little bow. "We were great builders and inventors."

"So are Singas," Stick brags.

The humana smiles. "We made things you cannot even dream of."

"According to the story, what you made was a lot of trouble," Zoya says. "You were the ones who caused all the bloodshed that drew Hasatamara from the sea in the first place."

"Which is why the Twelver commanded me to design a fleet of ships," the humana asserts. "They will allow us to invade in secret and with little bloodshed. Then we can destroy Hasatamara before he has the strength to escape his mountain prison. As the Twelver says, it is my chance to correct the humanas' mistake from long ago."

"I see her strategy," Anjali acknowledges, perking up. "She will load all the Jin and the Shifters onto the ships and sail them around the wall to the Great Mountain. I'll bet my tail and whiskers she will do it as Tamir launches his attack into enemy territory, when Singara and the castle are not well defended."

"That's why she's not worried about Tamir," I say, piecing it all together. "He's making it easier for her."

"She's not stupid, I'll give her that," Anjali says.

"Smarter than Daviyah, anyway," Stick jeers.

The Jin grumble and howl at that remark. "You will apologize, demonic—" one head of Yohan says.

"—for insulting Shakyah Daviyah," says the other.

Stick is defiant. "I'll apologize as soon as we stop getting called demonics!"

"Stand down, Stick," Anjali says woozily. "Don't mind him, Yohan. He has a mouth problem."

Both of Yohan's heads dip respectfully. "As you wish, Anjali."

I exchange a quizzical look with Zoya. That's twice the Jin have treated Anjali as their superior. Anjali couldn't care less. She's too interested in using every last bit of energy she has to uncover the Twelver's strategy.

"Am I right about the Twelver's battle plan?" Anjali questions the humana.

"You are correct," the humana says. "She might succeed, but as you say"—at this, he nods to Zoya—"it is very risky." The best way to overcome the demon is to use the Axis of the Ancients to summon the Four Guardians. I beg this young Shakyah to do everything in his power to help her. Bring the Red Firewing, find the Axis, and let us be rid of Hasatamara once and for all."

Now I understand why the Twelver sent me down here.

She knew these Jin would encourage me to help her. They are all desperate to go back to the Haven. Her strategy must look like the fastest route.

Perhaps I should.

If she can destroy the demon without shedding much blood during the invasion, why wouldn't I support that?

And yet, the Twelver is cruel. She holds her Jin captive far too long. Many have already become Shifters, whom she keeps as pawns in her plans. Alayah refuses to send her more Jin, and yet the Twelver still carries on.

Should I stand with someone who has been rejected by Alayah? Do I have a choice?

I barely know the Twelver, but Anjali is right. The Twelver is clever.

She might get me to help her whether I want to or not.

CHAPTER 19

All things bend toward good for those
who serve the Lord of Lights.
— *Sayings of the Ancients*

A MONSTROUS INSECT ADVANCES, climbing and slithering over the heads and shoulders of the other Jin.

"Magmar! Magmar!" it wails in alarm. "Magmar is coming!"

The creature has dozens of legs and a face without eyes. Two antennae swivel and lash above its head, scanning everything.

Latha cringes as though the name cuts her ears. "Magmar? Are you sure, Sentis?"

"He comes! He comes!"

The humana shudders. "May Alayah help us!"

"It is Alayah who sends him!" Sentis says. "As is true for all of us."

"Who is Magmar?" I ask.

Latha leaps from my head and changes into leo form, ready for battle. "He is the oldest Jin, older even than the Four Guardians, although not as powerful. And he is trouble."

"Trouble how?" I query.

"He is untrustworthy and unpredictable," she says. "He is the only Jin who is able to lie. What's worse, if he bites a Jin, that Jin will immediately become a Shifter."

That explains the heavy presence of fear in this chamber.

"Then he must be a servant of Hasatamara," I say.

"He is responsible for the existence of Hasatamara," Latha confirms. "That much is certain."

"Can't you chase him and his story away before he comes?" I beg Latha. "Like you did on the way into Elyon?"

"He is too strong for that," Latha laments. "He wants nothing more than to return to this world."

"He has arrived!" Sentis proclaims. Every wide-eyed Jin swings their gaze to me.

The feeling begins. Wind whipping in my head, heart pounding, and stomach churning as if I'm going to be sick. A jittery lump of fiction lands on my tongue and pushes against my teeth, demanding to be set free.

"Do not say his name after the Truth Telling, Lord," Latha warns urgently. "Magmar is harmless in the halfway state. But if you say his name, he will become real and turn us all into Shifters in a few minutes' time. Order him to disappear as soon as he arrives!"

My mouth opens, and the words spill out. The bright story vision overwhelms the glum cavern with light and life.

Long ago, at the dawn of creation, when no stories had ever been told, bright stars glittered in the sky around the light of Alayah. By day and by night, the stars shone down upon the earth.

One day, the great spider, Magmar, climbed a tree at the top of a mountain to get as close to the sky as possible. He asked Alayah about the stars.

"Each holds a different story," Alayah said, placing the words in Magmar's mind. "They are gifts for two-legged creatures who will be born many moons from now."

Magmar was sad because he had eight legs, not two.

"What is a story?" asked Magmar.

"A story is a vision that gives hope and courage, wisdom and guidance. They are my finest creation. One of them is about you, Magmar!"

Naturally, Magmar became more curious than ever. His desire to experience a story burned as brightly in his heart as the stars in the sky. He asked what he might do to receive a story. Once again, Alayah put words into Magmar's mind.

"Only the cleverest creatures can understand a story. Bring me a live python, a sprite, and forty-seven killer bees. If you can prove that you are more clever than they are by capturing them and bringing them here, I will reward you with a story."

Magmar immediately set about capturing these creatures, beginning with the python. He found the snake curled around the branch of a tree.

"Mr. Python!" Magmar cried. "Your wife tells me that you are not as long as her."

"Nonsense!" the python hissed indignantly. "Everyone knows I am the longest python in the entire world."

"Then we must settle the dispute once and for all," Magmar suggested. "I have just come from measuring her with this stick, and now I will measure you in the same way."

The python allowed Magmar to tie him to the measuring stick, because the only way to accurately measure a snake is to have the snake become completely straight. At that point, the snake was also trapped. Once the python was tied to the stick, Magmar carried him to his home, nestled in a cliff overlooking the sea.

To catch the forty-seven killer bees, Magmar filled a gourd with water. He climbed above the bees' nest and began sprinkling water from the gourd over the nest.

"It's raining! It's raining!" Magmar called as he sprinkled the nest. "A big storm is coming. Your nest will soon be destroyed! Save yourselves!"

When all the bees fled the nest, Magmar invited them to take shelter in the gourd, which was now empty. He counted them one by one as they entered the gourd. When all forty-seven bees were inside, he quickly sealed the opening and brought the trapped bees to his home.

To catch the sprite, who moved faster than the eye could see, Magmar had to be extra clever. He made a little doll molded from his own sticky webbing. He put the doll beside the sprite's tree home and placed beside it some sweet yam covered with the bees' honey. When the sprite saw the yam with the doll, she assumed the doll had brought the yam to her as a gift.

She ate the yam and thanked the doll, which of course did not reply. Curious, the sprite touched the doll's face. Because her hands were sticky with honey, and because the doll was made of sticky webbing, her hands stuck, and Magmar easily captured her.

Magmar took his captives to the top of the tall-est tree and presented them to Alayah.

"You have done well, Magmar!" Alayah exclaimed, dropping the words into Magmar's mind. "You have outwitted some of my most clever creatures."

"Will you share the stories with me now?" Magmar's eyes sparkled as he gawked at the count-less stars in the sky.

"I already have," Alayah replied. "And I will do so again."

As Alayah said this, a star fell from the sky and expanded into a vision. It was a tale about a giant spider who captured a python, killer bees, and a sprite and presented them to Alayah in exchange for experiencing a story for the first time.

This was not what Magmar expected. Feeling tricked, Magmar declared that he would no longer serve Alayah.

The dazzling vision disperses like morning mist. The Jin are as still as statues. Only their eyes move, anxiously searching the dim cavern.

"He will not arrive in the usual way," Latha reports. "He is a trickster at heart. Whatever you do, Eliyah, do not say his name!"

"Even if I accidentally say it," I say, "I won't allow

him to turn any of you into Shifters. I'll send him right back to the Haven."

"Do not be too sure about that," Latha warns. "He will not *want* to go to the Haven, so he will have little interest in obeying you."

A sudden yelp comes from the back of the cavern. A spooked Jin leaps into the air. This is followed by another Jin roaring and bounding away. And another. Something is plowing through the assembly, accompanied by cackling laughter.

At the moment when Magmar should burst into sight, all is quiet.

"Where is he?" I whisper to Latha.

Latha's ears angle forward. She holds her breath.

"Excuse me," comes a tiny voice to my right. "Do you know where I might find Shakyah Eliyah?"

Dangling by a single thread, no bigger than a pebble and no more than a whisker's length from my nose, is a spider. He is phantasmal, ghostly, and not fully in this world.

This little insect is the mighty and terrible Magmar?

"I am Eliyah," I say.

"A Shakyah who is also a Singa! What a good trick!" he squeaks. "Eliyah, do you know my name?"

"Do not say it, Lord!" Latha interjects. "Send him away! Now!"

"What's the hurry, Latha?" Magmar cackles as he climbs his web, getting bigger by the second. Soon he is larger than any Jin here, except the draycons. He clings to the ceiling. "When did the Jin become so cowardly and pathetic?" Magmar's voice booms around the cavern.

"Disappear!" I yell.

"You don't need to stay here like slaves!" he bellows, continuing to address the Jin as he fades away. "You can rise up and defeat the tyrant who calls herself the Twelver!"

"She is our only way back to the Haven," Yohan retorts.

"The Haven!" Magmar says in mockery. "The Haven is overrated!"

"Why is it taking so long for him to vanish?" I whisper to Latha.

"He is insolent," Latha sneers. "And terribly strong."

"Nothing to do in the Haven except sing praises to Alayah," Magmar carries on. "Why not claim this world as our own? Join me and we can rule it, together!"

"To join with you is to join with the demon!" Latha fumes.

"Oh, that is just an unfortunate rumor, Latha!" Magmar responds.

The gigantic spider is nearly invisible now. He releases his grip and floats downward.

Toward me.

"Remember my name, Eliyah . . . Magmar . . . Magmar . . . Magmar!"

He disappears right before impact.

Latha relaxes, but only a little. "Magmar is not to be trusted! He is still angry with Alayah and wants to rule this world again, as he attempted to do at the beginning of creation with disastrous results."

"Then why did Alayah send him?" Goram asks.

"Perhaps he was sent to deliver a message about rising up against the Twelver!" Yohan states.

"I rather like that idea," Mudra says to the approving rumble of many Jin.

"It is a foolish and dangerous idea!" Latha counters. "If you cut yourselves off from the Twelver and follow Magmar, you will become Shifters for sure, either from Magmar's bite or from too much time on earth!"

A thought bubbles up and spills out of my mouth. "If Alayah tricked Mag—"

The Jin gasp in horror, and I try again. "If Alayah tricked the ancient spider once, perhaps Alayah is tricking him again by sending him here. Maybe what the spider means for bad, Alayah will use for good."

"That is similar to one of the Sayings of the Ancients," the humana says. "Alayah is something of a trickster as well."

"Eliyah is right," Latha says confidently. "We must have faith in Alayah. Let us speak no more about Magmar. He is invisible but still listening to our every word. He waits to hear you speak his name, Eliyah, which I pray *never* happens."

"Leo!" Zoya calls. She crouches beside Anjali, who sits against the cavern wall, staring blankly ahead.

I've been so focused on Magmar, I failed to notice Anjali getting worse by the minute. I kneel beside her.

"You look terrible."

"Thanks," she mumbles. "I'll be fine. I just need to rest for a while."

"Not surprised," I say, scratching her ears. "When was the last time you slept?" Anjali closes her eyes and a tuft of orange fur comes off in my hand.

"Not sure," she moans. "Maybe never."

Latha shifts to squirrel form, climbs up Anjali's body, and stands on her snout. Latha checks her eyes and smells her breath as Anjali dozes off.

I've never seen Anjali as anything but energetic and sharp, ready to take on a dozen enemies at the twitch of a whisker. The dramatic change is disturbing.

"What's happening to her?" I ask.

Latha skitters down Anjali's body. "I have something to tell you, Eliyah. It will not be easy to hear."

"If it's about Anjali, just say it!"

"Anjali is more than she appears to be," Latha whispers.

"She's not your average Singa, that's for sure," Stick agrees.

"She is not a Singa at all," Latha adds with a shake of her tail. "Anjali . . . *is a Jin*."

CHAPTER 20

The most difficult cages from which to escape cannot be seen or touched. The most difficult cage is the prison of your mind.
— *Sayings of the Ancients*

WHAT?" STICK GASPS, nearly choking. "That's ridiculous! She's more Singa than any Singa in Singara!"

My mind whirls like a cub chasing his own tail. Anjali . . . *a Jin?!* How can this be?

"I know it is difficult to comprehend," Latha replies. "It will sound even more strange to Anjali. Alayah sent her into this world through you, Eliyah, disguised as a Singa. However, because the disguise was so complete, and because Anjali appeared as a very young Singa, not even she knew."

I study Anjali's peaceful, sleeping face. "When did she come? I don't remember."

"She arrived in your very first story when you were just a cub. You said her name and made her real. That frightened you and she fled. For years you never spoke the name of another Jin."

A hazy memory of the first Jin that came to me arises in my mind's eye: a little Singa appearing out of nowhere. That was Anjali!

"She was found and adopted by a blacksmith not far from the castle," I recall. "That's what a soldier told me on the way to the Academy."

"To be near you and protect you is all she ever wanted."

"She found a way." I sigh. "She was assigned to serve in the castle right after graduating from the Academy, which has never happened before. And if she's a Jin, that explains why she always wants to dive into me when I open the door to the Haven. She's been here so long."

"Too long," Latha says gravely.

"You mean—"

Latha nods. "You can see for yourselves she is not well. She has the signs of a Jin who is shifting."

"Is there anything we can do?" I plead. "What if I open the door to the Haven before she shifts?" I lift my chest and announce, "I am willing!"

The door to the Haven does not open.

"She must know who she truly is before that will be possible," Latha assures me. "Leave that to me."

"How much time does she have?" Zoya asks.

"Usually when a Jin shifts, the change is sudden and quick, as you observed with Tula," Latha says. "Anjali, however, is a very powerful Jin. The change will be slow and gradual."

"So . . . what? A week? A day?" Stick queries. "She's kind of important to us."

"She is important to all of us," Latha says. "I don't know how long it will take. But if she becomes a Shifter, she must be destroyed, and you must not stand in our way. It is a less pleasant way to send her to the Haven, but we cannot risk her becoming a servant of the demon. That would be catastrophic."

"Why take the risk at all?" Zoya insists. "Why not tell Anjali what she is right now and have Leo send her to the Haven?"

"Because I believe Anjali's purpose is not yet fulfilled," Latha replies gravely. "I believe you will be glad to have her at your side tomorrow, Eliyah."

"I'm glad to have her at my side every day." I watch Anjali's nostrils gently expand and contract in time with her rising and falling chest, the only signs that she still lives. I can't imagine going on without her. First Grandfather left me. Soon Anjali will as well. "If only I had known. If only *she* had known!"

"We must trust that this was hidden from you both for a reason," Latha says. "Let her sleep. You should sleep as well. We Jin will watch over her . . . very carefully."

. . .

In my dreams I see the Twelver as a giggling cub, chasing a Jin through the halls of the temple. The Jin is a quick six-footed creature who changes color and texture according to whatever background he encounters.

In her haste, the young Twelver almost crashes into a frowning elder.

The elder speaks using the Panthera's hand language. The scowling face and the sharp gestures suggest the elder is scolding the young Twelver for playing with her Jin. She wants the Twelver to send the creature back to the Haven.

The Jin, pressed against the wall and matching the stone surface, is practically invisible already. Only his bulging, darting eyes give him away.

The young Twelver sighs. "Time to go home, Nahum."

She spreads her arms and a beam of living light blasts from her stomach. The light expands, replacing her torso with a vision of the Haven: a beach and sparkling sea with thousands of beings flying around a bright swirling orb. All that remains visible of the Twelver is her head, arms, and legs. The elder kneels and chants something in the Old Language. Nahum joyfully detaches from the wall, leaps at the Twelver, and exits this world with a burst of light.

The vision closes, and the little Twelver's body returns to normal.

It is exactly what happens to me when I have opened the door to the Haven.

"I'm sorry, Amma."

Amma must mean mother or grandmother, just as abba means father or grandfather. She is too old to be the Twelver's mother. If she is the Twelver's grandmother, that makes her my great-grandmother.

The Twelver's amma smiles warmly. She lays a tender hand on the Twelver's shoulder and leads her to the Hall of the Guardians, communicating with her other hand as they walk.

The young Twelver's eyes widen as she reads Amma's hand movements. "My father liked to play with his Jin too?" she exclaims with delight. "Tell me more about Daviyah!"

The elder sits on a bench nestled between two towering bookcases in one corner of the hall. The Twelver climbs on her lap. The mark of the Green Draycon is visible on her upper back.

The elder's hands begin to speak.

The Twelver gently takes her amma's wrists. "No, Amma. I want to hear you talk about Daviyah . . . with your voice."

Amma hesitates.

The Twelver straightens her back. "It is an order from the Shakyah," she says with a playful grin. "Shakyah Suniyah."

Amma sighs and opens her mouth, preparing to make words for Suniyah. "My son, Daviyah, was brave . . . a fine leader," she croaks, "and impatient." She pauses to fill her lungs. "After being marked by three Guardians and having collected many Jin, Daviyah believed he could defeat the demonics on his way to Bad Mountain." Her jaw and tongue loosen, and the words come more easily. "He believed the Red Firewing and the other Guardians would come in time to destroy the demon. That is not what happened. Daviyah died, and the campaign ended just before the demon could escape."

"I will finish what he started!" Suniyah boasts.

Amma smiles. "Wait until the right time, little one. Wait and see if all Four Guardians will mark you. Trust Alayah, blessed be the name."

"Maybe there is a way to destroy the demon *without* the Guardians," the Twelver proposes, "before the demon has a chance to rise up. Maybe that is what Alayah wants."

"Now you *are* thinking like Daviyah!"

"Why didn't all Four Guardians mark any of the Shakyahs before?"

Amma lifts her hands. "Things happen in Alayah's time, not ours."

Amma gazes to the center of the hall, where there is a glowing, brightly colored staff in the stand I saw earlier. The staff is held upright, one end toward the floor and the other pointing to the ceiling. This must be the Axis of the Ancients! Each section of the Axis reveals some aspect of the Four Guardians: the metallic green scales of a draycon, the pattern of a black tortoiseshell, bright red plumage, and white striped fur. These four sections are not motionless. They are alive and pulse with intense power.

"One day a Shakyah is coming," Amma continues, "marked by all Four Guardians. That Shakyah will use the Axis of the Ancients to bring the Four from the Haven to destroy the demon. Maybe that Shakyah is you."

Suniyah's eyes sparkle. "When I see the Red Firewing, I will meet my abba, Daviyah, because they are one."

"Verily," Amma replies. "Daviyah's spirit dwells in the Red Firewing, like all the Shakyahs before him. You will meet him in this life or in the next. Be patient, Suniyah. The Ancients say if we trust Alayah with every step, Alayah makes the path clear."

. . .

"Demonics! Come with me!"

The Twelver's voice pushes the dream away. I awake in the crook of a Jin's arm. Her long fur drapes me like a blanket. Anjali is cradled in her other arm.

She is still here.

Still Anjali.

Daylight peeks through a crack in the cavern's ceiling and rolls across Anjali's face. Her eyes flutter open.

"Hey," I say. "Are you okay?"

"Not really," she groans. Her fur is almost copper. "I saw something while I slept."

My ears perk up. "What did you see?"

"A brilliant light and the Guardians, like in the Cavern of the Ancients," she says wearily. "But there were only three of them."

"Clear the way for the demonics!" the Twelver commands. "Today the Red Firewing is coming! Today begins the end of the demon."

The Jin drift apart, making a path to the far side of the cavern, where the Twelver waits with five Paladins.

One of them is Wajid.

Latha scrambles up my leg and clings to my back.

"I have a bad feeling about this," I say.

"Me too," Zoya agrees.

"Welcome to my world," Stick grumbles. "I've had a bad feeling ever since we left Singara."

Anjali struggles to her feet. "Let's get it over with."

We cross the length of the cavern, Jin once again bowing to Anjali as the Twelver lifts her voice: "Prajna! Doji! Ivran! Moriah!"

Wings rustle as four big ravens flap into the air.

"Fly quickly to the land of the demonics! Find out how close they are to launching their attack."

The ravens screech and soar through the crack in the ceiling.

"Enrik!" the Twelver calls.

The humana boat builder steps timidly into the empty path cleared by the Jin.

"Make an inspection of our fleet. Tell each crew to prepare. We must be ready to load and sail at a moment's notice!"

Enrik bows. "Right away, Lord."

"You four," the Twelver barks at us. "Put these on." The Paladins give each of us a white robe. "Lift the hood over your head."

I glance at Wajid as I slip into the Paladin robe. His downcast eyes avoid mine. His jaw is set.

The Twelver turns away, motioning with her tail for us to follow. We climb a ladder to a ledge some twenty meters up and march to a heavy wooden door. Wajid inserts a bone tool into the top and rotates it, and the door is unlatched. Daylight floods the area, bringing more color to our eyes.

And that's not all.

A massive drum pounds from somewhere above us, slow and steady, thumping like the heartbeat of creation. We're outside now, walking on the outer wall of the temple, marveling at the countless dwellings stacked up and down the riverbanks, as far as the eye can see. Streams of Pantheras pour into the main roads near the river. They are drawn by the drum, just as they were for the arrival of the Lost Paladin last night.

"I don't think the fact that there are demonics in Elyon will be a secret much longer," Stick murmurs. "We're basically dead."

He might be right.

Why else would the Twelver assemble the entire Pride like this?

The Twelver and our Paladin escorts take us from the outer wall into the temple.

Anjali struggles to keep up.

We enter the center of the building, where a winding staircase awaits. It spirals up and up and out of sight. This must be the way to the top of the tower, that curved stone steeple stretching far above Elyon and pointing to the sea.

Anjali pauses at the base of the steps, exhausted before she even begins to climb.

"Want to rest?" I ask.

"Nonsense!" she argues. "It's just a few hundred steps."

The drum keeps pounding as we go higher and higher. Occasional windows along the way offer views of the riverbanks, packed with Pantheras staring expectantly at the top of the tower. There must be hundreds of thousands. If Anjali had the energy, she would have made an accurate count already.

But I can say this much: They far outnumber the Singa.

The windows provide glimpses of a fleet of huge boats, dozens of them, docked on the far side of Elyon, all designed by Enrik.

Even now, Enrik is preparing the fleet to transport the Twelver's Panthera troops, Jin, and Shifters, who will have to be contained while onboard. She will sail them around the Great Wall as Tamir brings the Royal Army over the wall. No Singa would ever expect the enemy to approach by sea. For one thing, we hate being on water. For another, the sea coast of Singara is too rocky and treacherous to launch, or land, a watercraft. How the Twelver will manage it is a mystery. Perhaps even she is unaware of how difficult landing the ships will be.

Anjali quickly tires from the effort of climbing. Her legs wobble. She slumps against the wall.

"Keep going, Anjali," Latha encourages. "Do it for Leo. He needs you."

"What's happening to me?" she mumbles. "Why am I so exhausted?"

Zoya wraps one of Anjali's arms around her neck and shoulders. "Lean into me," she says. "I'll get you there."

The stairway is breezy and bright as we climb the final stretch. The top of the tower is nothing more than a wide platform, about fifteen meters across. Ten Paladins are stationed around the edges. A circle of elders gathers in the center. Abba was once an elder like them, before he challenged the Twelver.

I'm grateful for our robes. Otherwise our unstriped pelts would cause a hissing, fur-raising riot up here. And on the streets far below.

An enormous cone leans over the edge of the platform. The Twelver strides to the cone and speaks into the narrow end in the Old Language.

"Be-takh Alayah bechol leebeh-kha vehel bee-naht kha ahl teesha ehn!"

The cone makes her voice boom and bounce around the canyon of Elyon. The drums cease.

The whole Pride, including those at the top of the tower, answer as one living organism: *"Bechol dera khekha da'eh Alayah; ve-Alayah yeyahsher orkho teykha!"*

"What does that mean?" I whisper to Latha.

"Trust in Alayah with all your heart, and do not lean on your own understanding," Latha translates. "In all your ways acknowledge Alayah—"

"—and Alayah will make your path clear," Anjali mutters.

We stare at our quadron leader.

"She is starting to remember!" Latha whispers.

The Twelver waves her tail. Wajid comes to her side.

"Dear children of Alayah, the Twelver has good news." Again the cone sends her voice around Elyon. "Last night we celebrated the return of Wajid, the Lost Paladin! He came with a gift for the Pride."

Three Paladins shove us to the edge of the platform and tear the white robes away. Our golden pelts glow in the morning sun, in clear view of every set of eyes staring up at us. Alarm and outrage blow through their Pride like a hot wind. Here on the tower's top, the elders hiss and scratch the air with extended claws.

Only the Paladins stay relaxed, having already seen us last night.

"Be at peace, my children," the Twelver says into the cone. "We have nothing to fear from these demonics. They are a gift from Alayah. They bring the key for destroying the demon!"

She extends her arms triumphantly, as if the demon is already dead at her feet. A great cheer rises up from the riverbanks, swelling into an earth-rattling roar.

When the thunder of praise dies away, the Twelver bellows: "Today we welcome the Red Firewing, the fourth and final Guardian to mark the Twelver. But first we will witness the presence and power of the Green Draycon!"

The Twelver stands dangerously close to the edge

of the platform. She spins around and shuffles her feet until only her clawed toes hold her in place. Her body hovers over empty space, wind lapping the fur around her legs.

I hold my breath.

Our kind are skilled at landing on our feet from great distances. But the extreme height of this tower would kill anyone who fell.

Zoya appears hopeful. She would push the Twelver off herself if she had the chance. The Pride purrs in unison just as Abba's family did when the Black Tortoise arrived a few days ago.

Raising her arms, the Twelver looks skyward. Then she leaps into empty air and disappears under the lip of the tower.

I gasp.

The Pride keeps up their purring, unconcerned about their soon-to-be-dead leader.

A mighty roar shakes the tower and rolls around the river canyons of Elyon.

"Behold Jaden, the Green Draycon, one of the Four Guardians," Latha announces.

I peer over the edge of the platform and find the Twelver cradled in the front paw of a massive draycon, who glitters as though his scales are made of fine green jewels. He arrived just in time to save the Twelver from meeting her death on the stones of the temple courtyard.

Jaden is much larger than a regular draycon, so large he straddles the temple buildings.

"It is time," Latha whispers solemnly.

"Time for what?" I ask.

"Time to wake up Anjali," she says. Latha leaps to one of Anjali's drooping shoulders. "Anjali, what is your mission above all others?"

Anjali looks dreadful. Her eyes are glazed over. She's barely able to stay on her feet. "To . . . protect . . . Leo," she rasps.

"Yes," Latha concurs. "That has been your mission from the very beginning. And so it is right now. Now more than ever."

"What . . . do you . . . mean?" Anjali murmurs.

Latha stretches to speak directly into Anjali's ear. "You are more than you appear to be, Anjali. Much more." Latha concludes with words from the Old Language I can't make out.

A faraway expression settles on Anjali's face. Her eyes expand with realization.

The noise of the crowd fades. Lifted by the Green Draycon's head, the Twelver returns to the top of the tower and points at me.

"And now, the Red Firewing comes!" she shouts.

Wajid and another Paladin grab me by the arms.

Zoya lunges at them, but Wajid drives a swift back-kick into her stomach. She crumples to the floor.

"Stick, Latha! Do something!" Zoya wheezes. "Anjali!"

Anjali stares at her hands and arms as if seeing them for the first time. Wajid and the other Paladin lift me like a cub's plaything. My struggles make little difference. They dangle me over the edge of the tower where the Twelver stood only moments ago.

"What are you doing, Wajid?" I cry. "Put me down!"

"Have faith, Eliyah," Wajid says softly.

"Do it!" the Twelver commands.

The two Paladins pitch me over the edge of the tower.

I look back to find Anjali diving after me. She tackles me and wraps her arms, legs, and tail around my body as we begin a rapid plunge to the ground.

"What are you doing?!" I shriek, angry that we are *both* going to die now.

"Saving your life," she says, too calmly for the circumstances. "It's what I do."

She rolls so her back will hit the ground first . . . as if that would do anything to save either one of us.

Then something changes. *She* changes.

Anjali does not transform into a Shifter. Far from it. She becomes a different being altogether.

In a blink, I am no longer embraced by Anjali. I am enfolded in the arms of a creature with bushy white fur, partially tinted copper and marked by bold stripes.

Seconds later, we smack the ground of the temple courtyard not far from the Green Draycon's feet. The wind is knocked out of me, but other than that I am unharmed. And so is the beast cradling me in her paws. She picks me up in her mouth and leaps onto the outer wall of the temple in plain view of everyone in Elyon, including Jaden.

My rescuer lays me down and nuzzles me, purring. My whole body is smaller than her head. I startle and scamper away to get a better view.

Her features are like those of our kind, but more wild and animal-like. She is similar to the painting of the Four Guardians in the temple, radiant with life and strength like the Green Draycon, the Red Firewing, and the Black Tortoise. She is—

The White Tiger!

The Pride kneels on the riverbanks, purring and swaying.

"Anjali?"

"*Yes, Eliyah.*"

The otherworldly voice, which bears hints of Anjali's voice, fills my mind like Daviyah's. Words without speaking. The White Tiger's face contorts into something more like Anjali's face, but only for an instant.

"*I am the first of the Four Guardians to appear to you.*"

The unspoken words vibrate in my bones.

"It was Alayah's will for me to come as a Singa, to be your protector in this world."

Latha pops up behind the White Tiger's ear. Somehow she managed to stay with me on this near-death plunge.

Latha knew how it would turn out.

She knew Anjali was the White Tiger even when Anjali didn't know.

She knew Anjali was the first Guardian to come to me, long before the Red Firewing.

"You should kneel, Leo!" Latha recommends.

Kneel to Anjali? That's different. But Anjali is not only Anjali.

I drop to one knee and bow. The White Tiger's tongue brushes the top of my head.

"Rise, Eliyah, grandson of Daviyah. You need not bow to me a second time."

I stand, and the White Tiger rests her head on mine. The way Daviyah did. The way the Black Tortoise did.

My back tingles with warmth.

She's marking me.

It takes something out of her. When she's done, her fur is even more streaked with copper. She's shifting.

"You need to go," I say. "Get back to the Haven right away."

The Green Draycon offers a gentle roar that is more

like singing, Haven singing. The White Tiger responds with a melodic roar of her own. Jaden and Anjali grow larger as they sing. Eventually their bodies straddle the rivers and the city, blotting out the sky and dwarfing the temple tower. Elyon is plunged into shadow.

The earth shakes. The ground, the rivers, the sky, everything, bends unnaturally toward the two Guardians as if their combined weight is pulling our surroundings toward them.

If this is what happens when two Guardians show up, I can't imagine the result of all Four appearing together. This is why the Axis of the Ancients is so important. Somehow the Axis makes it possible for the Four Guardians to be on earth at the same time without killing the Shakyah or causing devastation to the world around them.

Aware of the danger they are triggering, the Green Draycon vanishes without a sound. The White Tiger scoops me up with one claw and lifts me to the top of the temple tower, where I stood only moments ago.

Stick and Zoya rush to my side. Everyone on top of the tower, including the Twelver, is too awestruck by the presence and power of the White Tiger to be concerned about us.

"Are you all right?" Stick asks.

"I think so," I say.

"And Anjali?" Zoya asks.

I look up. "She needs to go to the Haven as soon as possible."

At that moment, the White Tiger departs, and Anjali is at my side. Instead of her familiar unmarked gold coloring, her fur is white with copper undertones and marked with dark stripes. Her eyes quiver as she strains to keep them from rolling into her head.

As much as I can't bear the thought of being without her, she can't stay here. If one of the Guardians became a Shifter, that would spell disaster. There would be no chance of destroying Hasatamara.

Latha is perched on Anjali's shoulder.

"Lord Eliyah," Latha says, "I have fulfilled my purpose. I would like to go home now . . . if you are willing."

I open my arms. "I am willing."

Light shoots out of my chest and reaches for the clouds. It expands until the bright scene of the Haven is visible between my waist and head. The Paladins and elders around the tower dip their heads and avert their eyes.

"Come," I invite Latha.

"It has been a great honor to serve you, Lord Eliyah."

"It is I who thanks you, noble Jin."

Latha bows and leaps at my chest from Anjali's shoulder, departing with a flash.

Anjali stares longingly at the vision of the swirling

light over the endless beach in my torso. It's the same reaction she has had every time this happens.

"You don't need me to go there," I remind her. "You are one of the Four." I expect the door to the Haven to close.

It doesn't.

"Will I see you again?" I ask, fighting tears.

"I need time to heal. But I will return."

She reaches forward, over the vision of the Haven, and touches my cheek. She draws closer, as if to embrace me. When her chest touches mine, she vanishes in a silent explosion of light, knocking me flat.

And Anjali is gone.

CHAPTER 21

Nothing exists by itself. If you look closely at one
flower, you can behold the whole universe.
— *Sayings of the Ancients*

THE TWELVER makes a beeline for me, tail
lashing.

"So the White Tiger was the first Guardian to come
to you," she fumes, "*not* the Red Firewing!"

She was expecting to see Daviyah, her father,
and receive her fourth mark. Instead, the White Tiger
showed up, and I received my third. Her plan completely boomeranged. Now we have each been marked
by three Guardians.

"You deceived us, Eliyah!" she seethes. "You may
have blood from both Prides, but your lying, thieving
heart is from the demonics!"

"I didn't know what Anjali was. Anjali didn't know
what Anjali was!" I protest, knowing how ridiculous
that sounds.

"More lies!"

"How can I lie about something I know nothing

about? I never asked to be a Shakyah! But there is one thing I do know, Suniyah: You should send your Jin to the Haven! You are wrong to keep them here like prisoners! You are wrong to hold Shifters as part of your plans."

I didn't mean to use the Twelver's actual name. It just slipped out.

But it got her attention.

She was angry already. Now she looks as though she will combust from the rage. It isn't every day someone gives her an order, let alone uses her name. "Take them away!" she commands her Paladins. "Feed them all to our slaycons."

None of the Paladins move a finger in response. The Twelver's head swivels this way and that, searching for support. The Council of Elders hold their ground, looking slightly pleased.

"It is forbidden to disobey the Shakyah!" she screams at her servants in vain.

"It is also forbidden to harm a Shakyah," Stick reminds her.

The Twelver's face darkens. She glowers at Stick and extends her claws. Attacking Stick would break the rule against shedding blood in the temple, but she looks furious enough to do most anything.

"Touch him," Zoya dares, "and I will rip your arms off and beat you with them like a drum."

The Twelver grins. "You are welcome to try, demonic, and prepare to meet death at Jaden's claws." She saunters closer, taunting Zoya. "But death at the claws of a Guardian would be too honorable for you."

"Go ahead and attack her, Zoy," Stick encourages, glaring at the Twelver. "If the Green Draycon shows up, maybe he will give Leo his fourth mark."

That stops the Twelver in her tracks.

"Listen to me, Suniyah," I say. "Why does Daviyah keep his distance from you? Why do you think Alayah, blessed be the name, hasn't granted you a story in over a year?"

The Twelver doesn't answer.

"Because you lost their trust!" I answer for her. "Release your Jin! Let them all go! Send them to their Haven home, and perhaps Alayah will smile on you again. Maybe then the Red Firewing will mark you. Isn't it better to have the approval of Alayah than to command all the Jin in the Haven?"

"Of course you want them all sent back to the Haven," the Twelver scoffs. "You want to protect your Pride! But we have spent too long building an army of Jin to release them now. They will return to the Haven when the demon is destroyed!"

"Unless you die first," Stick chides, "like your father did in the Great War. Then they all return home automatically, don't they?"

The Twelver signs to the Paladins waiting at the edges of the tower. Eight come forward. Four lift Zoya by her arms and legs. She kicks and struggles without much effect. Four more pick up Stick, who doesn't put up any resistance.

"Throw them off!" she commands.

"No!" I scream.

The Paladins waste no time marching my friends to the edge of the tower and hurling them both into the air. Stick wails like a wounded cub.

I rush forward, but Wajid grabs me and pushes me roughly to the floor.

I'm powerless to save them. I sent Ursus and Latha to the Haven.

And Anjali is gone too.

I have only one option, one name to speak.

"Magmar!"

Everyone on the tower freezes at the sound of Magmar's name. The Twelver's face registers shock and disbelief.

The crowd of Pantheras on the streets of Elyon below breaks the uneasy silence with a collective gasp of horror. In the same moment, Zoya and Stick soar up over the lip of the tower, in a near reverse of being pitched off only moments ago. Stick is still wailing until he hits the floor with Zoya tumbling at his side.

I'm so relieved to see them alive, I nearly weep.

"I never thought I'd be happy to see that big ugly spider again," Stick groans as he sits up.

The Pantheras back away as Magmar's legs appear, pulling the rest of the giant spider's hideous body onto the top of the tower.

"Ha!" Magmar bellows, relishing the horrified expressions of the Twelver, the Paladins, and the council. "Oh yes. I am here! Magmar has returned! Thanks to Shakyah Eliyah!"

"You made a grave mistake bringing Magmar here," the Twelver cautions. "He is a servant of the demon and nothing but trouble. Send him away at once!"

"Trouble for you," Stick retorts. "Maybe not for us."

"You won't call any Jin to attack Magmar, will you?" I challenge the Twelver. "Magmar could turn them into Shifters with one bite. You're happy to keep a few Shifters locked up, but you don't want any heading for Bad Mountain before you're ready."

The Twelver lashes her tail.

"Magmar, get us out of here!" I command.

"Let's be clear about something right away, Eliyah," Magmar says in a measured tone. "You and I will get along much better if you don't order me around like some slavish Jin! In case you haven't heard, obedience isn't my strongest talent."

"Magmar," I try again, "would you please help us get out of here? Now?"

"I would be delighted, Eliyah," Magmar replies courteously. "But why don't I eliminate the Twelver and her pesky white-robed helpers first?" He takes a menacing step toward the Twelver.

"No," I say, to Stick's great disappointment. "The sooner we leave, the better."

"Suit yourself!" Magmar says. He scoops each of us up and delivers us to his back.

"You are a fool to trust Magmar," the Twelver warns.

"Is he less trustworthy than you?" Stick sneers. "Not sure that's possible!"

Jakobah says something to the Twelver in urgent hand gestures. I still don't understand their silent language, but he's clearly frustrated by our escape. The Twelver ignores him.

"You are free to go, Eliyah. And when Magmar betrays you, don't bother returning to Elyon. You have no home among the demonics and no home here. Go and find your mother if you can. But know this: You will never find your father without *my* help!"

"Where is he?" I can't help asking even though I know she isn't about to reveal his whereabouts now.

"Makayah is here, in the temple!" a Paladin shouts. It's Wajid! "He is another prisoner of this Shakyah who calls herself the Twelver!"

"Silence, Wajid!" the Twelver thunders. "Show obedience!"

"You are not worthy of obedience!" Wajid declares, pushing through the ranks of Paladins. "You have no respect for Alayah or the Jin. Wajid has given allegiance to Shakyah Eliyah!"

"Throw him off the tower!" the Twelver urges.

"Can't she think of another way to kill someone?" Stick wonders aloud. "Tossing enemies off the tower obviously isn't working out."

"No weapons or bloodshed in the temple," Zoya reminds him.

The Paladins close in on Wajid. Wajid rips off his robe to reveal forbidden armor and weapons beneath. He bounds toward Magmar. The giant spider bares his teeth, preparing to defend himself. For all Magmar knows, this Paladin is on the attack.

"Please let him come, Magmar!" I say. "He is our friend!"

"You see, dear Paladins and members of the high council," the Twelver taunts, "Wajid is a *friend* of the demonics! His heart has been polluted by the demon! He is no longer Panthera!"

Wajid pounces. Magmar lifts a leg as if to skewer Wajid in mid-leap. Instead, Magmar grabs Wajid around the waist and yanks the Paladin to his back with the rest of us.

Magmar is about to leap off the tower with his four passengers when a bird squawks. One of the Twelver's Jin ravens has returned. The silky black creature circles the tower and alights on the Twelver's outstretched arm.

"Speak your news," the Twelver commands, ears alert and ready.

"Tomorrow!" the raven says, tucking its dark wings. "Singas invade tomorrow! When the sun is high!"

Tomorrow! Tamir is moving quickly.

"Big fence coming down," the raven continues. "Singas come tomorrow."

The Twelver is delighted. "How fortunate! The demonics believe they are surprising us, when we will surprise them with a swift victory and death to the demon!"

"Without the Axis of the Ancients and the Four Guardians, you follow the Twelver to *your* death and to the destruction of both Prides," Wajid warns the high council and the Paladins.

"We have no choice!" the Twelver retorts. "The demonics are coming. We must prepare for war." She levels her gaze on me. "Beginning with the return of the Axis to its proper owner."

"I told you, I don't know where it is!" I yell.

"We will see each other again, Eliyah," the Twelver predicts. "Soon."

"Time to go, Magmar!" I say.

Magmar whirls and leaps off the edge of the tower. Stick screams.

Wajid wraps one arm around my waist. His other hand grips the hair on Magmar's back. Magmar plants a line of webbing on the side of the tower to slow our fall. He scrambles easily over the temple wall and bridge, then climbs up the sloping city of Elyon, rooftop by rooftop, as if ascending uneven stairs. Pantheras scatter like frightened mice as we barrel over their homes.

We surge through the farmland bordering Elyon and pause on the hill where we rested yesterday, waiting for night to fall.

From the hilltop, I watch the high ground of the river city, expecting to find a mass of warriors and Jin following us. But all is still around Elyon.

"Why did she let us go?" I ask.

"She believes we will lead her to your mother and to the Axis," Wajid says. "She will use her Jin to track us. Look!"

Six winged creatures rise up from Elyon and soar over the farmland, heading straight for us. They are the same type of Jin that took me into the holding chamber beneath the temple.

"Minokaws," Magmar says with disgust. "Their claws and teeth are sharper than their eyes and brains."

"What makes her think we will lead her to the Axis or to my mother?"

"Because, Eliyah," Wajid utters, "your mother *has* the Axis."

Breath catches in my throat. "What? She's the one who stole it?"

"Nice!" Stick says admiringly.

"Mira and Makayah stole the Axis one year ago," Wajid explains. "Makayah was captured in the heist, while Mira escaped with the Axis. Since then, the Twelver has searched for Mira without success. She holds Makayah prisoner, hoping to exchange him for the Axis. Wajid learned all this from the Paladins upon my return. Wajid attempted to free Makayah last night without success. He is very, very weak."

"I don't know how to find my mother and the Axis!" I exclaim, exasperated. "Where are we supposed to go?"

"Go wherever you like," Magmar says. "As for me, I will return to my ancient home. You are welcome there. It will provide you some shelter and protection from the Twelver's Jin."

"Before you take us any farther, Magmar" I say, "I need to know something. Is it true that you serve Hasatamara?"

Magmar exhales wearily. "I am partly responsible for the existence of Hasatamara. But I do not serve him. I do not serve anyone. Not even Alayah. I like my freedom."

"Won't you eventually become a Shifter," Stick asks, "like the others?"

"There is a way to avoid that," Magmar says, "but I doubt any of you would approve."

"Go on, please," I invite. "The more I know about all this, the better."

"To avoid becoming a Shifter, I only have to drink the blood of a Jin," he confesses.

"And then they become Shifters instead of you," I say.

"Correct," Magmar affirms. "It is true of all the Jin, but I am the only Jin willing to do it."

"Sorry to interrupt," Stick pipes up, pointing skyward, "but should we be concerned about *those* Jin heading our way?"

Wajid lifts his face. "They are not sent to do us harm," he assures us. "They are only sent to follow us and report our location to the Twelver."

"Do you want to come to my ancient home or not?" Magmar asks.

Stick and Zoya pull me close.

"Are you sure about this?" Stick whispers. "Going to the lair of a giant Jin-killing, blood-drinking spider no one trusts? What does that accomplish?"

"Maybe nothing," I admit. "But Magmar was sent for a purpose. We must have faith. Besides that, he's good protection against slaycons."

"That's true," Stick exclaims. "No slaycon would be stupid enough to attack him."

"We will go with you, Magmar," I say. "But how are we going to lose those minokaws?"

"We can't," Magmar says. "At least not during the day, even with the woods giving us some cover. We will arrive at my lair by night. The entrance is nearly impossible to find in daylight. With the assistance of night dimming their already-weak eyes, we will lose them easily enough."

"Lead on," I say.

Magmar's legs whirl, churning up grass and dirt as we bound through Panthera territory, heading southwest, through the woods in the direction of the sea, closer to Singara. The minokaws keep pace with us, soaring in wide, lazy circles overhead or waiting in the trees as we pause to feed on an antelope slain by Magmar and to drink from a warbling stream.

We exit the woods as the sun retreats behind the Great Mountain, which looms over the western horizon like a mighty wave of earth. Soft, salty air stirs in our nostrils. The soothing sound of surf caresses our ears. The ground levels to a plain peppered with boulders.

Magmar halts. "Not much has changed in a few million years."

"We are close to your home, then?" I ask.

"Very close," Magmar replies.

"And we are not far from our home," Stick says, gazing longingly at the Great Mountain.

Wajid searches the sky. The minokaws circle like vultures waiting for death to claim their prey. "The cliffs overlooking the sea are just ahead," Magmar says. "There is a gash in the cliff rock that leads all the way to the beach below. When night comes, we will make our way down that cleft to the sand, and into the entrance of my old home."

"And the minokaws won't follow us?" I say.

"They won't be able to see us, let alone follow us," Magmar promises. "As I said before, their claws are sharper than their eyes. If we stay still enough now, they might mistake us for just another boulder!"

Before the curtain of night drops, the six minokaws flap to the ground and surround us, baring their dagger-like teeth.

"I think they see us," Stick whispers.

"We can still lose them, but it won't be easy," Magmar warns. "We need to split up."

CHAPTER 22

You do not have a life. You are life itself.
Because life is eternal, it can never be lost.
— *Sayings of the Ancients*

I F WE SPLIT UP," Magmar explains, "the minokaws will split up as well. Their eyes are bad, but the fewer eyes on us the better. One of you will head east along the cliffs, and one of you will head west. You will find different paths down the cliff, moving from shadow to shadow to avoid the minokaws until you reach the bottom. Two others will ride me to the beach, traveling down the scar in the cliff rock. We will meet beneath the rocky overhang where the scar ends. At that point, we are only a few hops from the back door to my lair."

"It is a good plan," Wajid affirms. "Wajid will stay with Magmar and Eliyah. You two will run in opposite directions," he says to Stick and Zoya.

Stick bristles. "How come we have to be the runners?"

"Because," Wajid explains coolly, "from a strategic point of view, you two are the most disposable. Shakyah

Eliyah is the only one of us who matters, and Wajid has sworn to protect him."

"You hear that, Leo?" Stick vents. "Zoya and I are disposable!"

"Not to me," I say. "Your eyes are better than any of ours, Stick. You should have no problem finding a way down there."

"Let's go, Stick," Zoya says, sliding off Magmar.

"So we lose Anjali and now the Maguar is in charge?" Stick gripes.

"Make noise as you run," Magmar advises. "It will help draw them away."

"Will they attack us?" Stick asks.

"Without a doubt," Magmar says. "But remember, if you keep to the shadows, you will be invisible to their eyes."

Stick dismally surveys the barren landscape before him. There are precious few shadowy places to claim for camouflage.

Zoya roars and takes off running west. Stick groans and heads east, hollering bombastically as he goes. Two minokaws lift into the air after Zoya, while two others pursue Stick.

That leaves two for us.

"Our turn," Magmar announces. "Hang on!"

The giant spider waggles his Shifter-making fangs, howls, and charges one of the minokaws, who wisely leaps out of the way. Once again, Wajid curls a striped arm around my waist and grips the hair on Magmar's back to hold us both in place. We power for the cliff, and Magmar dives off the edge after planting a sticky blob of webbing at the top. The remaining two mino-kaws take flight and soar down the cliff to keep track of us.

The rapid descent is terrifying. The cliff is much higher than I imagined, ending in rocky sea coast at least one hundred meters down. There is no beach that I can see. Just waves lapping sharp boulders that stab upward from the water like rusty, broken blades.

A thick cord of web spools out behind us as the rocky shore rushes up. The web slows our free fall, and Magmar tucks into the gash stretching down the cliff to the sea. Frustrated, the minokaws screech and flap up and down the cliffs, searching for us without success.

Shrouded in the double darkness of night and the cleft, Magmar picks his way down. Salty droplets of surf sprinkle our faces.

"We are too soon," Magmar laments. "The water is high. The tide has not pulled the sea far enough away for us to reach the beach and the entrance of my lair."

"Can you swim, Magmar?"

"Like a rock, Eliyah. I swim like a rock with legs."

"What about minokaws?" I ask. "Do they float, especially when they are wrapped in webbing?"

"Excellent idea!" Magmar says, catching my meaning. "We shall find out!"

Wajid and I nestle into a ledge of rock inside the cleft and peer out to see how Magmar will trap them. The giant spider scampers out of hiding.

"Looking for us?" Magmar hollers to the minokaws.

The two flying Jin zoom toward their target, one from above and one from below. Magmar sprays a net of webbing and expertly snares them both as they soar too close.

"Ha!" Magmar cheers, followed by a surprised gasp as the bound and struggling minokaws nearly yank him off balance. He pulls them close and spools the beasts in layer after layer of webbing. He mercifully lowers his prisoners to the sea face-up, so they can breathe. "Minokaws float!" Magmar announces. "Come! Come!"

"The rock is slick, Eliyah," Wajid says. "Allow Wajid to go first to find the safest path. If you slip, Wajid will catch you."

Suddenly I see Kaydan on Wajid's striped face.

"Are you unwell?" he asks.

"You remind me of someone, that's all. Someone I lost."

"For those who trust Alayah, the Lord of Lights, nothing living is ever lost. That is what the Ancients say."

"I'm sorry I ever doubted you, Wajid."

"Come! Come!" Magmar cries again.

We creep down the gash in the cliff and find our way to Magmar. He has plugged and wrapped the mouths of the minokaws with webbing to keep them quiet but left their nostrils free. They ebb and flow, banging against the rocks in tempo with the tide. Their round eyes show fear and frustration.

"Not bad for my first raft!" Magmar exclaims. He reduces his size—a trick I witnessed when he first appeared in the Twelver's holding chamber—and hops to the floating minokaws to demonstrate their seaworthiness. "Please watch your step as you board." Although he's now half his former size, there still isn't much room left on this minokaw boat except directly beneath him. Magmar has two legs anchored to the rock to keep us from drifting under the cliff.

"Leo! Over here!"

It's Stick. He's crouching with Zoya on a small peninsula of rock about twenty meters off.

"There's our first stop, Magmar," I say.

Magmar studies the expanse of angry sea between us and my friends. "Too risky," he concludes. "These minokaws will keep us from drowning as we go under the cliff, but they aren't seaworthy enough to go out there. We'll have to leave them behind."

"That's not an option," I say. "Could I have a line of webbing?"

Magmar turns and produces a strand of webbing from the spinneret on his backside.

"This could be the end of you, Eliyah," Wajid says. "You might be pulled under the water or dashed against the rocks. Or both."

"That's why you're coming with me, Wajid," I say, wrapping the sticky web around my waist. "You know how to swim. Be ready to pull us in, Magmar!"

I leap into the sea. The water holds me in an icy grip, fingering its way through every bit of my pelt. A moment later Wajid is in the water, clutching me by the waist with one arm and fighting the current with the other. At first, we are beaten back, drifting under the cliff. Wajid roars and kicks up a storm to propel us toward Stick and Zoya.

Wajid flings me onto the shelf of rock where my friends wait.

"What took you so long?" Stick jeers.

"Zoya!" Wajid says at our feet. "Jump in and allow Eliyah and your brother to hold on to us."

"I can't swim," Zoya protests.

"That doesn't matter. We need your strength!" Wajid howls.

Zoya leaps into the water, and Wajid grabs her by the scruff of the neck. He locks one arm around her meaty shoulders.

"Fight the current!" Wajid instructs, letting go

of the rock. Zoya thrashes about in the water like an alarmed karkadann. She lacks the easy grace of Wajid in the water, but she's not sinking. "Now you!" Wajid calls to Stick and me.

I secure my line of webbing to Stick's waist along with my own. Stick's whiskers droop. His ears are pressed against his head.

"It's just water, Stick," I say, teeth chattering. "Salty, icy, miserable water."

"Can't wait," he moans.

I jump into the sea, taking Stick with me. We hug the broad backs of Zoya and Wajid.

"Let the current take you in!" Magmar calls, floating atop the minokaws. "I will meet you there!" He drifts under the lip of the cliff.

Above the roaring surf, we hear the unwelcome screech of a minokaw darting toward us, with another on its tail. All our hard work to stay hidden is spoiled. The minokaw latches on to Zoya's arm with its foot, digging sharp claws into her flesh.

She yowls.

Stick sinks his teeth into the minokaw's foot while Wajid sends three rapid punches into the minokaw's stomach until it releases Zoya. Wajid embraces Zoya chest to chest, to keep her from sinking, but he's struggling to stay afloat himself. And two more minokaws are bearing down on us.

"Take in as much air as you can!" Wajid barks. "We're going under. Magmar and the current will do the rest!"

With that, he vanishes under the water, taking us all with him. The dull roar of the sea echoes in my ears as the current sucks us beneath the cliff. There is a tug at the web around my waist. I hold on to Wajid tightly as we are pulled in and up. Breaking the surface, we find Magmar clinging upside down to a ceiling of rock, pulling the web line attached to me. Outside, the minokaws swoop, screech, and howl in frustration.

Magmar's minokaw raft floats nearby. The bound creatures hack and sputter as their heads bob in and out of the water.

"Why not set them free, Magmar?" I suggest.

The great spider considers the suggestion. "Why not, indeed?"

Magmar drives his two front feet into the minokaws' chests, killing them instantly.

"No!" I yell too late. "That's not what I meant!"

"They are free now." Magmar giggles. "Watch!"

The minokaw corpses fade into the ghostlike halfway state before exiting this world altogether, leaving nothing more than a heap of webbing. We were so busy avoiding these dreadful creatures, I forgot that they are Jin, kindred to the countless winged beings of light who sing praises to Alayah in the Haven. It pains me that

Magmar killed them, but at least he did not turn them into Shifters.

Magmar points to a hollow in the ceiling that resembles a gaping mouth.

"That tunnel leads straight up to my ancient home," he announces.

"Any time you're ready!" Stick yowls, desperate to get out of the frigid water.

One by one Magmar plucks our dripping hides from the water like someone pulling wet garments from a washtub and places us in the tunnel's opening. We huddle together, soaked fur matted to our bodies, shivering.

"Make way for me!"

We scramble deeper into the tunnel as Magmar joins us, maintaining his diminished stature. My fingers connect with a rough coiled-up object. I yank my hand away.

"What's wrong?" Zoya asks.

"I touched something," I say. "Something like a snake."

Stick directs his keen eyes into the darkness beside me. "That's nothing to worry about," he says. "Just a coil of rope."

"Someone has been here already," Wajid concludes.

"Intruder!" Magmar wails. "They will regret

breaking into the home of Magmar! Allow me to go first. I will deal with the trespasser!"

We lie flat as Magmar glides over us and zooms up the tunnel, grumbling curses against the unwanted guest.

"Should we wait here?" Stick asks. "Until he's . . . finished?"

"Might as well go up," I say. "It won't take Magmar long to neutralize any threats."

Our night vision is challenged by the deepening dark of this twisting incline. Meanwhile, Magmar's raging grows steadily louder. It sounds as if a full-scale battle is being waged up there, with objects crashing about. Dim starlight, coupled with fresh air, tumbles down the shaft as we approach the top.

Stick peers into Magmar's home and stops. "Leo, get up here quick! You're not going to believe this!"

I bound up the last stretch and crouch beside Stick on the floor of Magmar's lair, as Zoya and Wajid settle on either side of us.

His lair is a cavern that overlooks the sea illuminated by starlight pouring in through a wide opening. The cavern is adorned with furs, furniture, weapons, and tools, which a monstrously sized Magmar hurls outside, piece by piece, like unwanted toys.

"Out, out, out!" Magmar cries as he tidies up.

Stick points to some weapons stacked in the corner. "Look, Leo," Stick whispers. "Those weapons are Singa-made!"

"And that's a telescope," I observe, right before Magmar pitches the instrument through the opening. "And over there, on that table, someone is building a timepiece."

"I haven't felt so at home in days." Stick sighs.

"If all this stuff was made by a Singa," I say, excitement mounting in me like a wave, "that can only mean—"

"Your mother!" Zoya exclaims. "This is her hide-out!"

This little hidden cavern is where my mother lives! But where is she now?

Oh no.

Please, no!

"Magmar, was there someone here when you arrived? Another Singa?"

Magmar is too worked up to hear me. He sweeps the items on the table to the cave floor and flings the table outside.

"Magmar, stop!" I shout. "These things are my mother's. She's the one who's living here!"

"I don't care if the Red Firewing himself is staying here," he rages, carrying on with his housecleaning frenzy. "This place is mine, mine, mine!"

There's something like a doll tucked under animal

skins on a bed, which Magmar has not yet disturbed. I dash across the chamber to the bed, dodging Magmar's stomping legs. The doll is of a Singa cub. It's tattered and worn.

Suddenly the bed slides across the room as Magmar prepares to toss it out the window and down to the sea along with everything else. Wajid and Zoya each grab a corner of the bed, attempting to hold it in place. They both lift off the floor, but their combined weight is enough to slow the giant spider down.

"Let go, let go, let go!" he seethes.

I roar, "Magmar!"

Magmar hisses and drops the bed, sending Wajid and Zoya sprawling. He thrusts his face and hideous fangs a whisker's length from my nose. I stifle a shudder. With a small quick nip, he could remove my head.

"This may be your home," I say through gritted teeth, "but these things are not yours. They belong to my mother!"

"Neither she nor her things have any right to be here!" he thunders. "This is my home. MY home!"

"You have been away a long, long time, Magmar. Did you think it would stay empty forever?"

"What do you know of *forever*, mortal?" Magmar counters, shaking with fury. "From this cave I watched the sea for five hundred years, waiting for him to return.

Five hundred years would be forever for you, but it was not long *enough* for me."

He's calming down. I need to keep him talking.

"Waiting for who to return?"

"When he left, he was known as Helel." Magmar stares past me, out the opening to the sea, to another time, to another age. "When he returned, he was Hasatamara."

"Tell them the story, Magmar," Wajid says calmly, winking at me. He must know the story already. "It would be good for you to speak it and good for these demonics to hear."

I'm flooded with curiosity. Who is Helel and why was Magmar so afraid of him?

Magmar studies the floor for a time and shrinks until he is no taller than Wajid. "I don't care for stories, especially that one." He becomes so still, I wonder if he has dozed off.

"It was so long ago," he begins. "And yet, I remember it like it was yesterday."

I sit on the bed with Zoya. Stick and Wajid recline on the floor.

"It was in the earliest days of the earth, before the Guardians and the Jin, when no two-legged creatures like you, or the humanas before you, walked the earth. Alayah made two gold-skinned Titans. They were gigantic beings, impossibly huge and powerful. For them, trees were like blades of grass. And they were glorious, more beautiful than anything else in creation. To look upon them was to love them. That is how wonderful they were to behold."

Magmar's story does not spin into a vision. Nevertheless, he is a decent Teller, and his words drum up images in my mind.

"One Titan ruled the land and the other ruled the sea. They were brothers, yet each Titan did not know the other existed. The Earth Titan was named Helel. The Sea Titan was named Hydrus.

"Helel would set the length of the seasons and talk to the sun and the clouds to determine the weather. He created laws for creatures of the earth to follow. It was a time of great harmony and peace. All creatures respected and worshipped Helel as a god.

"Except me. I was jealous of him.

"I was not like other creatures, dull and slow-witted. I had already rejected Alayah, and I wasn't about to worship Helel instead. I wanted to rule the earth in his place, but I was no match for his size. In a contest of strength, he would crush me as easily as you might crush a mouse, though in terms of cleverness and trickery, I was his superior.

"One day, I paid a visit to Helel and asked him a question.

"'Your Holy Worshipfulness,' I said, knowing how

much Helel enjoyed being treated like a god, 'how do you know you are the largest, most powerful being on earth?'

"'I have been all over the earth and find no creature larger than myself,' Helel replied.

"'Ah! That's because you have only searched on the dry ground,' I said. 'There are creatures of the sea who are much larger than you. Why not go into the sea and have a look?'

"'No, thank you, Magmar. Alayah has ordered me to stay on the land. This is where I belong.'

"But I pressed on. 'Of course Alayah ordered you to stay on the land! Alayah does not want you to discover . . . *the truth!*'

"Helel grew thoughtful as the seed of envy took root in his mind. I left Helel alone but stayed close enough to see what the Titan might do. Helel asked the sun and the clouds if they had ever seen a sea creature larger than him. But they had never been in the sea and could not answer. Helel sat gazing at the sea for one hundred years, considering whether or not to search the ocean.

"I got tired of waiting. One day, I approached the golden Titan and asked, 'Will you die if you go into the sea?'

"'No, Magmar,' answered Helel. 'Unlike other creations of Alayah, I do not require food or air to live.'

"'Then what's the harm?' I said innocently. "You will be plagued with curiosity for eternity until you discover the truth. There is only one way to put your mind at rest.'

"'You are right, Magmar,' Helel determined at last. 'I will go.'

"He got up at once and walked straight into the sea. He soon found that the water world was much larger than the land. It took five hundred years to search every part of the sea for a creature as large as himself.

"Meanwhile, I made myself the lord of the earth, knowing Helel would be away for a long time. I hoped Helel would never return, because I was enjoying myself and because he would be very angry with me. I watched the sea from this very place.

"After centuries of searching the vast waters, Helel did find another gold-skinned Titan living in a crater in the deepest part of the water world. The Sea Titan, Hydrus, welcomed Helel like a brother, for that is what he was. At the sight of another Titan as large and beautiful as himself, Helel was overcome with jealousy and killed his only brother.

"By the time Helel came back to the earth, he was much changed. His brother Titan's blood had stained Helel's skin, transforming it from gold to copper, and distorting his once-beautiful features. He was covered in seaweed and barnacles. Few creatures recognized him. All avoided him. Although Helel was now certain that he was the largest creature on land and in the sea, his heart had grown dark and cold.

"Then Alayah put these words into the mind of Helel and into the minds of every creature so that all would know and understand: *'What have you done, Helel? Your brother's blood calls to me from the sea.'*

"'You deceived me!' Helel roared. 'You said I was the largest being on the earth!'

"*'No such thing was ever declared,'* Alayah replied, *'and now, because of your pride, your brother is dead. From this day forward, your name shall no longer be Helel. You will be called Hasatamara, which means The Accuser of the Sea, because you have accused me of deception. You will no longer live on the land you know and love. You will live in the sea in your brother's place.'*

"Hasatamara's furious wail shook the mountains. But he could do nothing to change his punishment. Alayah had spoken. Hasatamara was thrown into the sea.

"At that time, Alayah created the Four Guardians, who, together, are stronger than Hasatamara. The Four were made to guard the earth should Hasatamara ever attempt to return.

"At the end of the Humana Age, Hasatamara did return, drawn and emboldened by the bloodshed and violence of the humana wars. He rose up with a mighty wave and flooded much of the earth. Alayah sent the Guardians to stop Hasatamara, but the Shijin are so mighty and so glorious, their combined power nearly destroyed the earth itself. Instead, the Guardians attacked Hasatamara two by two. Hasatamara defeated the Red Firewing and the Green Draycon, but they also wounded and weakened the demon. The White Tiger, fighting alongside the Black Tortoise, barely managed to overpower Hasatamara and bury him beneath the mountain, where he is to this day, waiting for his chance to escape.

"That is why Alayah created the Axis of the Ancients. So that if Hasatamara ever found the strength to escape, there would be a way to bring all Four Guardians to the earth at one time without demolishing the very place they were created to protect."

"And what happened to you?" I ask.

"After Hasatamara was banished to the sea," Magmar goes on, "Alayah brought me to the Haven, where I could do no more harm, as it is impossible to cause harm in the Haven. But I was shunned by the other Jin in the Haven, which is why I am happy to take your side against the Twelver's Jin now. Alayah promised I would return to earth one day. And so I have."

"Since it is Alayah, blessed be the name, who decides when to send you to the earth and when to send you back to the Haven," I suggest, "you are not as free as you think."

"No one is, Shakyah Eliyah," Wajid despairs. "No one is."

"But your story continues," I say encouragingly. "Now you have the opportunity to make things right!"

"I have no interest in making things right." With each word, Magmar grows larger, until he reaches his preferred size. "I would like to see Hasatamara destroyed as much as anyone, but not because I want to reunite the Prides or any foolishness like that."

He still wants to rule the world. Not unlike Tamir. I hope they never meet.

"What do you think of the Twelver's plan to destroy Hasatamara by using a group of Shifters to dig their way into the Great Mountain?" I ask the giant spider. "She wants to expose enough of the demon's body for her Jin to make the kill, but not enough for the demon to escape. Could that work?"

"It could work," Magmar reflects. "But it is very risky. Better to have the Four Guardians do the job, which is why the Twelver is searching frantically for the Axis of the Ancients. Without the Four, it is nearly impossible to kill a creature as large and powerful as Hasatamara. As for me, I doubt that he can be destroyed, even by the Guardians. I believe he can only be defeated and contained."

And until a Shakyah is marked by all Four, the Axis is useless. Which is why the Twelver has a backup plan. She's not content to sit and wait for the Red Firewing to give her the fourth and final mark. Especially not with Tamir on the move.

An idea bursts in my brain. "If my mother stole the Axis, and this is her home—"

Magmar growls at my careless choice of words.

"Her *temporary* hideout," I correct myself.

"Then the Axis might be here somewhere!" Stick exclaims. "Unless Magmar threw it out already."

"If it's so powerful, it would be hard to miss," I say. "Let's look around."

Stick needs no invitation. He's already searching under the bed, one of the last things left in the cave after Magmar's rampage. Finding nothing, Stick moves on to inspect every nook and crack in the rock walls. Zoya helps.

"Maybe it's hidden in the shaft we climbed to get up here," Zoya suggests.

"Or more likely it isn't here at all," Wajid says. He hasn't moved one claw or one whisker to join the search. "Why would Mira risk having the Twelver find her hideout *and* the Axis at the same time?"

"Speaking of the Twelver," Zoya puts in, "won't those minokaws lead her here? Even if they don't find Magmar's home, they know we are nearby."

"We can count on the Twelver arriving by morning," Wajid says. "If not sooner."

Stick shudders. "Then why stay here? No Axis. Twelver on the way. Tamir about to invade. I'd say it's time to go!"

"No!" I snap. "This is closer than we've ever been to my mother. We're not leaving so fast."

"She might not be close by at all, Leo," Stick argues. "She's probably out hunting for you!"

"Silence!" Magmar insists. "Someone is coming."

CHAPTER 23

For Alayah every creature has the same name:
Beloved.
— *Sayings of the Ancients*

STICK'S EARS ANGLE toward the twisting tunnel that leads down to the sea. "Magmar is right. And whoever's coming up isn't alone."

"I will give these intruders what they deserve!" Magmar boasts. "My home is supposed to be a secret!"

"The scent is of demonics," Wajid whispers. "More than one."

"Maybe it's Mira!" I say, wanting to scurry down to meet her. "But what Singa would come with her?"

"Maybe it isn't her at all," Zoya considers. "Maybe it's two soldiers sent by Tamir to scout enemy territory before the invasion. We are close to Singara."

Wajid waves his tail for us to get back and draws two weapons. Stick, Zoya, and I hunker down behind a chunk of rock. Outside the opening, clouds block the starlight, making the cavern dimmer than ever. Wajid crouches in the shadows on the side of the shaft entrance, ready to spring up and attack. Magmar clings to the ceiling, melting into the shadows.

Two soldiers slip into the cavern, familiar Singa weapons unsheathed and ready. Magmar drops from the ceiling and quickly pins one intruder to the floor, while Wajid tackles the other. Wajid tussles with his opponent, blocking expert blows from Singa blades with his own weapons. Magmar wraps his soldier in a tight blanket of webbing. Wajid's challenger wriggles free and knocks Wajid to the ground, then swings a blade at Magmar. The giant spider dodges the attack and seizes the soldier by the throat.

"Who are you?" Magmar demands. "What are you doing here?" He could easily snap this Singa's neck.

"I could ask the same of you," the soldier responds, without a trace of fear. "I live here."

Magmar extends his hideous fangs, preparing to bite.

"Magmar, wait!" I shout.

My heart races. If this Singa claims to live here, she must be—

"Mira?" I say.

The soldier's eyes bounce to me. She studies my face as best she can in the scarce light. "Ma-Makayah?" she ventures, the name catching in her throat. A trickle of blood seeps from the corner of her mouth from the bout with Wajid.

I step closer. "No. I'm Leo. Eliyah. Your son."

Magmar releases her.

"Eliyah!" My mother sinks to her knees, as if my name is a weight too heavy to hold.

She draws me close, inhaling my scent as though it's her last breath.

"Is it really you?"

I nod, unable to speak.

"How long I have waited, only to find you here! This can only be the doing of Alayah, blessed be the name."

She spins me around to inspect my back. "Three marks!" she exclaims. "The same number as the Twelver. The time has come for the Guardians to choose who will bear the Axis."

Her eyes land on Wajid. She scowls. "Why do you come with one of the Twelver's servants?"

"His name is Wajid."

Mira rises to her full height. "Wajid!" Her posture and royal tone remind me of Grandfather. "Not Wajid the captive at the Academy?"

"The very same," Wajid rumbles, staring down at her. "Wajid endured much cruelty at the hands of demonics."

Mira lashes her tail and extends her claws. "And will you take your revenge on my son?"

"Wajid gave up everything for us," I say. "He was

captured after the Great War, risking his life to rescue Makayah."

"Then I give Wajid my thanks," Mira says, but the sharp edge to her words hasn't dulled much. "And you travel with the mighty and menacing Magmar," she says, as though Magmar isn't there, like Grandfather used to do—acknowledging someone's presence while dismissing them at the same time. "Is he the only Jin with you?"

"I sent all the others to the Haven."

Mira grunts her approval. "That is the right thing to do. And if you can only have one Jin, Magmar will do nicely. In fact, no other Jin care to be around him. That is a great advantage in itself."

"What do you know of me, demonic?" Magmar snaps.

"My mate has the blood of the Shakyahs in him," Mira declares haughtily, speaking directly to Magmar for the first time. "He is the son of Shakyah Daviyah, brother of the Twelver. It is their business to know about the Jin. I know you are powerful, Magmar, and good protection. But you are not loyal. You are selfish and serve no higher cause than yourself."

"I am not selfish," Magmar retorts. "I prefer to think of myself as—"

"That is my point exactly," Mira interrupts. "You prefer to think of *yourself*. But take heart. All is not lost.

Perhaps Alayah sent you to earth to change your reputation."

I can say this much after a few minutes with my mother: She is a force to be reckoned with. She is a master of verbal combat, like her father. In fact, the two of them are mirror images of each other, inside and out.

Mira shifts her attention to Stick and Zoya. "And who are they?"

"My quadron-mates: Zoya and Stick."

"Stick!" Mira decries. "What sort of name is that? A stick is a fragile, breakable thing, cut off from its source. Surely you have a proper birth name given by your family."

I have never thought to ask what Stick's real name is.

"He does," Zoya answers for her brother, who is too taken aback to speak, "but he goes by Stick because he has the sticky hands of a thief."

"I see," Mira says warily. "And where is the fourth?"

"She's . . ." My eyes well up. "It's not easy to explain."

Mira notes the grief contorting my face.

"I'm sorry for your loss, Eliyah," she says. "And yet, it defies all probability that even *three* of you survived. Shanti was wise to send you without weapons. Otherwise the Pantheras would have killed you as soon as they laid eyes on you."

"You have weapons," Zoya observes enviously.

"Do you think I survived this long in Panthera territory without knowing how to avoid them when I have to?"

"How is Shanti?" I say, fearing that he, too, has been killed by Tamir's soldiers.

"I am just fine, Lord!"

The muffled words come from my mother's companion, who is face-down on the floor, still bound and trapped by Magmar's webbing.

"But I would be better if I was cut free."

"Shanti!" Zoya and I rush to his side, bare our claws, and slice the webbing away. "What are you doing here?"

The shepherd is dressed in light armor like my mother and carries his familiar pole, slightly curved at one end, along with the standard Singa weapons.

"I came to bring you this," he says, presenting the pole as if it's the most precious thing on earth. "Behold, the Axis of the Ancients! The Staff of Sacred Power! The Prize of the Shakyahs! The bridge between this world and the Haven! The only way to harness all Four Guardians at once!"

We consider the very ordinary metal rod in his hands. It's the exact same staff he carried when we met him at the Border Caves. Nothing special about it.

Stick voices what we are all thinking: "Um . . . that old thing is the Axis of the Ancients?"

"It is asleep," Wajid explains as Shanti reverently

transfers the Axis to my hands. "When it is awakened, it will be unlike anything your demonic eyes have ever seen. It will become a living object with four distinct sections, one for each of the Guardians."

"If you had it this whole time," Stick says skeptically, "why didn't you give it to Leo before we left Singara?"

"I didn't know what it was!" Shanti declares. "Mira only told me to keep it safe. When she came to reclaim it this very day, and told me of its importance, I insisted on delivering it myself."

"He is as foolish as ever," Mira says, suppressing a warm smile. "And as persistent."

"Stealing the Maguar's most powerful object is daring enough to be called foolish," Stick asserts. "Why did you swipe it?"

"A year ago," Mira reveals, "when the Twelver stopped receiving Jin from Alayah, the Red Firewing came to Makayah and told him to take the Axis and save it for our son."

"And what made you decide to get the Axis from Shanti today?" Stick presses.

"I saw the White Tiger and the Green Draycon towering over Elyon this morning," she says, beaming. "I knew it was a sign that Eliyah had come."

"If it's asleep," I ask, "how do you . . . wake it up?" The Axis's metal is warm in my hands, like skin, and surprisingly light.

"There is a sacred word," Wajid intones. "When spoken by a Shakyah, the Axis awakens."

Stick's ears lift. "What word?"

"The word is passed from Shakyah to Shakyah. All that is known about the word is that it expresses the deepest desire of all creatures."

"Then the word must be 'food,'" Stick suggests. "Everyone desires food. Speaking of which, do you have anything to eat around here?"

"The Twelver is probably on her way," I tell Mira, ignoring Stick. "She should be here by morning at the latest."

"Excellent!" Mira pronounces. "She will awaken the Axis for you."

I cock my head. "She's coming here to *take* the Axis, not to awaken it."

"She will awaken it before she attempts to leave with it," Mira says. "But we won't make it easy for her."

"What do you mean?"

"She wants to meet her father more than anything else in the world, even more than destroying Hasatamara. She will use you, and the Axis, to get Daviyah to appear."

"She tried that already," I inform her. "It didn't work. The White Tiger came instead."

"That will change when she has the Axis. First, she will awaken it. Then she will order you to touch the

Red Firewing's section of the Axis and call on Daviyah. Because you have been marked by the Red Firewing, he will come."

"What if Daviyah marks her after he shows up?" Zoya considers. "That would ruin everything, right?"

"That is a risk we must take," Mira concedes. "However, I have a plan. Before Eliyah summons the Red Firewing, we will cause the Green Draycon to come and give Eliyah his fourth mark."

"This is starting to feel like a race," Stick says.

"Indeed, it is," Mira confirms. "And we must do everything in our power to make sure Eliyah gets to the finish line first."

CHAPTER 24

Never part with the truth unless it will save a life.
— *Sayings of the Ancients*

MY MOTHER'S BED, the one piece of furniture not discarded by Magmar, is far more comfortable than anything else I've slept on in the past week. Mira is wrapped around me. Her contented purr warms my pelt. With one finger, she traces the mark of the Red Firewing on my shoulder blades.

"It must have been hard to hide what you are all these years," she says.

"It was," I say. "The strange creatures, the fear of being caught, it nearly drove me insane. I hate to think what it would have done to Grandfather if he had found out."

Grief clogs my throat like a piece of stuck meat.

"Did Shanti tell you about Grandfather? That he's . . . gone?"

"He did, Eliyah," she replies gently. "But I have been grieving his loss for a long time. Was the Kahn good to you?"

"He was . . . everything to me."

"Raja was a great Kahn," she states. "Wise and intelligent. Kind and fierce. Strong and humble. A good scientist. And yet, he could be cruel and cold-hearted."

"He sent you away," I complain bitterly. "All my life he lied to me about you. He said you died. He had no right!"

Mira exhales. "He wanted to protect you from the truth about your father. He was furious with me for choosing a Panthera mate. He sent me away and kept you secured in the castle in case I ever attempted to return to Singara."

That's curious.

I always thought Grandfather kept me in the castle because he was concerned about my safety. Apparently, that wasn't the only reason.

"Did you ever try?"

"Once," she says. "Nine years ago. I dressed as a shepherd and went with Shanti to the castle gate to sell his flock. I caught a glimpse of you in the courtyard. You were only a cub of four at the time. I had to see you, to know you were alive and well, but it drove me mad with longing."

She squeezes me, as if pushing the painful memory away.

"Then, one year ago, the Red Firewing came to Makayah and me," she continues. "Daviyah told us to take the Axis and to keep it for *Shakyah* Eliyah. That was when we learned who, and what, you are. I made a plan with Shanti to get you out of Singara just before your thirteenth birthday, before your hunt. Shanti was to take my note to Galil, the one Singa I trusted to deliver the note to you. But Galil was also loyal to the Kahn. I waited and waited, but you did not come. It seemed our plan had failed."

"Galil gave me the note when Grandfather died," I say. "That freed him to tell me the truth about you."

"Then without the Kahn's death," she reckons, "you would not be here."

I never thought of that. But it's true. And there's this:

"You are next in line for the throne," I venture. "If we live long enough to get back to Singara, you should be the ruler, not me."

"Oh, Eliyah . . ." Mira sighs. "I have been away a long time. Everyone thinks I am dead, according to your grandfather's word. Despite all the pain Father caused, he still wanted *you* to become the next Kahn."

"I don't hate Grandfather," I confess. "I probably should for what he did to us, but I miss him too much to hate him."

"I understand that very well," Mira purrs. "Save your anger for Tamir."

"It's possible Tamir had something to do with Grandfather's death," I say.

"The Kahn dies right after the prince goes to the Academy? And who fills the power vacuum? It's not only possible," she scoffs, "it is highly probable. I grew up with Tamir, Eliyah. Power is all he ever wanted. Now that he has his heart's desire, he will use it to destroy everything. You must face him. And stop him."

·   ·   ·

I awake to words from the Old Language dancing in my ears.

Wajid stares outside, muttering a prayer as the first honeyed rays of sunlight spread over the surface of the sea. I'm still in my mother's bed. One of Mira's arms is curled around me. Her other hand grips the Axis.

Wajid's deep tones fill the cave, rising in volume and stirring Shanti, Stick, Zoya, and my mother.

Shanti stands beside Wajid to join in the prayer. Their voices intertwine like branches from two neighboring trees. When they finish, Wajid regards Shanti with surprise.

"Makayah taught me," Shanti explains, "long, long ago."

Mira gives me the Axis. "Time to claim your birthright."

She goes to the opening, scans the sky, and sniffs the cool, salty air. "The Twelver has not yet arrived. But she is close. Her minokaws are soaring overhead, searching the cliffs. You must show yourself, Eliyah, and draw her to you."

"How?"

"Go to the top of the cliff and hold the Axis high," Mira instructs. "The minokaws will spot you, and they will direct her."

"Wajid will go with you," Wajid offers. "The minokaws will attempt to take the Axis from your hands."

"And we will go too," Zoya adds, not about to be outdone by Wajid.

I look to Mira. "What about you? And Shanti?"

"Shanti and I will stay hidden until the right moment."

"Okay, let's do this," I say, masking my dread. "Magmar, can you get us up there?"

"Of course." Magmar squeezes his bulky body through the opening. "I will go up and drop a line for you to climb."

Stick watches him go. "Why didn't we enter this way last night instead of freezing our tails off?" He shivers at the memory.

"Then the minokaws would have found this cave immediately," Wajid explains.

"And there would have been no rest for any of us," Mira adds. "Magmar did the right thing bringing you up from the beach." It's the first kind thing she's said about him.

"There wasn't a beach when *we* got there," Stick grouses.

A silvery cord of web dangles outside the window, glinting in the morning light.

"You two go first," Wajid directs Stick and Zoya, "then Shakyah Eliyah. Wajid will come last."

"We're first again?" Stick gripes. "Because we are *disposable?*"

"Do you even know what that means?" Zoya asks.

"It means something not good!" Stick barks.

"Wajid," I say wearily. "Please go ahead of us."

Stick throws Wajid his signature smirk. Wajid doesn't give Stick the pleasure of expressing his own displeasure. He simply hops into the cave opening and climbs Magmar's thread.

"Zoya, I'm not sure I can climb up while holding the Axis."

Zoya beams. "I got you."

We climb to the edge of the opening and Zoya crouches down. I cling to her back, wrapping one arm around her neck while my other hand holds the Axis tight to my body. My legs are clamped on her waist. I entered the Royal Academy of War Science in much the same way.

"Ready," I say.

Zoya seizes Magmar's line of web and climbs. I gaze up, hoping the journey will be short, but the cliff is so uneven, it isn't clear how far we have to go. Mino-kaws circle in the sky, appearing like birds from this distance, searching the long stretches of cliff that extend for many kilometers along the sea. They haven't spotted us yet, but it won't take long.

I look down at Stick, climbing behind us. Seventy meters below him, sharp-edged rocks jut up like teeth around the roiling sea. My mother's belongings, pitched out by Magmar last night, have already been devoured and washed away without a trace.

I rest my head on Zoya's shoulders. Warm muscles ripple and flex beneath her pelt with each pull.

Suddenly, huge spider forelegs seize Zoya's arms and hoist us the remaining distance. We tumble onto flat ground beside Wajid. It's the same plain we encountered yesterday evening, desolate and lonely.

This is where I will face the Twelver. This will be our battlefield.

Magmar drops Stick beside us.

Moments later, the sky teems with minokaw screeches, louder and closer.

"Here they come," Stick says.

"We must prevent them from getting close to Eli-yah and the Axis!" Wajid instructs. He harvests rocks from the ground and loads them into his sack. "Get beneath Magmar, Eliyah!"

I scramble under Magmar while Zoya, Wajid, and Stick hurl rock after rock at the approaching minokaws.

The four Jin flap higher, out of range. One soars off while the other three swoop and circle in figure eights, marking the spot where we stand.

"That one will report to the Twelver," Wajid says. "She won't be far."

Not ten minutes later, the earth rumbles. Then it shakes. In the distance, a cloud of dust gathers as a small army of Jin rolls into view. They crest the plain and barrel toward us. With the Jin are a few dozen Paladins and many more warriors, dressed and armed for battle.

Leading the charge is the Twelver herself, riding atop the big bony head of Kaitan.

Zoya's claws are already out. She would like nothing more than to redesign the Twelver's face. But she would have to get through all her fighters first, not to mention the Green Draycon.

The Jin slow their stampede and trot ever closer. Fifty meters away, they form an arc around us, sealing off any hope of escape unless we want to dive over the cliff. Among the Jin, I recognize Yohan, Laylin, Akelah, Mizu, Kartik, Sunjay, Sentis, Timereth, Naraka, Mudra, Bazer, Dalami, Nimshook, Kumar, Zuman, and many others.

It's an imposing crowd.

The Twelver climbs down from Kaitan's head. She wears leather armor dressed with jewels, slaycon teeth, draycon horns, and firewing feathers. Two heavily armed Paladins take positions on either side of her. One of them is Jakobah.

Magmar hovers protectively over us, displaying his fangs to the Twelver's troops.

Magmar's threat is lost on the Twelver. She's focused on the Axis in my hands.

"You were right," I say with a shrug. "I found it."

"Where is Mira?" she demands.

"She's not here," I lie.

Grandfather used to say, "Never part with the truth unless it will save a life." That's why he lied to me all these years. He thought he could save me by burying the truth.

The Twelver raises a skeptical eyebrow and scans the lip of the cliff over our shoulders.

"You have done well finding the Axis for the Twelver, Eliyah," she says, slyly implying that I am about to hand it over. "Taking what does not belong to you is a grave sin against Alayah."

"Is it yours?" I ask. "Or does it belong to the Guardians? Perhaps we should let them decide."

"It was not given to the Guardians! It was given to the Ancients! It belongs to our Pride, not in the hands of demonics!" She takes a menacing step forward.

Magmar matches her advance.

"Back off, Magmar!" the Twelver warns. "This is no concern of yours."

"Unlike other Jin, I have no problem killing the Shakyah," Magmar threatens. "In fact, I would rather enjoy it. That would free all your Jin and make me the hero of the Haven!"

The two Paladins at the Twelver's side clutch their leader's arms to hold her back.

She scowls, shakes free of them, and takes another step toward us. "You are welcome to try, Magmar, and find yourself squashed like the pest that you are under the foot of the Green Draycon!"

I think she's bluffing. She wouldn't want to risk Jaden showing up and marking me.

"Bring the prisoner," the Twelver commands Jakobah.

Jakobah nods to some troops waiting a few meters off.

Two drag forward a mangy and beaten figure. His hands and feet are bound with rope. His head hangs limply to his chest. I would think him dead if not for the groan when they throw him to their leader's feet.

The Twelver studies my reaction. "Do you know who this is, Eliyah?"

"Makayah!" Wajid gasps, hastening to help him. Jakobah and another Paladin attempt to push Wajid away, but the Twelver holds them back. Wajid removes his canteen and tips it to Makayah's mouth, and my father drinks eagerly.

I want to rush forward and embrace him as well, but that's exactly what the Twelver wants me to do . . . right before she snatches the Axis from my hands.

Makayah struggles to lift his face to me. "Eli . . . yah . . ."

I close my eyes, doing everything I can to hold my ground.

"I have a deal for you, Eliyah," the Twelver says. "Give me the Axis. And I will release your father."

"No!" my father rasps, wincing. He's badly hurt.

Jakobah kicks Makayah, hard, causing him to vomit the water he's just consumed. Jakobah tries to kick him again, but Wajid grabs Jakobah's foot and tosses him aside. Jakobah lands nimbly, draws his club, and pounces back to Wajid.

Faster than thought, Magmar drives a leg at the airborne Paladin. Other Paladins and warriors hiss and prepare for a counterattack.

"Stop!" I yell before they cut Wajid to pieces or, more likely, before Magmar kills them all. "If anyone dies, the Twelver will not get the Axis!"

The Twelver's eyes shine. "The Twelver agrees with

Eliyah! No one needs to die today." She extends a hand. "Return what was stolen. Your father will be released. Then you may all leave in peace."

"Don't!" my father warns.

"Upon your word as a Shakyah," I press, "you will let him go."

"We risked . . . everything . . . to get it," Makayah labors to say.

"Upon my word as a Shakyah," the Twelver pledges, "I will release him to you."

I toss the Axis to the Twelver, counting on my mother and her plan. Besides, the Twelver is unlikely to awaken the Axis while it is in my hands.

"Take it," I say. "It's no good to either of us without four marks."

She snatches the sleeping Axis and holds it like a prize. "Which is why you will now summon the Red Firewing."

"You promised to release my father after I gave you the Axis!" I snap.

"But I didn't say *when*," she replies, grinning. "Before your father is released, you will bring the Twelver's father."

She wraps most of the Axis in leather until only the curved end is exposed. She holds the Axis close to her mouth and whispers a single word, too softly to make out.

Immediately, the Axis is transformed.

It is no longer a dull gray metal pole, but a living, pulsing shaft of vibrant colors. The leather hides most of the Axis, but its alien radiance cannot be contained. The uncovered section is wrapped in flaming feathers, as bright and as blazing as the Red Firewing himself.

I saw the Axis in my dream, but that was nothing compared to the real thing. The light grabs my eyes and holds me in a hypnotic trance.

I can't look away.

The Twelver also basks in the Axis's energy. She draws a long and satisfied breath, celebrating the return of the awakened Axis to her hands.

"That is the most amazing thing I've ever seen," Stick gushes.

"Come, Eliyah," the Twelver beckons. "Touch the Axis and know what it is to be a Shakyah!"

I creep forward, tugged by the Axis's allure more than the Twelver's invitation.

Before my finger makes contact, an arrow slices the air over my shoulder, blazing a path for the Twelver.

Instantly, the Green Draycon appears, towering, fearsome, and glorious. He hunches over the Twelver, shielding her body. The arrow bounces harmlessly off Jaden's gemlike hide, stopping it from piercing the Twelver's chest. The Green Draycon saved her, just as he did when she jumped off the tower. All the Paladins and other warriors drop to their knees in the presence of the Guardian. The Jin respectfully dip their heads.

"Mira!" the Twelver roars, pointing at the edge of the cliff behind me. "Bring that thief to me!" She wraps the Axis in a sheet of soft deerskin.

I whirl and see nothing except the rim of the cliff and the boundless sea under a dome of sky. My mother must have fired the arrow and immediately withdrawn.

On the Twelver's orders, four minokaws spring into the air and soar to the cliff. Magmar lifts his hind legs and spurts a stream of webbing, taking down one minokaw who makes the mistake of flying too close. The other three tuck their wings and drop beneath the cliff's edge.

The Twelver's face glows with anticipation.

The Green Draycon looms above her. With the Twelver momentarily distracted, I kneel at my father's side while Wajid cuts his bonds.

"Eliyah," he groans.

"I'm here," I say, cradling his head in my hands. His eyes brim and spill over. "You're going to be okay."

"Samen oto, samen oto, Shijin Jaden!"

The words from the Old Language seem to rise up

from the sea. Jaden, the Green Draycon, takes notice. He sways to the rhythm of the words.

"Samen oto, samen oto, Shijin Jaden!"

It's Mira and Shanti. The words from the Old Language have the intended effect on Jaden. The Guardian's eyes glow. His head angles to me.

The Twelver panics. "Find them!" she howls. "Find them and silence them!"

More minokaws take flight and dip below the edge of the cliff. Mira and Shanti will be easier to find now that they are speaking.

Meanwhile, Jaden's head glides closer.

"No, Jaden!" the Twelver screams.

She's afraid the Guardian will mark me.

He might.

"Samen oto, samen oto, Shijin Jaden!"

"Soon, Eliyah." Jaden's unearthly voice thrums in my head. *"Soon."*

And then, the Green Draycon is gone . . .

The chanting is replaced by battle roars as the unseen minokaws attack Shanti and Mira beneath the edge of the cliff. Moments later, two minokaws rise up. One has Mira in its clutches, dangling her over the sea. The other holds Shanti.

They are alive. Beaten and battered, but alive.

"Keep Mira where she is!" the Twelver commands the minokaws. "Bring the other one here. You lied to me, Eliyah," the Twelver fumes. "But what else should we expect from a demonic?"

The minokaw soars closer and releases Shanti near the Twelver, carefully avoiding Magmar.

Shanti immediately goes to Makayah's side.

"Shanti!" Makayah whispers. "Is it . . . really you?"

The Twelver is aghast. "You know this demonic, Makayah?"

Shanti rises to face her. "I rescued Makayah after the Great War and raised him until he was old enough to return home."

"Then you are the one who polluted Makayah's mind with demonic lies and introduced him to Mira!" She gestures to Jakobah. "Kill him."

Before Jakobah can strike Shanti down, Magmar lunges forward and snatches the shepherd away.

"You are a monster, Suniyah!" I say. "You kill without remorse. Even your own brother's life means nothing to you."

"A leader must make sacrifices for what matters most, Eliyah." She uncovers the Red Firewing section of the Axis once more. "What matters most right now," the Twelver says, "is to have a fully marked Shakyah who knows how to use the power of the Axis. Touch the Axis. Call on Daviyah. Or Mira dies."

Conflicting currents of emotion tug at me like a rip tide.

If I summon Daviyah, he might give the Twelver her fourth mark. With the Axis, she can summon all Four Guardians and destroy the demon. But her hatred of the Singa is so great, she won't stop with the death of Hasatamara. She would eliminate the Singá as well.

If I refuse to call on Daviyah, she will kill my mother, and neither of us will have the four marks needed to defeat Hasatamara. Meanwhile, the demon will be unleashed by Tamir's war, with no Shakyah to stop them. Both Prides will be destroyed.

I can't let that happen.

The choice is clear. She has won.

I seize the Red Firewing section of the Axis with both hands.

Instantly, I am fused to the thing. I couldn't let go even if I wanted to.

Bright flames lick my fingers and curl around my arms. My body sizzles.

"Call him!" the Twelver roars. "Say his name!"

The name is already swelling up in my mouth, like fiction desperate to get free: "DAVIYAH!"

There is a blinding surge of energy from the Axis. Fire blasts out from the Red Firewing mark on my back. The Twelver and I are thrown off our feet. The Axis leaps from our hands.

Then . . . nothing.

CHAPTER 25

Yesterday is a memory. Tomorrow is a dream.
Now is all there is. Now is the door to eternity.
— *Sayings of the Ancients*

DARKNESS, INKY AND INFINITE.

I'm drifting in warm salty water. Normally that would be unpleasant. This, however, is like floating on a summer breeze.

The sky lightens along the horizon. Dawn is about to break.

A wave carries me onto a boundless beach. Surf tickles my feet. A diamond of light rises into the indigo dome overhead, more brilliant than a hundred suns, light that does not burn.

Countless winged creatures circle the light, joining their voices in a spellbinding song. My body vibrates with the music until I feel as if I will lift from the sand and join them.

Instead, a blazing bird descends from the assembly, his bright wings filling the sky.

"Rise, Eliyah."

The familiar soothing voice, voices within voices, moves through my veins like blood.

Daviyah!

Then the Red Firewing is at my side, morphing between a giant flame-covered bird and a powerfully built leo. For a moment, or for an eternity, we do nothing but gaze at each other. Waves of tender emotions ebb and flow between us, like the surf at our feet.

"I know who you are . . . Abba, Grandfather."

"More importantly, you know who and what you are."

"What happened? Did the Axis kill me? Am I dead?"

"There is no death, Eliyah. Only transition."

"Will I stay . . . this time?"

"Is that what you want?"

"I want it more than anything, but I should go back. My mother and my father need me. The world needs me."

"You are the first to choose returning to the earth-realm after coming to the Haven."

"It is my home."

"Well said, Eliyah. Remember those words."

Daviyah spreads mighty wings of fire, lifts from the sand, and glides up into the light.

The sky deepens to purple as the light dims. Soon the Haven is out of reach and shrinking, pulling away.

I'm about to return.

"We could use some help back there!" I howl as the light dwindles to a distant speck.

"Help is on the way . . ." Daviyah's closing sentence is faint, like the last thought before sleep.

The sand under my feet gives way, and I'm sucked downward as if through a huge funnel. Then I'm falling, falling, falling, through bottomless space.

I smack the earth. My eyes fly open. I'm back in my body just after touching the Axis and being thrown to the ground.

It feels as if I was in the Haven for days, if not years. Here, only a second has passed.

The glowing Axis of the Ancients is less than a meter from my feet. The Twelver lies just beyond it, stunned and groaning, surrounded by chanting Paladins.

Stick's face hovers over me. Shanti is beside him. Then Wajid.

"Are you all right?" Stick asks. He's talking to me, but his eyes keep wandering to the Axis. "We thought you died."

"I might have," I say. "Did Daviyah come?"

"No," Shanti laments. Wajid and Shanti help me up. My mother is still in the clutches of the in-flight mino-kaw, dangling perilously over the rocky sea far below.

I nudge Stick. "Get the Axis."

I don't have to ask him twice.

Faster than a frightened mouse, Stick scuttles

forward and grabs the Axis, which is still partially wrapped in deerskin. As I reach to take the Axis, Stick is reluctant to let it go.

The Twelver sits up, searching the sky in vain for the Red Firewing.

"You failed, Eliyah," she says scornfully. "Daviyah has not come! He has abandoned his daughter, his son, his Pride, and now his demonic grandson! But the Twelver is a Shakyah of her word. Makayah will be released to you. But Mira will not. Mira will die!"

As the Twelver speaks, she signs to the minokaw who holds my mother. The Jin releases her.

"NO!" my father and I roar together.

Mira plunges below the edge of the cliff and out of sight. Magmar bounds after her, but he's too late.

Mira is gone.

I crumble to the ground, as though I have fallen with her, shattered by shock and grief.

An unearthly screech fills the air. Flaming wings erupt from the lip of the cliff. The Red Firewing rises like a mighty wave, holding my mother in one claw.

The Twelver's forces immediately fall to their knees. The Jin bow as low to the ground as they can, whimpering like cubs. The Twelver stays on her feet, face glowing in the Red Firewing's radiance.

The Red Firewing flaps to the ground and releases Mira. Flames shoot from his wings in every direction, flames that brighten but do not burn. Mira dashes to Makayah and me.

The Red Firewing extends his wings to their limit. Lightning stretches from wingtips to the clouds with a deafening crack of thunder.

The Twelver approaches the Red Firewing, more like a timid cub than a powerful leader.

"Daviyah . . . Father . . ." she begins.

"Samen ota, samen ota, Shijin Daviyah!" Jakobah bellows, still kneeling and keeping his head down. The other Paladins and warriors join the chant, inviting Daviyah to mark the Twelver.

"Samen ota, samen ota, Shijin Daviyah!"

The Twelver raises her arms expectantly as the chanting intensifies.

The Red Firewing sways to the rhythm of the chant, as the Green Draycon did. His eyes glow even more intensely. The words are having the desired effect. Then—

"Silence!"

Instantly the chanting ceases, proving Daviyah's word was received in the minds of one and all.

The Red Firewing tucks his wings and rests blazing eyes on the Twelver. In a blink, the Red Firewing vanishes, replaced by Daviyah in leo form, his red and gold pelt wrapped in living flames. Suniyah trembles as she looks upon her father's face. They stare at each other for a time, and I realize they are sharing mind-words between themselves and no one else. At last the Twelver lowers her head, shoulders slumped. Daviyah spreads his arms, and the Red Firewing returns, wings outstretched, absorbing Daviyah into itself. The Guardian tilts his beak to the sky and exits this world without a sound.

The Twelver's back is to me. Her tail droops. I don't know what was said between them, but one thing is perfectly clear:

The Twelver was not marked by the Red Firewing.

"The Guardians will not fight with us," she announces bitterly. "And yet the demonics will invade before the sun sets. We alone must protect our realm. We must destroy the demon without the Four! We have been preparing for years, and the demonics' attack gives us the perfect opportunity. And one day"—her words rise with passion, taking wings of their own— "you can tell your cubs and the cubs of your cubs that you were there when the demon was defeated. And once the demon is destroyed, all Jin will return to the Haven!"

The Jin respond enthusiastically. They would do anything to go home. The prospect of destroying Hasatamara as well only adds to their jubilation.

The Paladins, on the other hand, are less eager.

Some of them fought with Shakyah Daviyah. They

remember his failed attempt to destroy Hasatamara without the Four Guardians.

"If the Guardians will not fight with you," Mira declares to the Twelver, "then you have no use for the Axis."

The Twelver glares at the Axis in my hands. "And you will have no use for the Axis when it is asleep!" she responds. *"Yishni!"*

At the pronouncement of this word, the Axis's radiant colors are snuffed out like a candle. It's nothing more than a metal pole, slightly curved at one end.

"What good is it to you now, Eliyah?" the Twelver sneers. "You might as well return the Axis to us."

"I'm not giving up the Axis," I warn the Twelver. "If you want it, you're going to have to take it."

"Don't be a fool," she coaxes. "You are vastly out-numbered. Magmar is strong, but my Jin will eventually overtake him. Your parents and friends will all die, and the Twelver will still get the Axis. Why not skip all the needless violence and hand it over now?"

"Magmar can turn your Jin into Shifters," I remind her. "Do you want that many Shifters digging into Bad Mountain long before you get there?"

The Twelver lashes her tail. She turns to her Jin, who stand like statues in a half-moon around the Twelver's forces and mine. They have not moved a meter since they arrived.

The Twelver raises her arms dramatically. "Attack!" The Jin hold their ground.

"We will not attack Shakyah Eliyah," Yohan declares, speaking for all the Jin. "Not out of fear of Magmar, but out of respect for Shakyah Eliyah. He has allowed his Jin to return. Such honor must be honored."

The Twelver roars. "You will obey your Shakyah if you ever want to see the light of the Haven again!"

"You are *one* of the Shakyahs," says the other of Yohan's heads. "We will follow you to the lands of the Singa, we will destroy the demon if we can, and then you will send us home, but we will not put Shakyah Eliyah at risk."

The Twelver boils. "Get what belongs to us!" she orders her Paladins.

Her forces, at least seventy-five strong, draw weapons. However, instead of charging into battle immediately, the Paladins huddle to discuss their plan. Attacking a Jin as powerful as Magmar requires a careful strategy. The other warriors assemble into three battle groups. Each group subdivides into smaller teams of five warriors each.

Meanwhile, beneath the shelter of Magmar, Wajid, Mira, and Shanti draw their weapons. Shanti gives one of his blades to Stick and the other to Zoya. He keeps a dagger for himself.

"You need more than that!" I say.

Shanti winks at me. "Give me the Axis. They think the Axis is powerful only when it's awake. Allow me to show them what the Axis can do even as it sleeps."

I've seen Shanti wield the Axis as a weapon. He defeated Anjali with it in a few seconds.

Still, I'm reluctant to let it go.

It's not that I don't trust Shanti with this other-worldly object that is the key to saving our world. If Shanti has the Axis, he will be the focus in the unfolding battle. No doubt that is exactly what he intends.

"You were a father to my father," I say. "I owe you everything. But holding the Axis is like painting a target on your head. I can't let—"

"My dear Kahn," Shanti says, cutting me off, "if I died defending your life today, it would be the greatest honor of my many years."

Emotion dampens my eyes as I turn the Axis over to Shanti.

The Paladins separate to share their plan with the groups of warriors. They take up positions on every side, except behind us, where the land drops off to the sea. If they push us just ten meters back, we will be forced into an impossible defensive position.

My mother hands me a short blade.

"Fight for what is yours," she says. "Fight for your grandfathers, fight for your friends, fight for what is true, and nothing can defeat you, not even death."

"Wait," Stick entreats, "you're actually going to let Leo fight?"

"Of course," she says indignantly. "He is my son."

"They will not harm Eliyah," Wajid assures us. "It is forbidden to harm a Shakyah, and besides that, they do not want the White Tiger coming to your defense."

"Would she come?" I say hopefully. If Anjali arrived as the White Tiger, the battle would end before it began.

"Not likely," Wajid says. "Anjali almost became a Shifter. She needs time in the Haven to heal. Even so, the Twelver will not risk causing her to appear. That is why they will not use arrows or spears. Their attack will be up close, hand-to-hand, where there is little chance of putting Eliyah in danger."

"What about Makayah?" I ask.

"Wajid will guard him," Wajid declares. "Wajid failed to protect him once. Wajid will not fail a second time."

From the steely glint in his eye, I'm sure he's right.

"Attack!" the Twelver roars, now that her forces are ready.

There are three groups of fighters, each consisting of teams of five led by Paladins. The first group closes in on us from all sides. The two other groups of fighters wait with the Jin and the Twelver for their chance to join the battle. Since we are small in number, it wouldn't be practical to send all seventy-five at once.

Magmar keeps his position over us. He swivels this way and that, taking stock of his various targets.

"What fun this will be!" he says giddily.

He blasts the closest bunch of warriors with a stream of webbing. The team anticipates the move, lining up single file so that only the lead warrior takes the hit. Another cuts the sticky strand and coils the cord of web like rope. Magmar assaults the next team the same way, with the same result. And the next.

This is part of their plan.

"No more, Magmar," I warn him. "I don't know why they want your webbing, but it can't be good."

"Agreed," he says.

"Why not keep those other teams busy?" I suggest. "We'll focus on the web collectors."

Magmar leaps to a new team of enemy fighters, striking them with his powerful legs. The three teams who have collected webbing swarm him, while the final team of this group engages us.

My mother and Shanti pounce on the enemy. Shanti roars, whirls the Axis, and takes down a Paladin in no time. My mother meets two others, attacking them simultaneously with the blades in her hands. Then she and Shanti are fighting back-to-back, like half a quadron: blocking, striking, dodging, and leaping.

Zoya roars and rushes to assist. She's not an elegant fighter like Shanti or my mother, but she uses every bit of her size to get the job done. This team is soon defeated.

Wajid, Stick, and I keep our position over Makayah.

Magmar howls.

Our opponents have managed to bind most of Magmar's legs together with the webbing they have collected. He teeters and crashes to the ground, crippled and flailing. One brave Paladin blocks Magmar's spinneret by packing it with discarded webbing before he is kicked off the edge of the cliff by one of Magmar's free legs.

Now that the giant spider is restrained and subdued, the Twelver orders her Jin to finish the job. This time they do not hesitate; they know that Magmar's fangs pose a grave threat. Nimshook, Kaitan, Yohan, and three others charge forward and roll Magmar to the lip of the cliff, brutally stabbing and tearing his body as they go. Screeching with pain and fury and gushing blood, Magmar still manages to bite Nimshook.

Then a badly wounded Magmar tumbles over the edge to the sea, where he will surely meet his death on the sharp rocks.

"Magmar!" I scream in vain.

Nimshook thrashes about on the ground like a fish out of water. Her scaly hide turns copper. Her eyes roll up into her head.

The Jin need no orders from the Twelver for what comes next. They swarm the Shifter, slashing and stomping without hesitation or mercy. The Twelver's troops cease their attack and stand clear. When the Shifter is destroyed, and its ravaged corpse dwindles to nothing, the Jin march off the battlefield, sullen and heartbroken.

The Twelver's fighters, by contrast, roar and cheer Magmar's defeat and the Shifter's demise, giving them renewed vigor for the battle.

"Things just got a bit more interesting," Mira says.

"It's my fault," I lament. "I shouldn't have made Magmar separate himself from us."

"There are always losses in the calculus of war," Shanti counsels.

"I wish Alayah would send Leo more Jin right now!" Zoya says. "We need serious backup!"

The Paladins and warriors who overcame Magmar fall upon us.

We battle and brawl with blade, tooth, and claw. Many of the enemy are wounded and battle-fatigued from their bout with Magmar. As Wajid predicted, our opponents avoid me, focusing on Shanti, who wields the Axis with devastating results.

"Get Makayah out of here!" my mother yells as she clashes with the last remaining warriors of this group. "He's in too much danger out in the open."

"Zoya and I will take him," Stick volunteers, happy to do anything that will get him off the battlefield.

Mira points with her nose to a spot at the cliff's edge. "Behind those two boulders, there's a level place where you can lay him. My bow and arrows are there. Use them if there is need. Go!"

Zoya stoops to lift Makayah, who winces with pain.

"Sorry," Zoya says. "But this is no place for you."

They spirit Makayah to the boulders as the next wave of enemy fighters dashes toward us.

Anxiety and conflict dig deep trenches in Wajid's brow as he watches Makayah go.

"He's safer there, Wajid," I say. "I need you here. With me."

Zoya sprints back to our group. Wajid focuses on the advancing threat. These enemy troops are fresh and hungry for a kill. We are battle-worn and just hoping to survive. Each of them has a small bone dagger in hand.

"Those are throwing daggers!" Wajid exclaims.

"You said they wouldn't use flying weapons like spears or arrows," Zoya reminds him.

"She's getting desperate," Wajid concludes. "We must draw their attention away from Eliyah! We don't know if Anjali is strong enough to return."

Shanti leaps forward, holding the Axis high. "Is this what you want!" he yells to the approaching fighters. "Come and take it if you can!"

They fling their daggers at Shanti.

My heart drops.

Shanti manages to swat a few of the speeding weapons away with the Axis, while half a dozen others sink deep into his pelt. He gasps, wobbles, and flops to the ground. The warriors keep coming.

"Shanti!" I cry, bounding to his side.

Zoya, Mira, and Wajid fly past me and clash with the Twelver's troops.

Shanti is curled up on the ground, which is damp beneath his fur. I roll him over. His eyes are as gentle and wise as ever.

"Take it, Leo," he gargles around the red welling up in his mouth. "Become what you are."

"Stay with me, Shanti," I cry. "Please."

"Strength and prosperity to our Kahn," he gurgles before going completely limp. He stares at nothing.

"Dear Shanti," I say, closing his eyes. "Go to Alayah."

I slide the Axis from the old shepherd's hands as the battle rages on. Our opponents are pushing Mira, Zoya, and Wajid toward me.

I arc around the hissing mass of fur to assault our opponents from behind, swatting at their legs, beating their sides with the Axis. With Mira, Wajid, and Zoya attacking in front, and me from the back, we manage to hold them off. But Mira and my friends are tiring fast.

The Twelver releases the final group of fighters.

In a few heartbeats, I will be pinned between the second wave and the third. These new warriors will take the Axis from my hands and finish the contest. With Magmar dead, without any other Jin to call on, without knowing how to awaken the Axis, I am powerless to stop them.

The Twelver was right.

Not only Shanti, but everyone I love will die.

And in the end, the Axis will be hers.

CHAPTER 26

One tiny opponent is a nuisance. A million tiny
opponents are impossible to defeat.
— *Sayings of the Ancients*

THE FEELING BEGINS.

My heart pounds, not from fear, but from the lump of fiction rolling onto my tongue, accompanied by a violent wind howling in my head.

Stuck on the battlefield between two groups of enemy warriors—this really isn't the best time to be possessed by fiction.

Or is it?

I part my jaws, and the fiction takes over.

Once in a time long, long ago, a village was devastated by war and reduced to smoldering ruins. Those who survived were forced to leave and settle elsewhere. Soon a horde of mice happened upon the village and found it quite suitable for their needs.

The fiction vision extends all the way to the Jin standing fifty meters away. It's the largest vision I've ever produced, swallowing up everyone and everything in this waking dream.

The approaching warriors halt in their tracks and drop to their knees. Those entangled with Mira, Wajid, and Zoya jump away and kneel as well. Zoya wants to keep fighting, but Wajid holds her in place. The Twelver screams at her warriors, ordering them to ignore the fiction, press on with the attack, and rip the Axis from my hands. But the Pantheras only have eyes and ears for the story.

The battle has come to a full stop, as every enemy soldier settles in to receive the fiction.

> *The village was nestled on the banks of a lake, which made the land lush and fertile. Food was plentiful. In a few years' time, the population of mice multiplied into tens of thousands and then hundreds of thousands, eventually becoming a mighty legion. The mice lived peacefully until a herd of elephamuses came to that region.*
>
> *The elephamuses lived on the grassy plain not far from the lake. Every day, when the sun was high, the elephamuses would come to the lake to drink and bathe and lounge in the cool water. Because the rest of the lake was surrounded by woods, the*

elephamuses had to traverse the old village streets to reach the water.

On their way to the lake each day, the elephamuses crushed scores of mice underfoot. In less than a week of the elephamuses thumping their way to the lake, thousands of mice were killed. The mice were terrorized and grief-stricken. Something had to be done.

The mice called a meeting of their high council. The council decided to send a messenger to the elephamuses to explain their problem and plead for their lives. The messenger mouse bravely made her way to the elephamuses' lands and found the Elephamus Queen, who was attending to her offspring.

"Dear Queen," the messenger mouse began, "I am from the mice who live in the ruins of the village. Each day when your herd comes to the lake and passes through the village, thousands of us get smashed under their heavy feet. You are a mother. You can imagine how terrible it would be to lose your calves. Would you kindly change your route so that our offspring and elders and all may live? In return, we will help you in your hour of need."

The Elephamus Queen laughed. "You mice are much too small to be of any help to creatures as large and as powerful as us. Be that as it may, we will find a new way through the trees to spare your little lives." The messenger mouse thanked the Elephamus Queen for her kindness and returned home.

A few months later, hunters trapped most of the elephamus herd in huge strong nets. The elephamuses struggled to free themselves, but it was no use. Suddenly, the Elephamus Queen remembered the mice, who had pledged to help the elephamuses when needed. She summoned one of the elephamus herd who had not been trapped and sent him to the mice.

On hearing about the elephamuses' dire situation, the mice assembled thousands of their strongest jaws and set out to rescue the herd. They found the trapped elephamuses and wasted no time getting to work. They nibbled at the thick net. Eventually, the ensnared elephamuses broke through and got free. The elephamuses were grateful to the mice for their help and the two herds became friends forever.

The vision evaporates like morning mist.

No one moves.

I expect the Twelver to immediately get her forces on the attack. Instead, everyone is scanning our surroundings. I'm doing the same. We're waiting to see whether the fiction will bring an elephamus or a mouse.

Big difference.

But I'm not sure it matters. No names were given in this fiction.

Without a name to speak, I can't make any phantom fiction being become real and solid.

"It is an honor to serve you, Shakyah Eliyah," speaks a tiny voice.

There, perched on the tip of the Axis, is a single mouse: the messenger. She's no bigger than my finger.

Although the Twelver is at least twenty meters off, her keen eyes spot the minuscule Jin.

"So, Eliyah!" she cackles. "Alayah has chosen well from our perspective!" She raises her arms. "Finish them! Bring me the Axis!"

All her available troops and Paladins spring up and charge.

"Say our name, Eliyah," the little mouse on the Axis invites.

"What name?!" I beg.

"Our name is Legion, for we are many," she says.

"LEGION!" I cry.

The earth stirs beneath my feet.

The whole battlefield trembles and shifts like ripples of wind on water. All at once, millions of mice rise up from the dirt, announcing themselves with terrible squealing. The rodents swarm over the fallen and gather around each standing enemy. They scurry up their bodies, covering them from head to foot in a thick mass of gray mouse fur. The Twelver alone is untouched. The spooked fighters and Paladins roar and attempt to swat and shake the mice away, but there are too many of them. In thirty seconds, they are all immobilized and subdued.

But the mice don't stop there. The tiny tufts keep piling on, pulling warriors down, filling their mouths and ears, smothering and suffocating.

It is a sickening scene. These Pantheras will die in minutes.

"Enough!" I order the mice, wondering if they can hear me. "Let them live!"

Immediately the mice withdraw enough to expose the heads of their prey. Dozens of trapped enemy troops gulp air into starved lungs.

The messenger mouse climbs to my shoulder. She clings there, the way Latha would.

"Well done, little friend," I say.

"Suniyah!" I call over the horde of mice. "Do you surrender? Will you leave us in peace?"

The Twelver faces a hulking four-legged Jin with a boulder-like head and a long, thick nose flanked by two horns sticking out of its mouth.

"Kaitan!" she orders. "Clear the battlefield of these pests!"

It didn't occur to me during the fiction, but it's clear to me now—

"Kaitan is an elephamus!" Zoya observes.

Kaitan enters the battlefield, pounding the earth under heavy footsteps. The mice squeal in terror, peeling away from the Twelver's forces and scattering in all directions. Many are so frightened, they tumble right off the edge of the cliff.

"Get into position!" the messenger mouse instructs her legion. "We have a Shakyah to serve! Don't be afraid! That elephamus is no match for all of us!"

It's too late.

The panicked mass of mice is running wild as Kaitan carries on with his rampage. His goal is not to kill the mice—that would be impossible, not to mention forbidden. His goal is to send them into disarray.

It's working.

The Twelver grins. "Finish this!"

Her fighters bolt forward, nearly thirty in all.

We don't stand a chance. The mice were our last hope.

A resounding roar rises from behind the Twelver and her assembly of Jin, followed by dozens of new fighters streaming onto the battlefield. The Twelver is as shocked as we are by this unexpected onslaught. That means these warriors are not here by her command.

Leading the way are Kaw, Li, and Abba, followed by the rest of Abba's family. Even their younglings are dressed and armed for war, yowling ferociously.

Arrows whistle, and many of our surprised opponents fall like toppled trees. No longer in shooting range, Li and Kaw shoulder their bows and take on two Paladins each. They fight like mirror images of each other, drop-kicking one Paladin while swinging a weapon at the next.

Abba positions himself in a group of three opponents, whirling a bone blade attached to a three-meter strap. He takes down several foes with two swipes. His weapon never stops moving, finding targets at every turn.

Wajid, Mira, and Zoya fight on, fueled by renewed hope. I swing the Axis, tripping up enemy fighters and chasing Kaitan away. The messenger mouse clings to my shoulder, shouting at her mice to regroup. She rounds up enough of them to overwhelm three enemy fighters in the same way as before.

As the oldest one on the battlefield, Abba tires quickly. He drops his swinging weapon and bares two bone daggers. A Paladin and two other Panthera warriors close in on him. Wajid and Kaw hasten to assist, but they are too late. Abba receives several direct hits to his body and head. He staggers and collapses. Kaw and

Wajid overtake Abba's attackers, but not soon enough to save him.

When all the Twelver's forces are conquered, not only Abba but several members of his family are among the dead. They sacrificed themselves to defend a small group of demonics and the Lost Paladin.

Li drops her weapons and weeps over Abba's corpse.

"Thank you" is all I can manage to say.

Li speaks with her hands.

"Thank Abba," Wajid translates. "It was his idea to leave our camp and follow the Twelver from Elyon. He believed you might need help."

"He was right," I say. "I will never forget those who gave their lives today."

Throngs of mice gather into a gray pillar that towers over all of us. The messenger mouse, still perched on my shoulder, says, "If we have served you well, Lord Eliyah, may we return home?"

"You may return, Legion," I invite. "I am willing."

Golden beams spread out from my body as a view of the Haven opens in my chest. The Twelver's Jin roar and stomp their feet, longing to follow the mice home.

I place one end of the Axis on the ground and rest the other end at my waist. Immediately, the mob of mice becomes a long cord of gray, squealing with joy as they climb the Axis and exit this world.

It tickles.

The messenger mouse remains on my shoulder, waiting for each of her kindred to make the journey to the Haven. Finally, she alone remains.

"You are a good leader, mouse friend," I say.

"And you are a compassionate Shakyah," she replies with a bow. "That will soon be rewarded."

Without another word, the messenger mouse rolls down my shoulder and is swallowed up by the light. The vision of the Haven in my torso narrows, compressing the light into a thin beam until it is extinguished.

During the mice's return to the Haven, no one notices the Twelver making her way across the battlefield.

"Look at what you've done, Eliyah," the Twelver scolds, stepping over the bodies of the fallen. "So much needless death. Their blood is on your hands. If you hadn't stubbornly clung to something that isn't yours, something you know nothing about"—she pauses at the lifeless form of Shanti—"all these brave warriors would still be alive."

Wajid and Mira growl as the Twelver saunters closer.

"You launched this attack!" I retort. "Don't try to put the blame where it doesn't belong."

"You dare to lecture me about belonging? The Axis belongs to our Pride!" Her voice is slick with contempt. She's only two meters away now. "Who do you think you are?!"

My friends gather behind me, claws out, weapons ready.

"I am Shakyah Eliyah!" I roar. "I am the Kahn of Singara!"

The Twelver bares her teeth and leaps, aiming to snatch the Axis from my hands. As the leader of her Pride who has enjoyed the protection of the Green Draycon for most of her life, she doesn't expect resistance. Nevertheless, Wajid, Zoya, Mira, Li, Kaw, and half a dozen others spring to my defense.

Suddenly, the Twelver yowls and crumples to the ground.

"Wait!" I command. "She is wounded."

"By whom?" Zoya asks. No one has touched the Twelver.

The Twelver draws herself up. An arrow is lodged in the muscle of her shoulder. She rips the arrow out and hurls it to the ground. Blood flows from the wound. She covers it with her hand, astonished and embarrassed.

"Nice shot!" Stick cheers behind us.

We look to the boulders at the edge of the cliff where my father, bow in hand, is propped up by Stick.

Makayah drops the bow and collapses. Mira dashes to his side.

With one arrow, my father has proved that the Green Draycon and all the Guardians have abandoned the Twelver. She is as vulnerable as anyone.

Zoya, Li, Wajid, and Kaw hem the Twelver in, closing off any hope of escape. They grip their weapons, lash their tails, and prepare to end her life and her reign.

Not only that, killing her will send all her Jin to the Haven. I can feel all their eyes on me, leos and Jin alike, eager for me to give the order.

It would be so easy.

Just a thrust of a single blade.

And it would be wrong.

"Go back to Elyon," I tell her. "Help your Pride flee while you still can. Tamir's weapons are more powerful than you can imagine. If he finds your Pride, he will spill more than enough blood to free the demon. That is what he wants. If he doesn't find any enemies to kill, the demon will stay in his dungeon at the bottom of the mountain."

"We have been preparing for years," the Twelver boasts. "The demonics will find Elyon empty as we plunder their lands and destroy the demon without the Guardians." She glances at the sleeping Axis in my hands. "And you can do nothing to stop us."

The Twelver turns tail and marches back to her Jin, clasping her injured shoulder.

"You sure about letting her go like that?" Zoya questions.

"Not sure at all, Zoy," I admit, knowing that Grandfather, and most any Kahn before him, would have killed the Twelver in a heartbeat. "But I can't stomach the thought of executing her. She is . . . family."

"Leo!" Stick calls from the boulders. "You better get over here."

I sprint to where my father lies; Wajid and Zoya are at my tail. Makayah's breathing is shallow. Mira's watery eyes are fixed on her mate.

I take Makayah's hand.

"Father . . ." I begin, and immediately run out of words. There's so much I want to say, I don't know where to start. And now, it appears, we have no time at all.

"The door to the Haven is opening for him," my mother says.

"No!" I protest. "It's too soon!"

Mira's tail curls around my waist. "It's all right, Eliyah. He has suffered so much in his life."

"It's not all right!" I snap. "I want him here. With us!"

Stick has other things on his mind. "Does Makayah know the sacred word?" He's aching to see the Axis awakened again. "The word that speaks the deepest desire of all creatures?"

Zoya cuffs her brother's head.

"The word is passed from one Shakyah to the next," Wajid reminds us. "No one else knows it."

"And the Twelver wouldn't share a hairball with Leo." Stick snorts regretfully. "The word is probably in the Old Language anyway."

"The language does not matter," Wajid says, "if it is the heart that speaks."

"Then the Axis is useless to me," I lament, "and to the Twelver. The Guardians have abandoned both of us."

"Have faith, Eliyah," Wajid says. "The Guardians wanted you to have it."

"Yes," Makayah murmurs. "Have . . . faith . . ."

My father's words come as a surprise to all of us. Mira, Wajid, and I lean closer, our heads nearly touching as we hover over Makayah, longing to hear more.

Instead, his breathing slows to a trickle. His hand grows cold in mine.

Mira's tears drip onto her mate's lifeless face.

Scorching grief envelops my heart as reality settles in. Grandfather, Magmar, Shanti, Abba, and now Makayah, the father I only just met and will never really know: gone.

And Anjali. She's gone too. I might see her again

as the White Tiger, but will I ever have Anjali, the old Anjali, by my side?

"*Rise, Eliyah.*" A Guardian voice echoes in my head.

I crane my neck and behold Jaden, the Green Draycon, on the battlefield in all his towering and fearsome splendor. Li, Kaw, and the rest of Abba's family fall to their knees, eyes lowered.

"*Rise, Shakyah Eliyah,*" Jaden says again.

Fresh tears stain my muzzle as I stand and face the Guardian. "Can you bring him back? Can you bring all of them back?"

"*They are home now. Your story continues. Come.*"

Jaden's voice tugs at me like a magnet. My legs take me to him, moving of their own accord.

"*Samen oto, samen oto, Shijin Jaden!*" Wajid chants.

Abba's family chants along with him. Mira and Zoya join in.

"*Samen oto, samen oto, Shijin Jaden!*"

Jaden's eyes glow. "*Alayah is pleased with you, Eliyah. You have shown humility, bravery, and compassion, even toward your enemies. You are worthy of four marks. The Axis was made for your hands.*"

Jaden's mighty reptilian head lowers until a few glittering green scales of his chin rest on the fur between my ears. My back tingles with warmth as I receive my fourth and final mark.

In a blink, the Green Draycon is gone, and Jaden

appears in leo form. He is tall and powerfully built, covered in dazzling emerald fur. He rests his hands on my shoulders.

"The time is coming," he says out loud, "for two Prides to become one."

"How can I unite them," I ask, my voice cracking, "when my own heart is broken?"

"A broken heart is what makes a good Shakyah," he says, "and a good Kahn."

"How about telling him the sacred word?" Stick yells. "And giving him lessons on using the Axis?"

Zoya whops him on the side of the head, but the truth is, it's not a bad idea.

"You have everything you need, Eliyah," Jaden says, "The sacred word is already in you. Soon, it will be on your tongue."

And then he is gone.

CHAPTER 27

Trust takes months to build,
seconds to destroy, and years to rebuild.
— *Sayings of the Ancients*

WE BURY MY FATHER and Shanti together on the clifftop, overlooking the sea.

My mother weeps. Wajid chants prayers in the Old Language. I can't do either one.

Instead, I sit at the cliff's edge with Stick and Zoya, gazing at the blurry horizon where the sea merges with sky. The Axis is in my lap, and Shanti's cloak drapes my shoulders. There's a terrible aching rawness in my chest, but my mind races ahead, building a plan from the rubble of grief.

After Li, Kaw, and their family bury their dead, I send them to Elyon to convince as many as they can to defy the Twelver, abandon the river city, and flee east, toward the rising sun, to avoid Tamir. The less blood Tamir sheds, the better.

I have to convince a few others to leave as well.

I turn to Stick and Zoya. "I want you to go to Singara."

Stick perks up. "We're going home?"

"Not us. Just you two. Go through the Border Caves. Make your way to the Academy. Tell Alpha I'm coming. We will use the Academy as our base. It's close to the sea, where the Twelver will bring her forces."

Zoya's expression, as usual, hasn't changed. "What about you?"

"I'll come soon with Mira," I promise. "There's something I have to do first."

Stick's eyes drift wistfully to the Axis. He's craving to have it in his hands again, hungry to see it reawakened.

"You heard him, Zoy," Stick says. "Let's go."

As fascinated as he is by the Axis, he would rather scram before I change my mind.

Zoya doesn't move. She wants to stay with me.

"I'll be okay," I assure her. "I have the all-powerful, totally asleep Axis. Nothing to worry about."

Her dark eyes peer right through me. "You miss her, don't you?"

"Who?" I ask, although I know exactly who.

"I miss her too," she says. "Anjali always knew what to do."

My nose tingles. I look away, wishing Zoya didn't bring her up. I have enough grief to deal with.

"You're starting to remind me of her, though," Zoya adds. "Maybe she's not as far away as you think."

I blink away tears.

"Be careful," I tell Stick and Zoya. "I don't want to lose any more friends."

"I know Singara better than my own tail," Stick brags. "And we won't stand out like a purple karkadann as we do over here. No one will notice us."

"Good," I say. "Soldiers will be everywhere. If you're caught, Tamir will have your pelts."

"Speaking of Tamir, I've been thinking," Stick says warily. "Shouldn't we warn Tamir that the enemy will soon attack by sea?"

Zoya and I stare at him, aghast.

"Tamir is the enemy, brick brain," Zoya huffs. "You want us to help him?"

"We have important information about the movements of the Maguar," Stick says pointedly. "We owe it to our Pride!"

"We *will* warn them," I say. "That's why I'm sending you to Alpha."

"That's not enough!" Stick gripes.

"What would be enough, Stick?" I growl.

"I don't know . . . It's just that . . . I mean . . . What if . . ." he sputters, uncertain to speak his mind.

"What if what?" Zoya chides.

"What if Tamir is right!" he blurts out. "What if destroying the Maguar is the right thing to do?"

"I'm half Maguar!" I thunder. "Which half of me do you want to destroy?"

Zoya is boiling mad too. If she weren't related to Stick, she would fill his mouth with her fist.

Just then, an explosion rocks the earth.

From the direction of Singara, a sooty plume of smoke drifts above the trees. I didn't realize just how close we are to the Great Wall. But it makes sense that my parents would have their home as near to me as possible.

"It's Tamir. He's coming," I say, watching the smoke gather into a dark cloud. "You two need to leave. Stick, I'm asking you to trust me. We can stop Tamir and the Twelver. We can prevent a war. We can bring the two Prides together, and Hasatamara can stay where he is for another ten million years for all I care, but if not, we have the Axis as protection!"

"That's fantasy, Leo," Stick retorts, fuming. "No one in Singara wants the Prides to come together! Neither does the Twelver! It will never happen!"

"Come with us, Leo," Zoya pleads, disregarding her brother.

"Not yet," I say. "I have to face Tamir. I can't let him start a senseless war only to free Hasatamara."

Zoya is crestfallen. "You don't stand a chance

against Tamir and an army of Singa soldiers with exploding weapons."

"I have to try," I say. "All soldiers take an oath to protect the Singa-Kahn. Tamir isn't the Kahn. I am. They aren't his soldiers. They're mine. They will listen to me even if he won't."

"Don't count on it, Leo," Zoya warns.

"You're wasting time!" I snarl. "Go to Alpha now!" I regret that as soon as the words leave my mouth. Brother and sister exchange a bewildered glance. "Please, just go back to Singara. Go home."

The Axis quivers, nearly shaking itself free from my hands as it bursts to life. Dazzling colors illuminate four sections of the Axis, each reflecting one of the Guardians: blazing red firewing feathers, sparkling green draycon scales, white tiger fur marbled with dark stripes, and black tortoiseshell.

I stare at it, astounded and enchanted.

So does Stick. "How did you do that?" he asks.

"I must have just said the sacred word," I say, retracing the last thing that crossed my lips. "Home." Of course! Home is the deepest desire of all creatures!

Wajid and Mira draw near.

My hands are clutching the white and black sections of the Axis.

"Say their names," Wajid encourages.

"Anjali! Lamasura!"

The glowing Axis surges with energy. Light erupts from my back, pitching me forward. The Axis flies from my hands, just as it did when I summoned Daviyah. This time, however, I am not transported to the Haven.

I am transported onto my face. I come to all fours, spitting dirt.

"I see you are adjusting to the Axis's power."

Anjali's voice chimes gaily in my head.

"It didn't kill you this time."

I look up, and there she is, standing tall and strong with Lamasura. Both are in leo form. Anjali's white striped fur is a sharp contrast to Lamasura's pitch-black pelt. They wear bejeweled raiment more elegant than anything found in this world.

I scramble to my feet.

"Is it really you?" I blather. I want to embrace her, but I don't know if that's an appropriate thing to do to a Guardian.

"You called. We are here."

"Are you . . . better now?"

She smiles and holds out her arms to show the lack of copper tint on her fur.

"I'm sorry you got sick. I didn't know that you were . . ."

"It's okay. I didn't know either."

I have so many questions about what it's like to be a Guardian, about being in the Haven, and what it was like to learn who she really is. But I already know something about that. Her journey and my journey aren't that different.

"Would you do me a favor?"

Her white ears lift.

"Is it possible for you to look like the Anjali I remember? The Singa version?"

Anjali closes her eyes and inhales. As she breathes out, her pelt ripples as if stirred by the wind, replacing white striped fur with her familiar golden tones. She is just like she used to be, except she has no weapons, a rare sight for the old Anjali.

"*Better?*"

"One more thing. I know silence is the language of Alayah and all that, but could we just talk, like we used to?"

"As you wish . . . Leo."

Her regular voice is as delicious as Haven music in my ears.

Anjali's eyes bounce to my mother. "Aren't you going to introduce us?"

In my delirium over the Guardians' arrival, I have forgotten all about my mother. Mira's muzzle bears an impish grin as she watches me with Anjali. Wajid is on his knees, head bowed, showing reverence for both Guardians.

"Mira, this is Anjali, the captain of my quadron who is also . . . the White Tiger . . . and this is Lamasura," I stammer, totally unsure how to do this. "Anjali, Lamasura, this is my mother, Mira, daughter of Raja Kahn."

Anjali and Lamasura bow to Mira.

"It is an honor to meet Your Majesty," Anjali says.

Mira bows in return. "The honor is mine."

Anjali takes Wajid's arm. "Rise, noble Paladin. Those who have battled side by side do not need to kneel to each other."

Wajid returns to his feet, still averting his eyes from Anjali.

Anjali smiles at him. "You knew me before I knew myself, didn't you, Wajid?"

"Verily," Wajid says. "Yet some things are better left discovered for oneself, even for a Guardian."

"You are the very best of your Pride," Anjali purrs. "Alayah sent the most excellent of the Panthera to protect Eliyah when I could not."

Then she looks to Zoya. "And among Singas there are none finer than you, Zoya. Perhaps your good and trusting heart will rub off on your brother someday."

Zoya turns to Stick, but he's not there.

"Where is he?" I say.

Zoya whirls around, sniffing and scanning everything in sight.

"Stick!" she calls.

There is no trace of him. Not even a whiff of a scent.

"He's gone," I say. "But why? And where?"

"Not only him," Zoya groans. "The Axis is gone too."

CHAPTER 28

Victory comes to the one with the most courage,
not to the one with the most strength.
— *Sayings of the Ancients*

W HY WOULD HE TAKE IT?!"

"He's a thief," Zoya says, as if that settles it. "It's what he does."

"That's not the only reason!" I snarl. "You heard him. He thinks Tamir is right! If I don't have the Axis, there's no way to stop Tamir or Hasatamara."

She can barely look at me.

"Fan out!" I say. "We have to find him!"

"It's no use," Zoya says. "If he doesn't want to be found, he won't be found."

I know she's right. Nevertheless, Wajid, Mira, and I dash about, checking behind boulders and leaning over the edge of the cliff. We even search the battlefield to see if Stick has hidden himself among the dead.

There's no sign of him.

"STICK!" I roar.

A second explosion shakes the earth, followed by

another column of smoke climbing into the sky near the Great Wall.

"He'll probably go to Singara," Zoya says. "That's all he wanted to do since we got here."

"Then go find him!" I snarl. "Now!"

"Take a breath, Leo."

It's Anjali's voice in my head.

"You have already lost the Axis and one friend. Do you want to lose another?"

"I'm sorry, Zoya," I say. "I just don't know what to do."

Zoya shrugs it off. "Don't worry, Leo. I'll find him." She turns tail and bounds away. Mad as I am, I hate to see her go.

"It's possible the thief will take the Axis directly to Tamir," Wajid says, "to keep the Axis out of your hands."

That would be the ultimate betrayal.

"All the more reason to face Tamir with Guardian backup. The sooner the better." I remove Shanti's cloak and hand it to Lamasura. "You might want to put this on."

Lamasura receives the cloak with aching slowness and covers her tortoise-patterned fur.

I look to Wajid and Mira. "You don't have to come with us."

"I'm not leaving you again," Mira says.

"And Wajid has sworn in blood to protect you," Wajid reminds me.

An ashen cloud hovers above the trees, beckoning us to the Great Wall.

"Then let's go!"

In a heartbeat, Anjali morphs into the White Tiger—fearsome and powerful, twice the size of Wajid—and lowers her forelegs to the ground.

"I can get you there more quickly," she says. "Come."

I climb one of her legs to her back, waving my tail for the others to follow. Mira bounds her way up and settles behind me. Lamasura comes next, moving leisurely.

Wajid keeps his distance. "Wajid cannot," he says.

Like all Pantheras, Wajid worships the Shijin. Touching, let alone *riding*, one of the Guardians must be unthinkable to him.

As soon as Lamasura is in place behind Mira, the White Tiger snatches Wajid in her giant mouth and flings him overhead. The Paladin flips and lands deftly on Anjali's striped back, just behind Lamasura, trembling like a frightened fawn.

"Hold on," Anjali advises.

And she is off, galloping over the plain, soaring through the woods in the direction of the Great Wall, feet barely touching the ground. Moving at this unnatural speed is exhilarating. Neither Mira nor I can stifle a cry of elation.

Anjali slows as we near the Great Wall. The stone barrier, Grandfather's crowning achievement, is less than one hundred meters away. Anjali takes cover in a copse of trees, and we slide off her back to the ground.

Mira points. "Look."

We follow the line of her finger to a blackened section of the Great Wall. A hole, no bigger than a barrel, reveals a sliver of Singa territory beyond.

"He's blasting through," Anjali says, returning to her Singa form in a blink.

"What is 'blasting'?" Wajid asks.

"It's an explosion caused by a powder found in the deepest part of the mountain. Close to the demon."

"Demon dust," Wajid says with despair. "It has long been rumored that such an evil powder exists."

A third explosion sends an angry burst of flame into Panthera territory. Pebbles rain down on us.

When the smoke clears, we find that the opening is now the size of a small house. A cheer, rising into one collective roar of triumph, blows through the hole.

"Here they come," I say.

Soldiers pour into enemy territory. Each of them wears gleaming armor made of new metal, no doubt forged from the Border Zone Fence, which Tamir considered a waste. He was right about that much.

In addition to the standard blades, each soldier carries a long metal pole with a wooden handle at one end. These must be the weapons Tamir invented, which use demon dust to fire small metal balls at blinding speeds.

Atop the wall, larger versions of the same weapons roll into place, ready to fire at the enemy. These new weapons were cast from the metal of the Border Zone Fence as well.

I almost admire Tamir for accomplishing his plans so quickly. He is not only a great scientist, but he also designed a way to produce thousands of new battle tools in a matter of days. Or, more likely, he has been secretly preparing for months.

Soldiers spread out along the wall on either side of the hole, pointing their exploding weapons into enemy territory. They must expect the whole Pride to crash down upon them as soon as they bend one blade of Panthera grass underfoot. Knowing Tamir, he is counting on the dramatic booming entrance to draw the enemy to him.

That will be his first surprise about the Panthera.

The soldiers along the wall hold their positions and wait for ten heartbeats.

"Clear!" yells a commander stationed by the hole.

"Clear!" replies another commander from atop the wall.

A whip cracks, and a procession of karkadanns files through the hole, flanked by legions of soldiers. The karkadanns tow carts of supplies, food, weaponry, and barrels of demon dust. In a few minutes, thousands of soldiers are assembled, arranged in battalions, ready to fight.

A horn blares, and the senior soldiers cross into enemy territory. I can make out Dagan and the other generals, minus Kaydan.

Tamir is not among them. But his daughter is.

"Do you see the young general leading the others?" I whisper to Mira. "That's Amara, Tamir's eldest."

"Of course," Mira says. "The appetite for power runs strong in his side of the family."

"No surprise that Kaydan isn't there," Anjali observes. "He would die before giving allegiance to Tamir."

"The fact that Tamir sent Amara could be to our advantage," I suggest. "Singa soldiers are more likely to respect their Kahn than the regent's offspring, even if she is a general."

Mira nods. "It is a reasonable hypothesis."

"We not only have Anjali and Lamasura, but we also have you, Wajid," I say, gazing up at the massive Paladin. "Most of those soldiers met you at the Academy.

They were frightened back then. Now that there are no bars to protect them, they will be terrified."

Wajid grunts his agreement. "Demonics are easily frightened because they lack faith."

"All the same, Wajid," I continue, "you and Mira should stay close to me. They will not fire their weapons and risk killing the Kahn. That is punishable by death."

I wish I felt as confident as I sound. I have no idea if this will work. Amara could be so eager to use her new weapons, she might mow us down long before I can reveal who I am.

Mira squeezes my arm. "Father raised you to be the Singa-Kahn. He raised you well."

"Time to find out if that still matters to our Pride," I say.

Amara's forces push into enemy territory. The karkadanns lead the way. Their bulky armored bodies create a moving barricade protecting the swaths of soldiers in tow.

We emerge from the trees and walk single file, directly toward Amara and the army. I'm in the lead. Wajid is behind Mira, who provides little cover for the high and hefty Paladin. The two Guardians bring up the rear.

"Amara!" I roar.

"Halt!" General Dagan yells. "Prepare to engage the enemy!"

The Royal Army of Singara comes to a full stop. The front line of soldiers, eager to see and attack the dreaded foe, take positions around the karkadanns, pointing their exploding weapons at us.

"I am Leo, the rightful Kahn of Singara!" I declare, marching onward. "Drop your weapons!"

Many soldiers immediately lower their weapons. Others are just plain confused.

Amara bursts through the front line. "I give the orders here! That Singa is a Spinner and a traitor! He has abandoned his Pride and sided with the enemy!"

We're still advancing. Only twenty meters separate us from Amara and the Royal Army.

"You are wasting your time, Amara," I say. "The Maguar have left these lands. You came here for nothing."

"Nonsense!" she scoffs. "There is a Maguar with you now!"

"So you remember Wajid from the Academy?"

As anticipated, the soldiers recoil and hiss at the mention of the captive Maguar's name.

"We kept him in a cage for twenty-five years," I continue, still on the move. "But we did not damage his faith or his spirit. Our elders lied to us about them, Amara. They are not the enemies we thought they were."

"Stay where you are!" Amara roars. Her eyes sweep

the trees behind us. She fears this is an ambush. She's not wrong. I have two of the Four Guardians who are mightier than all the Panthera in Elyon.

I stop walking but keep talking. "The real evil lies beneath the castle of Singara. Has Tamir shown you the demon trapped in the Great Mountain?"

Amara startles. Her whiskers twitch.

"The demon feeds on violence," I warn. "The demon is the cause of the separation and hostility between our Prides. Your new weapons are powered by demon dust. You are playing right into the monster's hands. War will only help it escape and destroy everything. That doesn't have to happen. It *won't* happen if there is peace between the Prides."

"Fables and fantasy!" Amara exclaims. "Are you going to stop the Royal Army by infecting us all with fiction? You should have stayed away, Leo."

"I can't. Singara is my home. Tell Tamir the Singa-Kahn has returned."

Amara chuckles grimly. "No Spinner can be the Kahn. Seize their weapons!" she orders her soldiers. "They are my prisoners now."

Two quadrons shoulder their exploding weapons and bare their blades. Their movements are skittish and uncertain. It isn't every day they are asked to arrest the Kahn.

Anjali and Lamasura slide out from behind Wajid.

Lamasura sluggishly sheds the cloak to reveal her tortoise-patterned midnight pelt.

Amara's eyes land on Lamasura, expanding to their limit. "What abomination is this?!"

"Don't be afraid, Amara," I caution, looking at Lamasura. "Lamasura is a friend. She means you no harm."

"She is a mistake of nature. Like all the Maguar. Like you, Leo! They must be exterminated!"

Anjali growls. She's spoiling for a fight, ready to pounce as the White Tiger.

"Company C will have first blood in Operation Singa Storm," Amara proclaims. "Prepare to fire!"

Company C, fifteen soldiers in all, assembles behind Amara.

I recognize them.

They are Amara's company from the Royal Academy of War Science. Despite their two years of training at the Academy, they seem young and inexperienced, unsteady as they aim their demon-dust weapons.

Meanwhile, unhurried as the movement of the moon, Lamasura raises a hand.

"I am your Kahn!" I yell. "This is high treason!"

"Fire!" Amara commands.

The soldiers of Company C flick a switch on the handle of their weapons. Sparks fly. Fire jumps from fifteen metal tubes, accompanied by smoke and an ear-shattering boom.

Is this how it ends? All of us laid out on the ground, riddled with bloody holes?

The crack of the weapons firing is swallowed up by an even louder blast. The air ripples and everything around us stops, frozen in time, including Amara and all her soldiers. No, not quite frozen, just moving at less than a snail's crawl.

That means the blast wasn't from the exploding weapons.

It was Lamasura bending time, just as she did in Abba's camp. I check my companions. Mira is dumbfounded. Wajid dips his head in deference to Lamasura's power. Like me, they were not affected by Lamasura's spell. Amara's nearly frozen face is twisted with rage as she announces our execution.

Moving at a relaxed pace, Lamasura plucks from the air fifteen small metal balls slothfully carving a trail for us, one by one.

I release a breath I didn't know I was holding.

"She's handy in a pinch, isn't she?" Anjali says with a wink.

"Verily," I say, quoting Wajid.

Lamasura tips her hand, and the collection of metal balls patters to the ground around our feet.

"So what happens now?" I ask.

"What do you want to happen?" Anjali asks.

"I want to stop this war. If I can't, I'll need the Axis to stop Hasatamara. But I don't know how to do either one."

"You don't need to know how . . ." Wajid intones.

"I only have to be willing," I finish for him. "That's faith."

"Verily," Wajid concurs. "That is faith."

"Then let's go home, Son," Mira says.

"All of us?" I ask, observing Wajid's reaction.

How can I expect him to return to the realm where he was held prisoner and mistreated for so long? But how can I endure more heartbreak by leaving him here?

Wajid lifts his chin. "Wajid would follow you to the ends of the earth and beyond, Shakyah Eliyah."

"You too?" I say to Anjali.

"Me too," she replies.

"What about Lamasura?"

"She will hold the army like this until we are gone," Anjali explains, "then she will go back to the Haven. Unless," she adds with a sharp-toothed grin, "you would like the White Tiger to show up and wipe all these soldiers out first."

"These Singas are my soldiers, my responsibility, including Amara," I say. "Instead of wiping them out, what if the White Tiger takes all their demon dust, dumps it in the sea, and then joins me in Singara? But

I don't think the White Tiger should show up on the other side of the wall."

Not only would the sight of the White Tiger blow our cover and send the Singa into a fur-raising panic, I'm happy to have the old Anjali back for a while.

Anjali nods. "Then we return just as we were when we left."

"Just as we were . . . and not the same at all," I say.

Anjali smiles. "You are a bit taller, but have we really changed so much?"

"Maybe not," I say, "but the world as we know it will never be the same. One way or the other, everything is about to change."

FOLKTALE SOURCES

THE STORIES TOLD BY LEO and others are based on folktales from many cultures and traditions.

THE STORY OF LAMASURA is adapted from a Buddhist tale, "The Talkative Tortoise."

THE BRIEF STORY ABOUT THE YOUNGLING who breaks the goat's horn is a retelling of one of Aesop's fables, "The Goatherd and the Goat."

URSUS THE GRIZBEAR is inspired by "The Bear Legend" from the Cherokee tradition.

NO NAME'S STORY is based on the Turkish tale "No Name and the Squirrel." I was guided by Meltem Basel's version found at worldstories.org.uk/stories/bald-boy-and-the-squirrel.

THE STORY OF MAGMAR is adapted from a Ghanaian tale often called "How the Spider Obtained the Sky God's Stories."

THE STORY ABOUT HELEL/HASATAMARA told by Magmar is an original tale created by the author.

THE STORY OF THE MICE AND THE ELEPHAMUSES is based on an Indian folktale, "The Little Mice and the Big Elephants."

AUTHOR'S NOTE

All "Sayings of the Ancients" in this book are original with the exception of the saying that begins chapter 19, which is adapted from Romans 8:28 of the Christian Bible.

The words from the Old Language recited by the Twelver and the Panthera in chapter 20 are based on Proverbs 3:5–6 from the Hebrew Bible.

The Old Language is, for the most part, a phonetic rendering of Hebrew. I hope this reflects my great love for the beauty and power of the Hebrew language and inspires others to learn more about it.

Special thanks to the following young readers, who previewed a draft of this book. I am forever grateful for their feedback and enthusiasm:

NATHAN F. CRAWFORD
IRIS DOUGHERTY

Vivian Dougherty
Ethan Fitzgerald
Olivia Conway Hatcher
Ian Sinclair Wellman
Jason Zgonc

And deep thanks to my family for their patience and tolerance as I was pulled away into the world of this book, not always at the best time.

Praise be to God from whom all blessings flow.